DATE DUE			

Moths

Rosalind Ashe

Holt, Rinehart and Winston
New York

For Sophie

Library of Congress Cataloging in Publication Data
Ashe, Rosalind.
  Moths.

  I. Title.
PZ4.A8246Mo3 [PR6051.S47] 823'.9'14 76-4724
ISBN 0-03-016831-7

Grateful acknowledgment is made to Chappell & Co.,
Inc. for permission to reprint one line from "If Ever
I Would Leave You" copyright © 1960 by Alan Jay
Lerner and Frederick Loewe. Chappell & Co., Inc.
owner of publication and allied rights. All rights
reserved. Used by permission.

Printed in the United States of America

10 9 8 7 6 5 4 3 2 1

PROLOGUE

I could not stand the immolation of the copper beech: the sun is caught behind it and now the whole western sky is flaming with ragged crimson cloud, fragments of the monstrous bonfire. I closed the tall shutters against the glare, but still it trickles through the cracks and bloodies the mahogany.

This table, I suppose, was too big to go in the sale; like the cupboard upstairs, a beached whale in the centre of the bare master bedroom looking out across the Thames. And that cupboard was there when they bought the house: it has survived two auctions. They called it Moby Dick, and Nemo took it over. It is a poor deal thing, now one can see its back; its ridiculous crown of wooden bobbles can't fool anyone. Inside, it smells of her clothes and the musky Indian oils she got from small boutiques – where she probably bought the luscious poster of Che Guevara that James refused to have up in the bedroom. Now it is the sole occupant, curled and yellow in a drawer. Che lives.

Along with the fixtures and fittings – the extravagantly custom-built, aggressively masculine, walk-in cupboard that James had the builders construct for him, the deep white carpeting indented by departed furniture, the honeysuckle-tiled fireplace. You can't take it with you.

Someone took the bulbs, however. The chandelier above the stair-well is naked, and the ones I have bought with my provisions won't fit the tiny sockets. The handrail snakes down the graceful curve into the dark, a beckoning fading gesture. But I had rather face the passage between the bedrooms, even the twisting back stairs, than the hall with its padlocked drawing-room door. They had to do that: there

7

were so many sightseers with no real interest in the sale. Serious buyers were given a look inside.

But I have put a bulb in the kitchen which I have made my base. It was always the centre of the house, dominated by the black Aga, the heart – pumping out heat and food, and absorbing all the rubbish patiently into its central ring. James was intending to convert it to oil, but he left it too late. Now it is cold and grimy. I found some fossilized croissants in the back of it, relics of enlightened European man.

Those would have been for Sunday breakfast, with fresh orange juice, elaborate coffee, the *News of the World* and the *Mirror* as well as the usual solid *Sundays* – James insisted on balance, the 'tasties' as well as the 'tasteful'. All this in the 'Large light modern kitchen with polished stone floor and ample working surfaces; facing S and W. Eating area with open grate and breakfast bench. Aga and calor gas. The conversion has carefully preserved the original brick arches and pine shutters.'

Dark bare stifling kitchen, smelling of fly-killer – one has survived to do a dance of death behind the shutters. I must suffer its interminable sizzling: letting it out would let in the vision of the burning copper beech. Perhaps it was foolish of me to return.

But the time to retreat in an orderly manner has come and gone. I would be looking over my shoulder to see something I did not want to see. I would give myself away by my fumbling haste with the ignition. If I got as far as the holly tunnel and the distant white gate, would I come out on the other side?

Subdue hysterical thoughts. I must not let the beech's fire nest in my flax. I came back to the house I loved to have it to myself again. I found it first, before even Nemo and James, and together we disturbed the sleeping beauty. But I find myself attending a lonely wake.

8

Completing the full circle, perhaps I hoped to circumscribe the year's events with a magic ring – insulate them and render them harmless. Then I would pin them on the page, exotic moths. But of course you can't get back to the beginning: the centre has shifted, the circle does not meet, and now the things inside are flowing, pressing through the narrow gap, swarming, thickening the air, clinging, cloying, unbreathable.

Outside the kitchen door the weedy gravel curve is a darkening well, the tall L of the house cutting off the western glow. The yellow rose in the centre is almost over, but the pool of fallen petals holds the light as pale flowers mysteriously do, even when dark has come. How quickly the garden has submerged enlightened man's brief energetic rule. Wild peas have pulled down the ranks of white tobacco flowers I helped prick out in April: I can see them glimmering in the border at ground level; and bindweed has woven a cocoon round Nemo's prized Rosa Mundi. Sharp unsettled cries of settling birds come from the wood, and the warm air is stagnant and curdled; the weather is on the turn. Rusted bars of cloud have closed in over half the sky.

I

Nemo's mother was a blue-stocking *manqué* and christened her Mnemosyne, after the Greek muse of memory, and so as to recapture, perhaps, the honeymoon on which she was conceived. But everyone shortened it to Nemo, so she ended up as Latin instead, the Latin for 'no one'. James called her Mo, but that had an aura of Wimbledon and frilly knickers, and I thought the Latin for 'no one' was better. At least it was wide open to other meanings: and I am not the first to find such haunting negatives full of vague suggestion. She dwelt among the untrodden ways, one felt; quoth the raven nevermore. Good reverberative stuff – intriguing, to put it at its lowest.

She was dark and fey and in her early thirties when I met her, when I met them, her and James, looking round the house. Unlike me, they were prospective buyers: they had collected the keys from the agents; and I – and an anonymous carload of sightseers with children – took the chance to see inside the house while we could.

She was unremarkable, I suppose; rather untidy, in dark glasses and faded trousers. I was so intent on the business of entering and opening up the house I already knew so well from the outside that I barely noticed her then.

We trooped through the hall and made straight for the 'receps' so highly recommended on posters and in the particulars. The big bell-shaped drawing room was in darkness, pierced by white light slanting through the cracks in the shutters, that muddied into slices of bright dust as we moved through them. James and I worked at the catches and forced them open, and the folding leaves clattered back into their niches. Then another, then another, round the great bow.

Blinded by the incoming light, I turned to see the room we had woken. Almost a third of the wall space was absorbed by those soaring casements. The proportions were immaculate; there were fine mouldings and an austere marble fireplace. Uncluttered, a bowl of light, the room was as noble and bare and beautiful as I had known it would be.

'I won't spoil its bareness,' she said.

So then I looked at her. She was standing in the dusty sunbeams staring up at the pure curve, her sunglasses in her hand, and her eyes were golden – coruscating with swarming specks of light like the small rare beetles that gild the corpse of an Amazon explorer. I knew very well that in shadow, and on her passport, her eyes would be 'brown': a poor two-dimensional sort of word, applied indiscriminately to those dead beads set into some faces like pairs of currants, as well as to those peat streams floored with mica pebbles, and dark Jamaican rum filled up with crushed ice, and the zircons, and chips of iron pyrites – aptly named 'fool's gold' – that spin through my mind in the suspended second, as if I were a drowning man.

I suppose I fell in love – became obsessed, anyway. I date it from then. All at once, frightened by the impact, of her voice echoing my thoughts, her eyes making a troubled hive of my brain, I left them. I went to discover my house and to be alone.

That, in brief, was our initial encounter; and it would be unfair to myself and to the truth – the reason for writing this – if I did not admit I was in a vulnerable frame of mind. One obsession breeds another and I was already fanatically involved in the place itself; for finding it had been just such another blinding encounter, and in the space of about ten days had developed into a passion.

The Dower House at Sutton Hamden had been widely advertised. Large posters, bearing a medium-sized, medium-grey photograph and a lot of information, had been up on several hoardings in Oxford – outshone by, but outliving, the week's gaudy films. 'This unique Georgian residence . . . four recep . . . six bed . . . scope for modernization and renovation . . . Walled garden with serpentine feature, orchard, wood; seven acres in all . . .'

The grey photograph was effective, haunting by virtue of its very faults. It tugged at the eye like the smudged portrait in a newspaper that one senses immediately is a blow-up from a school group or family album, and that spells, without the aid of a caption, 'No other available picture' or 'Missing, presumed dead'. Flat and uncontrived, hastily – even furtively – taken, in a poor light, the poster showed little more than a Georgian bow front, a blasted acacia tree, curved steps disappearing into long grass. Noble and forlorn, good lines, sad eyes. I had noticed it many times: it was to be auctioned in July.

I wanted no house. My rooms in College were extremely comfortable: by the time they reach forty, bachelor dons have usually feathered a snug nest, part of the vicious circle that keeps them bachelors. But driving back from London through Sutton Hamden one warm evening in June, I passed the poster again, this time surmounted by a large red arrow. It took me several minutes to turn in the lay-by, get back across the rush-hour stream and into the lane, by which time I was cursing my curiosity and thirsting for my cool rooms and a drink.

The Dower House was posted again at the fork in the lane, which narrowed, pressed in on by bolsters of cow parsley. Soon it degenerated into a pitted track, and disappeared at last under a tunnel of holly that scratched along the car roof and made me duck involuntarily. All I could see ahead was a section of pink brick and a mess of yellow roses.

I emerged into the sun, and the secret garden opened up to me, curving away on either side and closing its arms again around the old house. There were noble ancient trees that kept their distance – acacia, tulip, cedar – and then an inner ring where the L of the house was continued by overgrown box hedge. This in turn had as its centre a wide circle of grass in the gravelled drive, and a straggling rose tree shed its petals into the bowl of a broken fountain. All this before the gravel was silent and the car door slammed; then, after the traffic and din, the astonishing quiet as I stood and gazed round, and gradually became aware of the sounds of the wood below.

They drew me along a path that led between the tall Georgian wing and the strangled herbaceous border, all willow herb and wild sweet peas, out on to the west lawn. There was the bow front of the poster – not grey but faded golden plaster that seemed to gather in the sunlight and hold it like honeycomb. Beyond, the Thames, improbably blue, wound through the view and disappeared behind high hollies and beeches in the steep wood, where a dense undergrowth of laurels and rhododendrons clothed the slope and lapped the edges of what had been a lawn.

Columbines sprouted and flowered between the steps, and I sat on the hot stone and leaned back against the curve of the house. I could make out a pair of double-sculls, delicate waterboatmen shapes, scratching the surface of the far-off river, and caught the metallic bark of an invisible coach distorted by the loud-hailer. Louder and nearer was the purr of wood pigeons, almost continuous, and now and then a woodpecker's brief Morse, and the off-key June call of a cuckoo, quite close at hand.

I felt no impulse to explore further. This was no fumbling hasty flirtation. This was love, and however short the affair must be, I would draw out every moment of it. For this place was mine until the auction. There would be time to find out the hidden places of the garden and the wood, the orchard and the serpentine wall. Now I simply wanted to bask in the sun and my new passion, to plight my troth.

I remembered a case of white wine in the boot of the car, and fetched a bottle, which I took back to the steps. I opened it with my gadgety penknife and tilted it to my mouth. It was too warm, but it was like supping liquid sun, looking up the barrel of the bottle and watching the bubbles break through.

Gradually the shadows lengthened across the grass, chilling the shaggy stones: I corked my bottle and rose. Now pheasants were churring domestically down in the spreading beeches, and the cuckoo had closed in, haunting me from the top of the tulip tree. The broad border was still in sunlight, and over it a cloud of insects simmered like a heat haze. I unwound a sprig of lavender from its swag of bindweed and put it in my buttonhole. Stopping to look at the two wings of the house – the grey-gold Georgian stucco, its pompous porch flaking under the damp load of honeysuckle, and the older kitchen block of humble brick – I was struck by its dual nature. It would be an expansive versatile house, I felt; and I was moved both by the neglected beauty of the place and by its potential as a way of life, a self-sufficient paradise I would never want to leave.

I travel light, even counting the hoarded treasures and comforts of my college rooms. No ties – *frei aber einsam*. I never get involved; but I decided to indulge in a brief affair with this secret place. Tomorrow I would return, as soon as the morning's teaching was over, with work and a picnic.

I drove away slowly down the gravelled track, watching the pink brick and the yellow roses growing smaller in the mirror. Then I was enclosed in the dark holly tunnel and found myself outside in the lane, like Alice, full of wonder and disbelief.

2

There was very little about the Dower House in the Victoria County History to add to the passing references of the handbook on the Great House nearby. Mention was made of the 'crinkle-crankle wall' and of the 'oval room' – the bow-ended drawing room, presumably, looking out over the Thames. But one might hazard a guess that the wood below the house was the furthest extremity, perhaps the Wildernesse itself, of Capability Brown's grand garden scheme. The wild west lawn was a platform that fell away with dramatic steepness unnatural to that part of Oxfordshire, forming a self-conscious vantage point as marked in Michelin guides, and the oldest trees, cedar and acacia, were set to frame a water-colourist's view up the Hamden reach to the fabled spires.

I found, however, references to famous visitors who had mentioned or stayed at the Dower House: Oliver Goldsmith, Boswell, the actress Sarah Moore; and there was an allusion to a fire, the occasion for some rebuilding. My house, as I now thought of it, was interesting enough, mysterious enough, to justify my interest, if not my passion. That, I determined, should be deliciously unreasonable.

In England, hot clear weather is most likely to be the euphoria of fever – unhealthy flush, overbright eye – that precedes the spasm, the storm. Day after day of sun is something we are unprepared for, like all extremes in a sensible moderate-minded country: 'set fair' is a term the English use cautiously, and do not really understand.

But the sun that flowed down my tilted wine-bottle when I plighted my troth to my house, and had built up in the stone I sat on like a storage heater, was in its third day, and continued for three miraculous weeks. Water, and the choice in iced lollies, ran short; baths in College were rationed. Undergraduate plays in College gardens lost their premiums on rain-insurance but played to full houses through the warm midgey evenings. At Commem Balls the expensive striped tents were abandoned: both groups and dancers performed tieless and shoeless on the immemorial lawns.

Most of the exams were over: only a few of the more obscure sciences still drew in their clutch of students perspiring in subfusc, and through the open windows of the Examination Schools filtered the cries of the free, hailing one another from open cars and bicycles on matters of tennis, of punts, of strawberries.

I still had two-thirds of my normal tutorials to keep me in College. I was forced to decree that the academic gown should not be worn over the bare male torso; and I found it hard to expand in depth and with full concentration on the longer poems of Milton to the girls I was paid to instruct, as they lay back against my cool leather chairs in bright wisps of clothing over which the obligatory fustian was little more than a couple of titillating black straps. I switched to Marvell and Herrick: consistency, if not high seriousness, lay in their 'sweet disorder in the dress' and 'green thought in a green shade'.

Each day as soon as I had dispatched my duties I escaped to the old house at Sutton Hamden, stopping only to get pâté or salami from the delicatessen in the covered market: I even bought an insulated plastic picnic bag to keep it cool, along with the butter and bottle of beer. I took a folding wicker bed-table acquired long ago in an auction because it was pretty. I had never found a use for it; but now I set it across my knees as I sat on the south steps, and spread out my books and goodies. The sun arced over and sloped down the western sky, and I moved to the broader columbine-fringed stones that overlooked the Thames.

As I got to know the garden, my desire to explore the house itself increased; but it was an ultimate, a crowning goal, and I enjoyed a constant state of expectation suitable to a man in love. I knew that one day, perhaps tomorrow, I would walk in and open the shutters and watch it waken, and it would be all mine. But on the severely practical level it was a matter of monopolizing the keys for a day – and I was assured by the agent that they were in increasing demand as the auction drew nearer – or being on the spot when serious buyers arrived with the keys and ingratiating my way in. This was not the scenario I had planned, and twice I turned away the chance.

Once I returned from a walk down to the river and found the front door open; but the lilac E-type parked before it, and the sallow toddler that stood scratching with a nail-file at the crumbling stucco, made me head for my car and back to College. Another time as I sat eating my salami on the south steps, two large cars arrived, and a well set-up middle-aged couple, with the agent, did the usual round. The agent nodded pleasantly at me as they passed. I heard the rich booming voices of the solid prospective buyers condemning the old brick wing – 'That of course will have to come down' – and the agent's smooth agreeing murmur. I was so incensed, even alarmed, that I nearly bit through the neck of my beer-bottle; all at once they were monstrous. As they passed back, red-faced blue-haired aliens, I heard them talking in a strange tongue of four-car garages, and a shooting syndicate – to cope with the pheasants in the wood. Then I heard them unlocking the front door. I could not bear it – I gathered up my books, my unfinished picnic and fled. I did not go back for three days – thinking it preferable to kill my love than witness something worse than death.

But of course I returned. I told myself I had always known

18

it was a doomed passion – mine for such a little while: it was contrary to all the rules laid down for those who love and move on, to agonize over who should have it afterwards. Sitting at my desk in College, or even working in a deck chair in the formal garden, littered with tanning bodies, I knew just how far the shadow of the tulip tree would have reached across the shaggy lawn, and how the crushed wild camomile would give out its sweet-and-sour scent now the sun had touched the western side. I went back.

By this time I knew the garden well. I knew the border was full of promise under the wild sweet peas and white nettles; and I had waded through the deep orchard grass and found a pair of old beehives and a small chicken run on the far side.

The walled acre itself was virtually impenetrable. Here the sun and the high sides had acted like a pressure cooker. Above a kitchen garden gone mad, giant cow-parsley towered with spreading umbrella flower-heads of extra-terrestrial proportions. Gooseberries, loganberries, arti-chokes, rhubarb were there, glimpsed or guessed at, but all as safe as Princess Aurora, guarded by the all-encompassing brambles – and, no doubt, the basking adder. It was real adder weather.

The wood was another world. By this time the house had been empty more than a year, and untended for many more: the Wildernesse had been neglected so long that a genuine wildness was returning to it. Man must have planted those oppressive evergreens and laid out the winding paths that threaded them; but they had flourished monstrously, outgrown their strength, fallen, taken hold and grown again, fighting upwards to the light. Down here you could still make your way through. For under the gloom of laurel and rhododendron no weed took root; only a few pale ferns sprouted in the black leaf-mould. The winding tunnels were low, and blocked in many places by huge tree-trunks, spongy with age – almost mould themselves – richly matted with acid green moss and shelved with scarlet fungus. And always there was the sweet carrion smell of Dead Men's Fingers, growing somewhere deep in the laurel thickets. It was, I suppose, an ecologist's paradise of its kind, where the diversity of life-forms worked away like a restless yeast at every level in the steamy shade.

There was something, even then, that was vaguely threatening about the wood: you felt, like Grandmother's Footsteps, it might be a little closer when you turned round again. So, though I explored the Wildernesse, I preferred the upper garden and its level distances, the fragile plume of the tulip tree, the long walk with its wavy wall and arching sprays of ancient scented roses, even the prodigal walled garden. And it was all mine, just for a while.

Then came the time when, late one afternoon, two cars drove ahead of me up the lane into the holly tunnel and parked round the gravel circle. The Boyces had the keys, the other car was just a coincidence of sightseers; and then there was me, jealously guarding my domain. But this time I did not look too closely at the invaders. This time I was determined to break into my house.

So we opened the shutters, and saw the bare beauty of the rooms, and the woman spoke, and I looked at her eyes for too long. I fled from the drawing room, got well away from them to the old wing and found myself in the farthest corner of the L, where the small unshuttered cottage windows looked out over the northern valley.

Not since I was seventeen had I suffered such a *coup de foudre*. Here I was at forty, secure enough, rich enough, neither to toil nor to spin too arduously where need for female society was concerned, here I was tangling eyes with a woman, middle-aged – well, thirty-five, perhaps – married, who had barged into my sacred preserves with her hairy husband and spoke as if she already owned the place.

And this was no stranger on a train: the chances of my seeing them again were manifold.

For the sake of the house I would worm my way into their shortest list of favourite people. Fresh views opened up: I would not have to relinquish my paradise. I would see it in all its seasons, being coaxed into order. The fine old trees would spring from closely mown lawns, the deadwood disappear from the thickets, the pruned espaliers bear fruit once more. The big kitchen, I thought, as I pressed back the stiff brown-painted shutters, would be bright and warm and she would move about it in a Liberty-print apron making sense of it all. But I seemed to have lost my thread of concentration. She was now impossibly mixed up with the house; and I realized with sickening certainty that I was going to fall in love.

I went from room to room, opening the doors and peering in unseeing, until I came back into the 'grand' wing, five steps up to accommodate the higher ceilings. I could hear voices and footsteps downstairs, and children in the garden. I did not look into the master suite – already it was Theirs; but I found a shuttered bedroom on the west side that felt still undiscovered. As I closed the door behind me against the sounds of intruders, a car drove away and for a moment I feared, and pretended to hope, it had been the woman and her husband. Then I tried to forget they existed, tried to recall the anticipated excitement of breaking into my house. Surely this was enough to quicken my pulse and make my knees weak at the turn of the stair. Now, all powerful and all intent, I would open the view I had never seen, the full upstairs view of the west.

The catch was both ingenious and stubborn and I bruised the heel of my hand knocking it upwards, while the half-inch of sun through the crack burned and dazzled me. I flung the shutters back and pushed up the heavy sash window. The air flowed into the stuffy room, a rich tide of late philadelphus and early honeysuckle and sounds of the wood pigeons. Then the door behind me opened. She came in and stood at the window beside me: together we saw the view from upstairs – from a high place we surveyed the kingdoms of the earth.

Here all at once we were above the trees. Now we had dazzling glimpses of a sloping mustard field; and the long blue ribbon of river laced its way through the tree-tops, continually visible until it disappeared round the curve of the hill. Only the old acacia stood higher than we did; the sparse delicate branches sprang from a massive trunk so grey and so deeply chasmed with age it was more like an outcrop of stone, an Old Man of Hoy, not twenty feet from our window. I wondered about its life expectancy – or, rather, I wondered if she would have it felled; and sensed that it was another test she would pass if it was put to her – like the bare drawing room. So I remained silent until we both felt the silence must be filled; just social pressure: and she broke first, as women do, as Nature rushes into gaps. Still looking at the view she said:

'Do you come here often?'

The conventional dance-floor opening gambit was so beautifully selected and delivered with exactly the right primness, cutting through all the red tape about the scenery and the weather; and it tacitly admitted This is an Encounter – which I liked best of all.

'Well I do, as it happens,' I said. 'I come here almost every day.'

'You will be a serious rival, I can see that. Have you had surveyors, building societies – ?'

'Oh no – I'm not interested in *buying* it,' I said. 'I'm just very taken with the place – I'm enjoying a brief doomed love affair with it before it goes to auction. In fact, this is the first time I've seen inside it, thanks to your keys. So it's just an absurdly emotional sort of voyage of discovery.'

'Well, imagine what it is for me. It's come to you gradually – I'm going through it all in one day.'

'You rather like it, do you?' I was sitting on the broad sill looking back at her. She stood in the middle of the room, her arms folded tight as though to contain her excitement. Her eyes were brown; her face, dazzling in animation, now was solemn and awed.

'Yes, I like it, much too much. James – my husband, downstairs – has warned me so often not to get worked up about houses, and specially when an auction is involved. We've looked at dozens now, and he relies on me to see what he calls home-potential – his department is the "investment quotient". But what do you *do* when you simply fall in love with a place? I don't know,' she went on, pacing and hugging her arms. 'It hasn't happened before like this. I just – well – belong to it.'

'Yes,' I said. 'You get beyond feeling possessive: you feel possessed.'

She stepped forward into the light and the eyes she turned on me with sudden concentration were gold again, swarming, addling my brain.

'How you must hate people looking round,' she said. 'Wondering who's going to bid the highest.'

'I only want it to go to someone who feels like I do about it; then I shall go on my way.' I got up, alarmed at the speed of sympathy, feeling the need to break it; but I turned at the door. 'I'm putting my money on you,' I said, and left. I felt rash, committed, drunk on those fermenting golden eyes.

I went along the landing and down the curving staircase. The husband was in the hall. He had taken up a corner of the tattered linoleum, but put it back hastily and straightened up when he saw me.

'It's all right,' I said. 'I'm not a rival purchaser – just wanted to see round the place.' He looked relieved.

'Well, give us a hand here – I think there's a rather fine floor under this that the particulars don't mention.'

Together we peeled back the cracking lino: in places it was stuck tight with mildew. There was parquet beneath; we could see it was in a pale wood, even through the dirt, with an austerely handsome border in a darker grain. Satisfied, he let the corner drop back and stepped it firmly into place.

'That's the sort of thing I like to know about – but there's no need to advertise it. I suspected the floors might be rather good. Altogether pretty sound, structurally, I'd say, though the kitchen wing needs a lot doing to it. Have you seen it? Dark and damp – it amazes me really how dry these reception rooms feel, considering –'

Then I told him about the Victoria County History and the mention of some rebuilding during the Regency, which had included something of an innovation in damp courses. We went back into the drawing room to a trapdoor he had noticed in the floor – the dull gleam of the sunken brass handle had caught his eye. With my penknife we worked it free of dirt, raised it and lifted clear the square hatch. Below was perhaps four feet of space running under the joists. He was jubilant.

'This would make the heating and electrical operations a very different matter,' he said, brushing off his trousers. He went out into the hall and called: 'Mo, come and look here –' Mo. Not the name I would have chosen for my projected sonnet sequence. But his enthusiasm was infectious; and while I resisted the excitement of shared discovery as much as I could – it made me feel like a collaborator – still I was well aware that it was just this sort of thing that, for him, might tip the balance in favour of the house. I wanted her to have it and live in it: with my hot tips from the VCH, I was a Greek bearing gifts.

We introduced ourselves then; and while we put back

the shutters he told me he was the new Economics Fellow at Crispin College, starting in October; now they had moved from London into a rented flat, and were looking at houses, in between his freelance articles and the usual trips to Rome, Geneva, Brussels in fringe EEC activities – he was a ready talker, probably not much of a listener, but likable enough. At the front door he stopped and called again: 'Nemo!' She was coming slowly down the curling stairs in the shuttered gloom; but I knew she was not feeling her way – she was caressing the silken banister, right down to the final snail-shell curve. We went out into the quiet L of shadow that smelt of honeysuckle. I could not let her go yet: the sun would be low and yellow on the western steps, the pheasants beginning to settle in the wood below.

'I've got some wine in the car,' I said, 'if you don't mind the lack of glasses. You ought to see the best part of the day.'

So we spread ourselves out among the columbines and the smell of crushed camomile and passed the bottle round. She sat looking at the view and the sinking sun; it shone into her eyes, and I watched them sizzle. James scribbled in a notebook.

'I estimate something in the neighbourhood of ten thousand to put it right,' he was saying, 'structurally, decorationally and service-wise, excluding frills.' He looked up, put away his calculations and pronounced.

'It's unique – the site alone is worth between five and ten. That'll put up the price; but the state of the brick wing will put off a lot of private buyers. Not the developers: they'd bulldoze it anyway just to fit in another dwelling unit. It really turns on that old wing: if you're determined to save it, Mo, well – it could cost anything. On top of the central heating, plumbing, rewiring . . . Maybe it's just too much to take on.'

She was watching him closely now, and cutting in with practical points about lath-and-plaster, rolled steel joists, plastic membrane. It took me by surprise, how down to earth my sunbeam dreamer could be. No talk now of being in love with the place, no hint of obsession – it was a secret bond. Or was she embarrassed now, I wondered, by her outburst? As if in answer, she suddenly turned and smiled sweetly at me for no reason at all, except that James was saying 'Oh, absolutely –' and tilting back the wine-bottle. Reason enough, come to think of it: she had as good as persuaded him, in his own language and in the only terms he knew, while all around us the darkening garden and the facing golden walls spoke softly of mystery and the things of the heart. We finished the wine and watched the light go; and the wild white flowers on the edge of the wood and in the border became luminous in the dusk. Then we said good-bye, I wished them luck, and we went our separate ways.

I only went back to the house once more before the auction, but it had changed. It was no longer just mine. Even the little vine I had rescued, now carrying a tassle of embryonic grapes, obscurely disappointed me without Nemo there to see. Latin for no one. So a pedant could cuckold the hairy James and claim truthfully, 'I have been to bed with no one.' But it was poor barren humour, a court-jester on an off-day. Mnemosyne. Memory, haunted by. Ridiculous name. I did my rounds, and sat down with my books. A car came up the drive, and I pricked my ears; but it wasn't the Boyces. I found I couldn't settle to anything. I could no longer enjoy the place for itself, for myself: for now I minded too much about the outcome of the auction. I might have been high on the Epsom downs, listening to the larks and watching the milling race-course through field glasses as if it were no more than a pretty kaleidoscope: but I had abandoned the long, the philosophical view, and now stood sweating on the crowded rails, with all the money I owned on one horse.

3

I did not see the Boyces again before the great day; I even resisted telephoning the agents until five o'clock. 'Oh, very exciting, sir – a very good crowd. It fetched just over forty –' My heart sank: I knew that was well above the sort of figure James had mentioned. 'Bought by an academic gentleman like yourself, sir, I understand – a Mr James Boyce –'

Then I telephoned James in his college to offer up my congratulations. He was very affable and gave me a fifteen-round account of the auction, culminating in the coolest knockout in the history of the ring.

'– And I just said, quite quietly, you know: "And fifty." And this other chappie got the idea, *finalmente*, that I wasn't going to give up – and that was it.' It reminded me of John Ridd's great confrontation with Carver Doone: 'He could see from my knitted muscles . . . but most of all, from my stern blue eyes that he had found his master . . .'

I was going to Spain for a short holiday and had to refuse James's pressing invitation to join them and a few friends on Saturday to celebrate with a picnic. Never mind, I thought: my horse has won; and I was happy to have the pay-out deferred. I promised to go out to the Dower House on my return.

As I look back on it, sitting alone now at the big kitchen table, and trying to see an order in events – a pattern that I should have perceived at the time – there was more than just its own intrinsic significance in the first visit I paid to the house after my holiday. It was an afternoon of cloud and sun – the rains had come and gone in my absence – and Nemo was measuring for carpets and curtains while James went round with a builder. For me it was my first visit knowing that the place I loved was going to stay in my life. What part it was going to play I did not attempt to define – though that day, I now realize, I might have felt the first chill of misgivings.

Knowing they could do little to the house itself before the full-scale building operations, Nemo and James had started on the garden, and had called in a tree-surgeon and his gang as first on their list of priorities. The giant cedar of Lebanon had been scaled and put in order, dead branches removed, and a tall fir tree that had fallen against it, spoiling and blocking one long sloping entrance to the wood, had been sawn up and stacked. The old acacia was trimmed, lopped, strengthened with a bolt; and while they were there the gang had opened out the view to the Thames. It was only a start, but already the place felt cared for. 'Those big trees are really the feature of the garden, as I see it,' James said.

'They are in our care now,' said Nemo: 'we've inherited them – and they'll be here long after we've gone.' I think they were both not a little awed by the sudden reality of what they had taken on. James was full of the 'challenge' of it – and busy justifying, for his own peace of mind, his over-bidding; backing his hunch. Nemo, on the other hand, was like a child who had been given not a new toy but the whole shop: still stunned by the miracle – and the responsibility. 'D'you realize, Harry,' she kept saying, 'this is ours? It's *all ours?*'

I left them and went round the grounds to see what had been done. Now all the lawns had been treated to a first rough cut; and someone had started attacking with an auto-scythe the edge of the waste of nettles that menaced the long walk. There was a rough-hewn track all round the walled garden, and two dead fruit trees in the orchard near the beehives had been felled. It was all very green and lush after the rain, with the smell of cut grass and crushed nettles.

Then I went down into the wood, through paths where the laurel and rhododendron had been trimmed back with secateurs just enough not to whip coldly across the face or catch at the ankles; and other ways that had been opened. I took the long way round by the boundary fence, down under the yews and twisted hollies to the little iron gate that led out to the ferry path and the river; then turned back under the huge copper beech, and arrived for the first time at the clearing, the centre of the Wildernesse to which all the paths led.

It was oppressively still, turning what was, after all, a bright open space into something like the bottom of a well: the wind passed above, but down there the air was unmoving. The towering hollies to the north and the copper beech marking the western boundary formed a dark backdrop, a protective screen, and two tall macrocarpas, lush with the emerald fur of new growth, marked out a sort of stage. Round me the foxgloves were nearly over, and a fork and wheelbarrow showed where Nemo and James had started weeding. Yet there was something already unhealthily over-tended about the place. In spite of the scattering of nettles that flourished there under the open sky, it had obviously been kept clear over the years; the foxgloves had been sown along the sides, and azaleas set round the lower edge. Nemo had told me of these. 'They'll be spectacular in the spring, like a ring of fire,' she said.

I found the clearing strangely claustrophobic, and sensed an unease, a restlessness in myself that was at odds with my joyous voyage of rediscovery. Why should I feel moody and disturbed when the house I loved was safely in Nemo's hands, and Nemo herself so warm and welcoming? I enumerated my blessings and started back through the dark everglades, found a new path and came out in the small clearing made by the removal of the fallen fir tree. Here the sawn bole was neatly stacked under the cedar, the fresh damp sawdust powerfully resinous; and now the view was clear up the steep grassy slope below the west front. I looked up under the black dragonish shapes of the branches and saw the house from a totally new angle. The shock of discovery halted and held me.

It was not just that the slate-blue cumulus cloud that had covered most of the sky suddenly threw the building into glaring relief, the lurid sunlight turning the faded gold of the walls to a deep unhealthy orange. It was a different house from here, tall, menacing, desolate – a stranger to me, staring out with blank bloodshot eyes across the darkening land. Now, from this angle the old acacia that had been struck by lightning reared lopped branches against the threat of the sky, isolated by the line of view from the softer shapes of the lower trees. The total effect was shocking; it was both alien and sinister. There's more to this place than meets the eye, I thought, in spite of myself. I would not say I was given to idle fancies, yet at that moment the house's intrinsic age seemed more like accumulated knowledge. It will be like marrying a woman with a past, I thought; she may never speak of it, but it is always there. And sometimes, in a light like this, you will catch her remembering.

Then a faint shiver of breeze, the first cold breath of the gathering storm, rustled the top branches of the evergreen wood, and I climbed the slope into the sun.

That evening, while the rain lashed at the windows, and the trees, with all the weight of high summer, tossed and roared in the wind, we built a fire in the morning room, and by its light, and that of two candles Nemo had fixed with wax to the mantelpiece, we ate our cold *quiche* and drank our wine. There was no electricity yet, and we wound up the gramophone and played through the odd selection of heavy old seventy-eights inherited from Nemo's nursery days – the Intermezzo from *Cavalleria Rusticana, Pale Hands I Loved,* the *Light Cavalry Overture* and the *Daring Young Man on the Flying Trapeze.* There was not enough light even for James to continue with drawing out his large squared-paper plans, and he gave up and relaxed. He had found an old car seat in one of the outbuildings, and stretched out on it luxuriously with his feet in the grate. Nemo lay on her stomach on the picnic rug, propping her chin on her arms and watching the logs crumble, and I put a packing case against the wall by the fireplace and watched them both in the firelight. They talked desultorily of plans and dates and projects: Nemo seemed determined to move in and camp before the builders arrived at the end of September. They would clean up the kitchen and get the old Aga going; the electrician promised to come and test, and if need be, patch up any usable circuits.

'If we could have enough to plug in my power drill – and a fridge,' said James.

'And a record-player . . .' said Nemo.

I remember it as a rather special evening. For I was still curiously shaken by the new angle I had seen of the house, that glimpse of its dual personality – though I said nothing about it – and the stormy evening, however shuttered and firelit, had done nothing to dispel it. But now, with Nemo, it felt more like a dare than a threat. After all, had I not sensed, on my first encounter with it, that it was a house of many moods and for all seasons; and on my first meeting with her, that she was the chosen person to live out my dreams? Now that the wild neglected spirit of the place was showing its claws, should I doubt that she could tame it?

But before we left, when we were fastening the shutters in the big drawing room by the light of James's powerful gas lighter, I remember feeling quite distinctly I was shutting something out, something that was more than just the draught that whistled through the broken pane and between the overlap of the sashes, and blew out the fierce hissing flame: something that pushed as I pushed. James swore and flicked at the lighter without success, and we finished fumbling in the semi-dark. He kept up a running commentary on the advantages and drawbacks of double-glazing; but Nemo stood near the fire and was silent. I think she had become aware of the darker side, of that dual nature, before I did; and I felt from that evening it was something to do with the wood. I knew she had been down there many times – was, I thought, inordinately fond of it: she who on her own admission was readily susceptible to the nuances of atmosphere and suggestion, which I was not. I told myself, driving home, that it just happened to be the 'weather side'; exposed as it was to the north and west, you felt in those rooms you were on a headland – the nearest windbreak was the distant line of Wytham.

Yet the wood certainly had a way of pressing in on you. The laurels were lapping over the lawn before James cut them back; and in the evening the pleasing sounds of the roosting pheasants soon gave way to the monotone of owls, sudden sharp cries of pain, and the endless dry rustle of the tallest hollies. Sleeping in one of those west-facing rooms with the window open wide, as I did later on that autumn, one's dreams were constantly invaded by that restless flood of sighs and screams and whispers – just bloody Nature, as my father would say; but what is background music to the peaceful heart can turn nightmare where there is the least hint of unease.

4

It was late in August, when I had finished with the reading party I took to Scotland, that I was summoned to the house for supper – a proper meal, James told me on the telephone: they had moved in, and now, though they still had no drinking water, the solid-fuel range was in operation and some electric light from a couple of runs of good cable. Heating was still confined to open fires; fortunately there was firewood and to spare, for the summer that started so gloriously was ending with unseasonable chill, its passion spent too soon.

Oxford seemed empty, except for Parks Road, where there were always scientists – glassy-eyed, observing neither the customs of the seasons nor those of day and night – and there were the maples. These, the barometers of autumn as the North Oxford prunus is that of spring, were already on the turn; and driving out to Sutton Hamden I saw a sulphurous breath had touched the elms, and all the oaks were dark and rusty. My tulip tree bore one brilliant yellow branch, high against the sky, the border was full of ragged Michaelmas daisies, and the apples were ripening.

On all sides I saw the change effected not by the seasons but by human hand: clipped hedges, close-mown lawns, urns of geraniums and newly planted trees dwarfed by hefty stakes. The gravel circle where I parked – there were three other cars – was clear of weeds, the honeysuckle had been lifted and trained back against the house, and a white-painted bench set against it, for drinking one's coffee in the morning sun. The place was not simply coming to life: it was being lived in.

Nemo was cooking at the Aga with Frazier, the small white dog, at her feet, while people stood round drinking. James came in with an armful of logs for the fire in the brick hearth on the other side of the kitchen, where they had arranged an assortment of stools and benches round a large Victorian mahogany table, this week's bargain. 'I really wanted pine,' said Nemo, 'but it was so cheap – and two of the leaves come out, with a lovely handle to crank it open. It was terribly scabby when James got it; he's been scrubbing and polishing like a maniac – actually it's quite a lovely piece of wood.' (It is, but it looks sad and heavy now, with the lot number still stuck on it for the auction last month; and the elaborate legs have gathered dust.)

Leaving the supper in a warm oven and James pouring drinks, Nemo took me on a tour of the house. Nothing basically was changed, but it was as if it had been filled in by a child with a box of new felt pens. Brilliant rugs were spread on the bare swept boards, pictures hung wherever an old nail had been and posters were arranged over the patches of damp. A big oval looking-glass propped on the drawing-room mantelpiece repeated and extended the vista through the morning room and into the garden, and in the kitchen, neatly stacked under the blackened brick arches, were saucepans, biscuit tins, coffee-pots in primary colours. The sombre green dresser was hung like a Christmas tree with mugs on glinting brass hooks, and covered with bowls of fruit and paper fans and postcards; and there were jugs-full, jam-jars-full, egg-cups-full of flowers tame and wild in every room. Of course there was furniture too; not enough to clutter the main lines, but it, and the firelight, and the candles softened the gaunt elegance of the old rooms with their brown paint and their drab peeling paper hung with the shadows of absent pictures.

'You were the right person for this place, Nemo,' I said as we stood together in the bow end of the drawing room, looking out at the mown lawn spreading from the urns of geraniums and at the sunset Thames beyond. 'Do you feel that, now you're here?'

'It's much more complicated than that really, isn't it?' she said after a pause. 'A house and garden that have been so long on their own have grown, well, not just neglected, but somehow independent. Does that sound ridiculous? I feel one has to approach it with caution, almost – and subdue it by degrees – which is why I was so intent on moving in before James started tearing it apart. He would like to get it all done, right down to the last door knob, in one clean sweep, as if it needed sterilizing before we could use it. I believe if he had his way, and unlimited money, he would smooth it all out – plaster the uneven walls and replace the worn flagstones – renew these shutters, even, where the cross-bars have swung across over the years – see? – and chewed into the wood. It's just age, after all, like lines and wrinkles – as I said to him. He said, "Who wants lines and wrinkles?" . . . I don't know, Harry. I *hope* I'm right for the house. It's right for me, I feel. But then we're only an incident in its life, really.'

Semantically, I could not justify the impression I had that 'we' did not include James. Physically, I could. It was tacit in the way the slow golden glance slid over me as she said it, like the lozenges of sunlight on the old blue tiles of the fireplace, bringing them momentarily to life. With a conscious effort I stuck to the train of thought.

'More of a turning point, Nemo,' I said. 'You've persuaded James to buy it, and beaten the developers; you've saved the brick wing, and you've given the whole place a new lease of life. As for its wild side – well, I for one hope it always keeps something of that. I don't believe even James would be able to subdue it completely; and if he did, it would simply wait, and win in the end.' (I did not mean to be fanciful, or sinister. I only meant to align our sympathy with the house against James's blind reforming energy. But we were all blind then, and the glib words were prophetic.)

We heard James calling and started back to the kitchen, with Frazier leading the way along the passage.

'Here James is going to have The Billiards, he says.' Nemo opened the door into the long sombre room where generations of dead dowagers had dined. 'He wants proper lights, you know – to catch the curling cigar smoke and the gleaming mahogany – and heavy curtains and naughty busts. I'm going to contribute a keen little waistcoat so he can be like those Wolverhampton worthies one sees playing on the telly – perhaps some really fancy braces for hot weather . . .'

Now I see that period when the Boyces were camping in the house awaiting the builders as Before the Fall. In such a time-scheme the first clang of scaffolding marks clearly the flight of innocence, the beginning of change. But I know very well that change was already working away. For their tragedy was propagated, like fungus, underground, with a secret cobweb-like motion. Fungus can creep through a brick. And the timeless spore had long lain dormant. It simply began to move.

All I can claim is that this was their happiest time, when Nemo and James played at the simple life. It must have felt real enough, gathering wood early in the chill September mornings to light the fire they ate their breakfast by; carrying water by the bucket from the one good well; scrubbing out clothes (those that did not go to the laundrette) in the shallow trough in the scullery; keeping the oil lamps clean and trimmed; scraping the dirt of centuries out of the corners of cupboards; mopping the uneven stone floor of the kitchen with water heated on the range; and bathing by candlelight in two rusty inches of it. But it was all a game, a time-trip into the hard life and hard-won pleasures of another period, and arcadian only because it was temporary.

Nemo might, I think, have been happy if time had stopped altogether. Each gently busy day was perfectly satisfying. Feeling both pioneer and provider, she would tunnel through the jungle of the kitchen garden, with Frazier in pursuit, to forage for windfall apples, for herbs and blackberries. The discovery of a cache of dusty stoneware jars in a shed, of an overgrown potato patch under the nettles, of a rickety carved wooden stool inside the chicken house – these had become the events in her life; and she took her time, even over the chores, as if savouring the true flavour of each moment.

James indulged her, and when she went and sat on the steps to peel her windfalls or hem up an old curtain he came round with a can of beer, and, weary of mowing or nettle-chopping, lay back and gazed out over his broad acres, all seven of them. James, so restlessly energetic, always looking for new worlds to conquer, seemed to have paused in flight and caught the mood, of leisurely pioneering and assumed simplicity. If anything he over-played the part. He rather fancied himself as a D. H. Lawrence figure, in his Army Surplus boots, two days' stubble and a red neckerchief, the hairy forearms scratched and beaded with blood from grappling with the brambles man to man. His only concession to the supper was that the torn shirt was clean; but the wives there that evening seemed to like it well enough.

I felt he not only over-acted: he over-verbalized. And this was perhaps the only jarring note: I could see how frequently he threatened to spoil Nemo's fragile world by exposing it to words. Not simply an academic disease, it chiefly sprang from boredom, I think. His restless ticking nature soon tired of the common round, and he had to play word games to divert himself, to divert others. For him to enjoy or even, it seemed, to experience the day's little victories, they had to be clothed in words, set out for display as by some tireless press photographer – 'Hold that!'

This evening he and Bob MacLean were batting words about as if they were disposable plastic shuttlecocks; or, alternatively, building card castles of projects, of imagery, of fantasy, each too busy with his own to pause and admire the other's. Bob, a science-fiction writer with a sweet admiring wife, was another word merchant, and one of James's best friends. They were very good company, James the best of hosts, Bob the life and soul. But I felt, and sensed that Nemo felt, it was never enough for them that the sun was setting, that the honeysuckle was sweet, that the stew was good.

It was a side of James that I had not really seen before. Admittedly the other two occasions had been dominated by concern with the acquisition of the house. Perhaps Nemo and I had not been the right audience to spark it off; for I guessed that on this occasion it was both a party trick and the accumulation of high spirits.

I was glad that he was happy: he had every possible reason to be, in my opinion. I only wondered what he was like when they were alone together; for Nemo was not a batter of words – though she had an instinct for the apt, and I knew from our first encounter she could talk compulsively, but always *im*pulsively. I imagined they would speak mostly of practical matters. Nemo was deeply practical; you could tell by the way she moved and handled things. She played the old black range like an organist; and whether she was wielding a hod or chopping chives, whether she was trapping a butterfly fluttering against a pane or hurling a dead rabbit over the hillside, she did it both gracefully and capably. James achieved less but with more effect: he even stacked plates dramatically, and when he brought in a bucket of water he became a Water-carrier, with flair. Don't call us, we'll call you, I felt. Meanly.

No – they were happy. And the next incident did not cause even a ripple at the time: it was accepted, in all its strangeness, as another discovery, a bonus, like the secret potato patch, or the case of wine beneath the firewood in the cellar. Something for Nemo to revel in, for James to tell his friends.

Now, as I knew from the Victoria County History, Sarah Moore had taken the Dower House for five weeks one summer in the 1820s, to enjoy the country air. She was reported elsewhere as saying: 'That beloved Dower [Bower?] is the sweetest spot, my spiritual home.' So when Nemo told us about her Happening in the wood, I suggested it was the ghost of Sarah Moore's music box that she had heard. For what more natural than amateur dramatics *al fresco*? The clearing might have been designed for just such an occasion; and though they would probably have imported musicians for the actual performance, a music box might very well have served for rehearsals.

Though we felt alike in our passion for the house – such a powerful bond that I wondered sometimes if in other circumstances I would have fallen in love – I still could not share Nemo's feeling for her magic circle deep among the evergreens. I cannot put my finger on just why I did not like the clearing. It was certainly a 'fine and private place', as I admitted to Nemo: and she resented the allusion; for it had become her favourite haunt.

It was down there one evening – it must have been late September – that it happened. They had only been camping in the house for about three weeks, and in that time had seen wind and rain and early frosts. Now they were enjoying an Indian summer. This was a clear golden evening: it had been my day in London, and I remember resenting the waste – except that I met James on the train and came back with him.

Apparently Nemo had been pulling up nettles and willow herb; she fetched a glass of wine and a cigarette to take back to her special log, where she sat surveying her handiwork and watching the sun go down behind the copper beech. That is when she heard it; and when we arrived she came up out of the wood, glass in hand, though the sun had long gone and it was chill and nearly dark. She said: 'I was waiting to see if it would come back.' And then she told us.

She was sitting there at the head of the clearing, and the dog, scuffling about under the laurels, gave two short, sharp barks. In the silence that followed she heard a music box. It was very clear and tinkling – about four and a half bars of a sugary little minuet – and then it stopped. She was so surprised she just sat and waited for more, waited for someone to step out into the circle. Nothing. No rustling, no retreating footsteps. The dog ran back to her bristling, his ears flat. She stood up and called. No answer. She went quickly down between the two tall macrocarpas to the place it had come from. Nothing. She even searched around among the fallen leaves – feeling a bit foolish, she said. She went back, sat down and waited, hoping it might come again, until it was cold and dark, and she heard the car.

Her cheeks were bright. She drank down the whisky James gave her and shivered. He said:

'What you heard was the Tonibell Ice-cream van across the river in Little Hamden.'

But she stuck to her story, and told it without any posturing or elaboration – no attempt to impress – a story so simple and factual, almost flat, that we found ourselves accepting it. 'It was precise,' she said, 'as close sounds are. I heard how the notes were made, and that irregularity, almost hesitance, as if it needed rewinding . . . I'll try again tomorrow.'

'Are you psychic, Nemo?' I asked.

'Not that I know of –'

'No –' James was serious – 'she's supersensitive, I'd say, but not psychic. A bit over-imaginative at times, perhaps.'

'I didn't imagine this, James. It was there.'

5

So it was an inexplicable fact; and we talked it over solemnly, as only sceptics can; of the possibilities of wave-lengths as yet untapped, of imprints recorded by past occasions, of Sarah Moore and amateur dramatics. James clearly liked the idea; it was added to his *hauspiel*, and he grew impatient with those well-meaning excitable friends who said, 'But of *course*! I always *felt* you had a friendly ghost.'

Then October came; bad weather moved in, and with it the builders. I saw less of Nemo and James. Term had started and I was busy in College. They dropped in one Saturday for a drink, the car loaded up with sinks and tiles, and James gave me a progress report while I watched Nemo on my window seat outlined by the light.

'– Taking far longer than we thought. Yet where there is only decorating needed, it seems Mo can't make up her mind –'

There was a tight-drawn thread of strain stretching between them, tempting to pluck: I felt the unworthy stir of hope, and disliked myself for it.

'How is it, Nemo?' I asked. 'Making it all come alive?'

'It's at its worst, actually – it can only get better.' She smiled wanly. 'It was so lovely, somehow, before. That's all gone.'

'Mo feels we're spoiling it. "Unreverberative" – that's the new word.' He made it sound as if words were his preserve.

'Talking about reverberations,' I said, 'has Sarah Moore wooed you again with her music box?'

Nemo looked up, startled. James answered for her.

'No. Been down to that damn wood almost every evening. Not a sausage.'

'No, but I think she's round the house now,' said Nemo.

'Friendly?' I asked.

'More like whiney: unexplained cold draughts and a sense of outrage,' said James sourly. 'Drink up – we've got to get this stuff back.'

I went down with them to the car, and they told me they were planning a house-warming party for New Year's Eve.

'Not that it'll be anything like finished by then. There'll be the kitchen and drawing rooms anyway – if Mo can get a move on with ordering covers and curtains –'

'Well, at least there'll be *acres* of bare floors to dance on –' she said; but James was already backing noisily out of the quadrangle.

I decided then I must put a merciful end to the passion I had for this woman: the warning bell for me had been that inner quickening on witnessing their dissension. I would detach myself; three months in the States – where I was going in January – should help. Till then, with at least an attempt at detachment, I would study their differences; and I set myself to observe, as an exercise, those very divergences in their natures, in their backgrounds and their basic interests, that proved so disastrous in the events that followed.

James Boyce was one of those academics who seem to use their universities more as a club. He must have put in a certain amount of teaching; but he was always paying flying visits to Rome or The Hague, and he dabbled in more than one business in London under the vague title of Consultant. Very seldom, it seems, was he called upon to give lectures at Bangor or St Andrews, the accepted outlets of colleagues with less urgently relevant subjects than the Economics of Transport.

James was Nemo's senior by ten years, and a self-made academic of enormous ambition, now crowned by double success: a fellowship at an Old University, and a smart marriage. She was the last of a line of penniless aristocrats, and had the nerves, beauty and, in company, the assurance of the acceptable few; there was also a slightly fey eccentricity stemming from the period, the year even, of her début – the start of the era of Sensibility, before that of the Permissive had taken over, torn off the flood-gates and carried them out to sea. In California, or on another social rung, she might have turned flower-child, perhaps Jesus-freak. As it was, she had an altogether unusual charm, a strong reaction against the twinset image of her class, and more than ten years later she still carried the stamp of originality that it had all been about. She dressed more casually and unconventionally, listened to further-out music, and had a more independent line of thought than one would expect from an under-educated débutante. She trod the razor's edge of the trendy, picking the best from each passing craze and adding it to the collage of her life. She had a lot of odd friends, most of them younger than herself; but now, buried in the country and absorbed by the house, she was suddenly cut off from them. Sometimes she went to London to see them: I think that until then they had probably been the most formative element in her life.

Thus James had picked her not only from a different world but another generation. It was his one great imaginative leap: installed, she became just another of his well-made objects. (James minded about quality: he left taste to Nemo. He took pleasure in something being 'well made' – it was one of his favourite stances, and led to the justification of the stainless-steel trolley, and the condemnation of a Staffordshire fairing.)

They were an odd couple, but one could not call them ill-matched: their very contrasts made a pleasing whole, I suppose. And, seeing them at parties and dinners that winter, I had to admit they looked well together. He had the build of a rugger blue, and the sideburns and carefully chosen shirts of a dandy. Women said he was sexy, and I think, as he passed forty, and the slightly roué, mysteriously powerful man-of-the-world image increased, so did his attraction. They said it was something to do with his puffy eyes – 'like André Previn', I was informed; and I heard the Boyces described, certainly with envy, as 'the thoroughbred and the prize bull – both fine specimens, but understandably without issue'.

They had been married three years; she had been married before, and divorced, both in her twentieth year. Now the Dower House, perhaps their one real common interest and child-substitute, nevertheless made the difference more marked. Here James was even more purposeful, restless, critical, domineering; and as his hard-edge confidence increased, Nemo's sensitivity seemed to blur and soften. She seemed to grow more imaginative, more suggestible – too much alone. I even said as much to James.

'No, dear fellow,' he said. 'Just bored.'

So I stood back, when I might have helped them. If only I had not been so busy cultivating my detachment, so assiduously protecting my bachelor freedom from a grand passion. Even when I weakened and went out to the house to help plant trees or hang pictures, and I came nearer to a real understanding of Nemo and James, I was too involved in thinking 'how much better *I* know her'. I should have seen the importance of contact between them; I should have convinced James that the time for bluff scepticism was past, persuaded him to use his propensity for words in the cause of actual communication. Perhaps I am trying too hard to believe that those disasters that are unnatural can be averted – a comfortable theory, but highly questionable. Either way, the comfort is cold.

One of these visits I remember, when Nemo and I seemed peculiarly close: I was out there so late helping them to plant a dozen little eucalyptus trees that we worked on until after dark, and made ourselves scrambled eggs in the warm kitchen; and they insisted I stay to breakfast to admire our labours in daylight. Afterwards, back in College, and for many days, I thought about those precious hours, counting them over like a gold-hoard: Nemo looking at me across her hot chocolate as she cradled and blew on it – a look that seemed both at the time and on reflection as exclusive and as devastating as a kiss. Nemo making me a hot-water bottle, or lighting my candle – the flame leaping back from her golden irises – and avoiding my eyes: Negative Capability. And in the morning, after a night in which, almost deliberately, I woke many times and savoured being in my house, and the night sounds, and Nemo sleeping only yards from me, I awoke to the sound of her pulling back my curtains, the vision of her holding out a cup of tea. Then going round the garden with her before breakfast in the chill dewy stillness, the end of the Indian summer, seeing the sun breaking through the early mists and coming back with our arms full of apples.

It was then that I chose to present her with the marvellous camellia I had bought. James was not down yet: I still had her to myself. I fetched it from its pile of sacking in the boot of the car.

'Oh, Harry,' she said, standing in the kitchen door with the steaming porridge saucepan, a Delphic oracle. 'It must absolutely go in my magic circle.'

And abruptly all the sympathy, all her awareness of me, seemed to cease, to be transferred to the glossy camellia and its future. It is the only time I have felt jealous of a plant.

Then James came down; he and I breakfasted quickly and left. But even mulling it over, alone in my rooms, I was too busy treasuring, and extending, the moments I thought of as 'significant' to see that this last was the most significant of all.

During that time there was only one other occasion of any significance: early in December I was drawn out to christen the newly finished kitchen with a champagne supper, just the three of us – 'like that first time,' said Nemo, 'in the morning room, d'you remember? with the old gramophone. When the weather broke.' And I remembered what the kitchen had been like then; now the old brick arches and walls were brilliant white, the York stone floor sealed and polished, and there were tailor-made cupboards and spotlights and a streamlined sink.

It was quite late when Nemo started to question me about Sarah Moore, and changed the subject abruptly as James came back from walking the dog. Anyway, that was the evening he lugged the old looking-glass up from the cellar.

'There,' he said. 'See anything funny about that?'

'Oh, James, it's all different out here in the light – that's not fair –'

'Well, it's a bit odd,' I said, feeling my way. 'From here it looks more like dull silver than glass.'

'It's just very dark and mildewed,' said James; 'but Mo said she saw something strange in it.'

'What was it, Nemo?'

'Well –' She hesitated. 'Just myself, of course. A woman anyway. There was very little light down there and it was covered with dust. Just me, but I seemed to have a sort of hat on.'

'Arl of a quiver she were when I come 'ome,' said James in his darkest Loamshire.

'Perhaps you saw something behind you,' I said to Nemo.

'*What do you mean?*' she asked, almost under her breath.

46

'Well,' I went on quickly, 'an old lamp-shade? A bag hanging from a hook? Something that in the half-dark would merge with your reflection and look, well, like a hat.' It ended lamely and we left it lying where it fell.

'Come and see the billiards room,' said James. 'Not that it's there yet, but it's a darn sight more there than Sarah Bloody Moore.'

6

The invitation to the Boyces' New Year house-warming party arrived just before I left College for two weeks and Christmas at home. I was tempted to telephone my acceptance, so that I might wish Nemo a happy Christmas, but I resisted and confined myself to putting both on a card: I allowed myself the gratification of trudging through the sleet to the Ashmolean to get it. I knew Nemo had a special weakness for Samuel Palmer.

When I returned to Oxford I did telephone the Dower House. A strange voice answered. 'Mr and Mrs Boyce aren't back yet . . . Oh yes, they've gone abroad while we got on with the decoration. I'm one of the painters . . . Saturday, I think they said –' and he took my name down. 'Mr Boyce asked us to look after phone calls for him. Very particular he was.' I was highly impressed by the efficiency of it all; and, sure enough, James telephoned me on Sunday, only two days before the party. I congratulated him on what could only be superb organization – ten out of ten for cool, I said, flattering the ageing trendy in him.

'All fixed, Harry old thing. Nothing but the best. Disco, caterers, florists forcing their lilies for us, *fraise-de-bois* sorbet jetting in from Paris, France – you name it –'

'And how was the skiing?'

I heard all about the depth and texture of the snow, the attractions of the chalet-birds, the joys of the *cuisine*. And Nemo?

'Oh, flourishing, flourishing – a bit upset about Frazier – did you hear? He was discovered in the wood – yes, dead. No marks or blood or anything: just natural causes, I suppose. Mo says "highly unnatural for a dog in its prime just to go and die", and wants an autopsy, but I'm overruling that – there's enough to do without holding an inquest for goodness' sake. Oh, and by the way, she wanted you to bring over some of your golden oldies to plug the gaps in the disco feller's repertoire –' I was going to be in London next day; so we arranged I should come out to the Dower House on the morning of the party.

It was mild and grey and muggy: no white Christmas, and no hope of a white New Year. Aconites were already out at the edges of the wood – its green depths looked even glossier against the bare tracery of the trees beyond, and seemed more in keeping with the close hot-house weather.

James took time off from his impressarial duties to show me round the house, then left Nemo and me and the coffee in the morning room to go through the records I had brought. She wanted to tape a few tracks from my Cole Porter and Temperance Seven.

She closed the doors between the sitting rooms and went and sat on a stool by the french windows. Thinner, brown from her holiday, she looked more beautiful than I had prepared myself for. But when she turned her head to me she was preoccupied and unsmiling.

'Harry, before you start, let me just play *you* something. Actually it happened about three weeks ago and it's been bothering me. I wanted you to hear it. It was all a bit odd: I was taping a repeat of that fantastic Prom, mostly Liszt – that very late way-out Liszt, Clouds and Lugubrious Gondolas and things. I left it recording and when I came back and replayed it, I could hear this sort of Voice Over, in the short gaps between the pieces. It's difficult to make out as it's very high and squeaky and there's quite a lot of coughing and audience noise as well – and when I played it again to see if I'd been hallucinating or something, it was even fainter, so I scribbled down what I could. I've got it

here. It doesn't make sense. No – I want you to listen first
and see what you make of it. You'll have to use the head-
phones, and I'll turn it up as loud as I can. I just hope it hasn't
gone: I didn't dare play it over again. Here. It's very short,
and then there are some other bits later on.'

She fitted the ear-phones on me and I nodded. She
switched on the tape and kept the volume low. When the
last notes of *Nuages Gris* had faded she turned it up and my
head was filled with the crashings and rustlings of an
audience at ease. Then I caught a whisper, high and scratchy,
like a twig on a window-pane.

'– Candles at the windows . . . pale squares . . . I am the
only candle left alight in the wood and I am burning low
. . . winter coming apace . . . I am going to need a new
coat . . . fur is warm – flesh is warmer –' (The first notes of
one of the *La Lugubre Gondola* pieces. Nemo turned it down
and ran the tape on to the next pause; then, high above some
noisy coughing, I heard it again.) 'The dog's hair stood up
like holly and it circled barking . . . I cannot feel the holly
when I go cautiously barefoot . . . the house was frightening
at first so changed . . . but I have found a looking-glass that
knows me . . . I have not changed –' (and something more
that I missed in the opening of *Unstern*. Nemo spun it on,
then –) 'At sunset the copper beech was like a fired galleon
in one of Mr Turner's fantastic paintings . . . she sat in the
circle and watched it burn . . . perhaps I speak too high . . .
shall I dance for her . . . music poured from the bright casements when the wind was loud . . . passing above . . . wild
music for a wild night –' (Now the piano started again, so
soft, so low I could still make out the whisper.) 'When the
gale shifted round only the pulsations rhythmical reached
me, through the ground . . . the soft loam, laurel roots . . .
dank drum, dripping – I get no rest when the music . . .
rest . . . no . . . one more little life and then rest . . .'

It had faded away.

'There's another short bit, at the end of the *Totentanz*, the last thing in the concert: the tape ran on and you can hear the voice again – this time more like giving orders –' Through the end of the clapping I made out '– Brambles nettles . . . and sow digitalis . . . but beware of willow herb a pretty mongrel thing . . . tend the ring of fire . . . burn the fallen giants across my path . . . trace dead fingers and *cut them out*' (almost a shriek) 'I need a royal way fit for a queen . . . the awnings, banks of lilies, and always music . . . to direct my feet . . .' Then just the hissing of the tape.

I opened my eyes and took off the head-phones. I found my hands were shaking. Nemo was silent, watching me. I took a drag of cold coffee and said, as lightly as I could, 'Well, Koestler was righter than he knew –'

'How?'

'Oh, just one of his book titles – *The Ghost in the Machine* . . . Yes, that is strange. I probably missed quite a bit of it – it seemed so disjointed. And I don't see – what did you manage to write down?'

Together we looked through her scribbled notes and Nemo pointed to the passage about the dog, and the sun setting.

'You see? That sounds like the time I heard the music box –'

'Yes – and it says "shall I dance for her" –'

'Then that looking-glass –'

'What happened to that?'

'Oh, James gave it to one of the workmen when I wasn't there. He said it was past saving, even re-silvered.' She was silent; then: 'Well at least you're not laughing at me –'

A van came up the drive.

'That'll be the florists.'

'Banks of lilies?' I asked casually.

'Yes, Harry.'

'And awnings?'

'James is supervising those now, pavilions, really – more fun than a straightforward tent, don't you think? Almost like extensions of the house. We're having braziers and benches – and these awnings have an extra flap, all looped up and tasselled, like El Cid or something, that we can let down if it gets really cold. One out here, from the french windows –'

'But, Nemo,' I said. I took her by the shoulders to stop her pacing and made her look at me. 'What are you trying to do?'

'I don't know. What I'm told, I suppose. Just ideas for the party, Harry – James was rather impressed by me being so definite about it all. So I thought I might sort of – set the stage and, well, see what happened.'

James appeared with a tub of lilies in his arms outside the french windows and we opened them. The watery sunlight was almost warm.

'Where do you want these, Mo?'

'Oh how lovely – Goodness! don't they smell strong? Terribly sweet – they'd be overpowering indoors. Out here, I think – two banks, well, rows of them, either side of the windows, like a path on to the lawn –'

And below the lawn the wood shimmered, luxuriant, timeless, evergreen and very still in the steamy grey light.

I didn't have a chance to speak to her again. She was needed by the furniture movers, the caterers, the discothèque. I didn't even have time to play through my Temperance Seven for her; I just left the records in the morning room, beside the head-phones.

7

So we come to the night of the party.

There was a huge crowd there when I arrived about ten. The buffet supper had started and I only saw Nemo in glimpses, flitting about in a silky gold and white striped dress with flowing sleeves. The food was superb, and, in spite of the hordes of Beautiful People, Nemo's London crowd – whom I had rather dreaded – there were inevitably lots of my Oxford friends, and I began to enjoy myself. There seemed no end to the champagne. But I remained unattached and drank sparingly; I was on watch, though for what I did not know.

It must have been well after midnight, after Big Ben and the kissing and letting the New Year in: the dancing was at its height, and I looked into the big drawing room. It was dark except for moving oil patterns of light from a projector, sliding over the big looking-glass and across the ceiling. The place was packed – and the morning room beyond it – the music deafening. I left my glass at the makeshift bar in the hall and edged into the room.

A step-ladder had been left in one corner under an extra loud-speaker that had been rigged up at the last minute, and I made my way slowly round the jostling floor to the foot of it. A couple had already taken refuge on the bottom steps; below dancing level they had found a form of privacy and were indistinguishably enlocked. I climbed round and over them to the top: it felt quite firm with the added weight at the base, and I made myself comfortable on the little platform with my shoulder tucked into the corner of the wall. From this position I had a good view of the dance, and a novel one: as if, having fought amidst murderous breakers, I had escaped the undertow, dragged myself on to a ledge and looked down, battered but safe, over the wild waters.

There was so little light that it was almost impossible to pick out individuals. The beat was compulsive, a seemingly tireless crescendo like the famous *Bolero* in hard rock, and even more nakedly sexual. Yet it could never be an orgy, I thought as I watched: people are never so alone as when they are carried away by music. Each was a private, narcissistic frenzy, rapt, panting, devoted to the spasms of their individual bodies. They weren't even showing off: it had passed beyond that.

At this point the disco men started messing about with the lights, as if to screw the jaded senses up one more notch. Till then the oily light had simply changed colour, amber and crimson giving way in rotation to frosty blues that, from my Dantesque position, had the effect of a hasty conducted tour through the several circles of the Inferno. Now they put on a 'black light' – an ultra-violet bulb that illuminated a weirdly specialized selection of fabrics and features: only teeth, nails and eyeballs glittered, and various man-made materials or specific dyes. One discreetly patterned dark shirt became a blaze of electric snakes; an innocent white blouse that had been washed, presumably, in a certain detergent, was all at once transfigured, disembodied, writhing on its own. But more than anything, the room became a jungle scene of teeth and claws and eyes.

And then the white strobes started. They flashed rapidly on and off, alternately illuminating the crowd of writhing figures, the ecstatic upturned masks, with a blinding naked whiteness, and plunging them back into the jungle darkness of the single black bulb.

At first I tried to shield my eyes from the flickering images. Once I had forced myself to watch, I found it hypnotic. It was a refinement of tortured grotesquerie that

Dante and Goya had not dreamed of – the alternation of life and death, white and black, a landscape of arrested spasm, of frozen gesticulation, where the puppets were jerked mercilessly, mindlessly and precisely by a machine no one could stop.

Then I saw Sarah Moore – or what I know now was Sarah Moore. At the time I realized – and it was an extreme shock for a confirmed sceptic – that I was seeing what is called a ghost. None of my misgivings had prepared me for this; yet I had no doubt at all that it was supernatural, and so I continued in the face of all the level-headed explanations I had to confront afterwards. Heat, they said, drink, turmoil, mind-blowing noise and, above all, the tricks that prolonged strobe-lighting can play with the retina – all these they ranged against me, heartily, humorously, rationally. Alas, I had no other witnesses, no one to back me up; in a roomful of people totally absorbed in passionate activity, I had been the sole observer.

Even the discothèque men, I found, had lashed the tiller: they knew that this peculiarly extended, frenetic, cumulative number took up the whole side of the LP, and were having their own little rave-up, close enough to the turntables to be in control. But the window had been opened earlier as the heat built up, and they both remembered stopping in mid rave to shut it – the heavy sash window – because they had felt so cold. Quite suddenly they warmed up again, and let in the fresh air once more when they went back at the end to switch to the slow convalescent cling-music that came next.

So I suppose that's the nearest I came to having a witness. For I too felt a chill that turned the sweat on my forehead to ice, as I crouched on my perch up near the ceiling where the heat had gathered in a tropical miasma. I was hugging my goose-pimpled arms to me, and turning to find the source of the draught, when I saw.

It was just a pale thing that advanced steadily where all else was bobbing and twitching, that shone evenly when all around was juddering black and white. 'Shone' is misleading: it did not so much shed light, as leave a luminous smear on the crowd as it passed straight through. Starting by the french windows it moved smoothly, and fairly swiftly, across the milling floor towards the corner of the big inner drawing room where I sat; and as it approached I could see it was a woman in a long flowing dress – I remember describing it as 'sleep-walking gear', and this may have been something to do with the way it moved, that unhesitating, indeed that obscurely purposeful, ridge-pole glide that one dare not interrupt.

I watched mesmerized as it approached through the dancers, steadfast and luminous. They were jerky pasteboard figures from an old silent film, a series of stills, by comparison with this constantly visible thing, solider than they – this pale comet whose slowly fading track marked the line of a regal progress.

Two yards from the foot of my ladder it stopped and its glow seemed to concentrate itself on one other figure, to share its corrupt light. It was Nemo. Then the ghost stepped forward and disappeared; and there was Nemo, still dancing, but now she was distinguished, outlined clearly as with a shining snail-track. I do not think she paused in her rapt Bacchanalia, though the strobes would have masked a hesitation; but she had changed her rhythm to half time, and, as I watched, she started to move in a solemn courtly parody of a sarabande to the fast hard rock music, that had reached its ultimate crescendo and become just a repeated pounding scream. For the last minutes of frenzy the strobes were cut, and the black light alone illuminated the climax of the dance. After the staring white, the blackness was absolute, but as normal vision returned and jungle of teeth and eyes took over, I found her again in the whirling crowd. No one else had noticed – why should they? – the priestess-like figure in their midst. Yet they had made room for her, and it seemed to me that she still held an afterglow, now only a pallid limning, distinct from her photo-negative companions. Her partner, intent on his own gyrations, abandoned his isolation for a moment to grab and spin her slowly turning figure, and as he became absorbed once more in his dizzy Black-and-White-Minstrel Hallelujah thing, I saw his hands and sleeves glittered where he had touched her.

Then suddenly, mercifully, the music ceased, low lights came on; a slow melody seeped in to tend the wound the final scream had made. Limp puppets drifted away in ones and twos; others flopped towards each other and stayed propped and shuffling in the gloom. Nemo danced on alone, altering the rhythm of her formal dance to fit the soft syrupy beat. There were fewer couples now and people began to notice her: even in the half-light she stood out, swaying her arms in slow gracious gestures in her cleared space. 'Weave a circle round her thrice, Close your eyes in holy dread . . .' Then James broke away from the huddle and led her from the room.

At this I too came out of my trance. I climbed down the ladder, and I seemed to be trembling a lot. I got out into the hall, where the bright lights and the drinks were.

'Feeling all right, sir?' the straight-faced waiter asked as he poured. But before I could answer, I passed out.

I found myself on the sofa in the study where we had left our coats, with two of my colleagues standing by; the barman and a cosy unknown girl were fussing round me.

'No, sir,' the barman was saying. 'And I should know. No, I'd say he was taken ill, sir. Could be the heat – very close evening –'

'How are you, old man?'

'Fine,' I said. 'Extraordinary thing to do. Did anyone else see it?'

'See what, old man?'

'Well, I suppose, for want of a better word, the apparition –' I found myself embarrassed; others were there now, and I looked round desperately for someone who had been dancing, but, as I said, it had been hard to distinguish people. I tried to make light of it, dipping into my brandy for the bravado I did not feel.

'I just saw a ghost – that's all. You were probably all too busy twisting and shouting.' One of the young men who ran the discothèque came out for a breather and a drink, and I buttonholed him. '*You* might have seen something – or felt it, even. Didn't you feel the cold?'

My only witness. He sat down to compare notes, and the others drifted away, drawn by shouts and singing from the other end of the house. We were still talking – I was trying to take in, as well as to describe, what had happened, when my friend came back.

'How is Nemo?' I asked. 'Where is she?'

'Why, she's fine – and furthermore she's going to do a fire-dance, she says. It's getting somewhat wild in there – all those young things egging her on. My old nanny would say "There'll be tears before bedtime". Someone was drinking champagne out of her shoe. I think this is where Margaret and I toddle off: she's pretty tired anyway – the kids get up so early; and I've got a normal working day to face, New Year or no. Anyway, this isn't really our scene, as they say. Good party though – James certainly knows how to do things – just that the younger element is getting a bit out of hand and our hostess has suddenly kicked over the traces and seems to be the centre of it –' As he talked he was getting his coat and putting it on. 'I was going to suggest we gave you a lift, old man. Better to slip away and give them a ring in the morning –'

I found my coat and followed him obediently, glad to be set upright and given a direction, for I was quite drained of energy.

'Ah, there you are, my dear.' His wife had joined us. 'I was just saying to Harry, no need to hunt out our hosts. Better to slip off and give them . . . Quite – getting a bit out of hand. But a very good party, as I was saying to Harry –'

The fresh air, even that clammy overcast night, made me feel better.

'I'll be able to drive,' I said.

'We'll follow you then, old man. Just to make sure.'

My car was parked by the old wing, and I stopped and looked through the window into the big kitchen. It was crowded and noisy and dark, except for candles; and above the swaying shoulders of those nearest me, I could see across the room to where Nemo was dancing on the big mahogany table. She was wearing a mad blonde wig, stuck all over with lighted sparklers, and she was doing the same formal dance with snaking arm movements, to the rhythmical chanting of the wild upturned faces round about.

Then I heard the peep of a horn and turned away. I drove slowly back into Oxford, with my kind friends just behind. I did not want to stay. I wanted quiet and time to think. I had tried to sort out my impressions with the very sleepy sympathetic young disco player; but, muddled with comparative theologies and perhaps a joint or two, he had been all too ready to believe in a mystical happening. I needed to talk to another sceptic like myself. Most of all I wanted to talk to James, but that would have to wait.

When I got back to my room I made myself sit down and write as clear a description as possible of all I had witnessed – from which I have taken this, and, I trust, kept it pure from hindsight, remained true to the comparatively innocent eye I had then. I know it gives no impression of the speed with which it all happened, and that afterthoughts were already intruding. For example, I knew afterwards, but did not know at the time, that I was very frightened; that, starting with the sensation of cold, I experienced a sensation – physical – of evil so strong that it had produced a state of shock. I replayed the scene for myself as precisely as I could and compared it with the words with which I had tried to pin it down. It *sounded* almost beautiful – mysterious, thrilling in the tell-me-more-ish sense. It had in fact been horrible, unearthly, impossible, wrong. And as certain as I was that I had seen it, I knew that it was malevolent, and I knew also that it was continuous; I had almost said 'alive'.

8

I was tired, but I could not sleep. As soon as I closed my eyes
the image of the luminous figure returned to me, imprinted
on my retina as if I had been staring into a naked light bulb;
nor did it fade: it seemed tattooed on my brain. Once when
sleep at last began to draw me down, blurring senses and
thoughts, and I felt myself gradually, gratefully beginning
to float on the tide, the bright image rushed toward me
with a terrible speed – an optical trick: it simply grew larger
in three or four swift ghastly jerks – and I sat up screaming,
but it came out as a whimper. After that I left the light on.

I tried to read; I was so drowsy that I kept drifting off and
starting up again as the pale shape materialized on the
printed page. Desperate for sleep I buried my face in the
pillow, but it was there too. Never had I longed so for total
blackness, the black of a newly wiped blackboard, of a coal-
mine, of a night so starless you cannot tell the earth from the
sky. I shall never be afraid of the dark again, I thought; and
I realized that to close one's eyes is no escape. There is that
ceaseless floating plankton of light particles, like a random
scanner of the life processes – Keats described it as 'to see the
spangled gloom froth up and boil'. It is a restless peep-show
we have learned to live with. Now that 'spangled gloom'
persisted in boiling and congealing into one shape. I wondered if this was what it felt like to go mad.

Then it came to me as an inspiration, like the Only Real
Truth one scribbles down, half awake, knowing that tomorrow it will change the world: I was being haunted. This
was it. I must sit up and wait for the dawn when it would
go. I stumbled out of bed and dressed, lit a fire, made

coffee, and when I had pulled back the curtains, I sat down by the fire to watch for first light. But New Year's night is one of the longest in the year; by the time the sun rose I was asleep in my chair. And when I was woken, I found the imprint had gone: I could remember it well enough, but I could not see it. So perhaps I was right. There is no way of knowing.

I had two busy days ahead packing up for the months away and preparing my room for my opposite number in the exchange. There was only one other thing I had to do: I must thank the Boyces for the lovely party.

My pressing need to tell James what I had seen had seemed a little foolish in the morning light. I decided simply to send a note of thanks and drop the whole thing. Something deep and selfish, the mainspring of survival, told me to cut loose and look after my own future – busy myself with travellers' cheques and lecture notes and useful letters of introduction. The Boyces' ghost was none of my business, Nemo was not mine to worry about, and, either way, I must be off. 'A superb evening', I wrote in my neat italic. 'How lovely the house was looking: you really have made it come alive.' A Freudian slip? I let it stand, and dropped the card into the Lodge post-box.

There were various telephone calls inquiring about my health – friends who had been at the party, and a colleague who had heard I was unwell. Then James phoned about five o'clock. It had just grown dark – the hour when one remembers dreams; and as I drew the curtains I had been thinking about my night fears, and of Nemo. Had she too been haunted? So James's voice was something of a shock, and I cut across his inquiries.

'I'm fine – How's Nemo?'

'Well, funny that you should ask – not too good, actually. Persistent headache, quite bad. The doctor says it looks like migraine. Certainly not a hangover, anyway. She's very depressed, too – and yet she was in terrific form last night – absolute firecracker.'

'Maybe it's some sort of reaction. Look, James, where are you?' I could hear traffic in the background.

'I'm just returning the punch bowl we borrowed from College – I'm in our Lodge –'

'Meet me for a drink?'

'Why not? I've got a few things to see to first. The Turf in about half an hour?'

I knew that before I left for the States I must tell James about the ghost: if it had harmed Nemo in some way it was the least I could do. I had not had time all day, perhaps deliberately, to put my thoughts in order; now, as I went out through the gate and walked towards Holywell, I tried. As an isolated incident, and especially under the conditions in which I witnessed it, the apparition seemed freakish and little more. But in conjunction with the other unexplained incidents, the music box, the looking-glass and, above all, the tape, I felt it should no longer be ignored. Yet I dreaded the business of exposing my fears to James; it was only his apparent, and untypical, concern over Nemo that pushed me into it. I decided to try him with my account of the ghost, and if he listened, tell him more. I must sight-read it from his reactions – far harder than playing it by ear.

While we were getting our drinks I thanked him for the party. 'It really was brilliantly organized,' I said; 'did you and Nemo enjoy it?'

'Oh, absolutely – that's what caterers are for – they take all the *angst* out of it. Yes, I had myself a ball. Feel a bit flat now, of course – and Nemo isn't exactly the best of company at present.'

We found a table and settled ourselves.

'James,' I said. It sounded wrong already: if there was anything he hated, it was 'being intense'. I supped my beer and started again.

'A funny thing happened last night on the way round the dance floor – actually I was up on a ladder at the time – thing is, I saw a ghost.'

'Ah,' said James, leaning back luxuriously. 'Tell me all. I needed some light relief. Was it Sarah Moore in full regalia?'

'Well, yes – could be,' I said, laughing nervously to keep him with me. 'It came in at the french windows and walked – well – moved –'

'Very good, Harry – keep that in.' He went through the motions of working a clapper-board. 'The Haunted Dower House, Take two –'

'No, James, really. It came quite close to where I was perched, and stopped in front of Nemo and then disappeared.'

'And where was this exactly?'

'Just to the right of the drawing-room fireplace.'

'And then what?'

'Nothing more – that's when I felt ill – actually I passed out – and then I went home. But I was worried about Nemo.'

'Oh come on, Harry – ghosts don't give people headaches. I'm sorry you felt so rotten though; are you really OK today? Oh, good. Well, Nemo will be fascinated to hear about the apparition –'

'She didn't see it, then?'

'No – she'd certainly have been full of it if she had. Ever since that damn music box, she's fancied she might be sensitive to the supernatural. I've often considered bribing a Tonibell man to say he took his ice-cream van down the Ferry path and got stuck – it would have saved a lot of trouble. Perhaps it's best now to play it the other way: just admit we've got a ghost that even old Harry the Unbeliever could see, and incorporate it into our life-style, as they say. My, my – when she hears this she'll be putting out a glass of Madeira and a *petit four* when she feeds the cats of an evening.

64

A bit of a blow for her, though – not seeing it. She'll never get over that.'

I tried once more. 'So she didn't even behave strangely? Nothing odd at all apart from this headache?'

James looked at his watch. I had lost him.

'No, Harry old pal – not a thing. I told you, she was in terrific form – absolute life and soul – even when things got a bit hairy later on, she was in the thick of it –' He was finishing his pint and getting up to go.

'And this headache?'

'Well, as you said, reaction. It's been quite a strain for her, this party; and the holiday wasn't exactly a rest. You know the skiing scene – late nights and early mornings. She's simply overdone it. And I must get back, actually, and see if she feels like some food now. She'll be as right as nine-pence – or approximately four new p – you'll see – Oh, but you're off aren't you? Tomorrow? Sorry about that, but don't worry dear chap. Have a super time in the States – all those adoring bobby-soxers sitting at your feet – squealing and fainting when you say: "Of course, 'The Mariner hath his will' is a sexual image" in your deep thrilling voice –'

We walked together up the Broad to where his car was parked. I felt worsted. I knew I had been poor company; now I was numb, and at the same time full of rising panic. But I heard myself wishing him luck with the house, and some more, about how I would look forward to seeing it in April when I got back from Princeton.

'Thanks, Harry,' he said, 'and for the drink *and* for the smashing ghost story. Made my day, that has –' He let in the clutch, steamrollered his way into the line of traffic, waved triumphantly and was gone.

I do not come well out of that interview, on re-reading. It is difficult to put across the special sort of childishness of dons together, a form of arrested development that makes serious, or rather, real, conversation almost impossible: you can be serious about an Old High German vowel shift, or a legal quibble, but concerning life's troubles – sickness, anxiety, love, fear – there is a conspiracy of silence. Words are toys; one must amuse or shut up. I had tried; I had gone to the edge of embarrassment and drawn back. Luckily I had come up with a good yarn and so might be forgiven. On the telephone James had sounded anxious, and so I went and stuck my neck out – only to find he was merely flat and fretful. Nemo's mysterious and unaccustomed headache did not worry him: it put him out. My ghost story had genuinely diverted him; already it would be being fashioned into something with which to bait Nemo, something on which to dine out – and well worth the time spent on having a pint with lugubrious old Harry.

I made myself dine in College as I had planned. Two of the company had heard about my bad turn, as well as my insistence, on coming round, that I had seen a ghost; and I found myself being as hearty as James about it all, making a good story of it. Our end of the long table enjoyed an exhilarating skirmish on the subject of the supernatural: my manifestation seemed a little flat, it was generally agreed, and they embroidered on how M. R. James might have presented it. Several far better experiences, albeit second-hand or hearsay, were produced over the port and a good time was had, and seen to be had. I was tempted, in my cups, to cap their stories with an account of the tape. But some instinct held my tongue. It was my last evening with my colleagues for three months: I did not want to strike the wrong note and spoil the fun.

No tungsten images troubled me that night. I slept well, finished packing next morning and took a train up to London in the late afternoon. There is a short space between cuttings, just after one has sped past the Little Hamden halt, from which one can see the Dower House crowning its long woody spur. The cedar stands out boldly, and this evening the west front was caught in the light of a low sun emerging like a bronze penny from a bank of cloud. I always associate the house with sun – sun as Hitchcock uses it, as a cover, a front for something else; and I swear that day, in the distance, it looked like a haunted house: just a brief lantern-slide, then click, and the scrubby slope of the cutting took its place.

9

I was spending the night at my club, as I had an early start, and would have to be at the Air Terminal by eight. Determined though I was to put Nemo and the Dower House behind me now, I could not resist ringing up a friend whom I knew to be a member of the Garrick: there were a couple of portraits there I wanted to see.

Till now, my desultory researches on the actress Sarah Moore had produced little enough. Indices yielded up the odd page number, where I would find either her name in a list of other minor actresses of the Regency, or at best a line quoted from a contemporary critique of a play in which she had appeared, apparently in a secondary role. Earnshaw, the diarist, was the most helpful: he was an inveterate theatregoer. He said she was an 'incomparable' Lady Macbeth – the only reference to her in a leading part – and added: 'It is perhaps unfortunate that Mistress Moore will go down in History, if she goes at all, as a society beauty rather than as a Thespian. She is too wilful and impatient to court her Public; for what can the greatest Impressario do for an Actress who will not repeat a performance? And they say it the same with her Lovers –' And elsewhere: 'To Devonshire House. A great crush. The Incomparable Sarah Moore has access even here! The Beaux Monde gathered round her like moths at a candleflame. The Belles Monde not a little put out!' I liked that. But it was only from a catalogue of theatrical paintings that I discovered there were two portraits of her hanging in the Garrick.

They were quite hard to find. The larger was in the corner of an inner dining room; it was by Raeburn, very stylish in a large grey velvet hat with plumes. Her hair was pale and elaborately frizzed and curled, her thin red mouth smiling smugly between broad high-coloured cheeks. I did not think her beautiful, but she might have been quite amusing, with her patches and her beady sidelong glance. The other we found in a passageway, a small drab oil by an unknown painter. Here she was dressed for the 'out damned spot' scene in *Macbeth*, shrouded and nun-like with melodramatic eyes rolled up in ham horror. But I observed numbly that the clothes were right: it was my ghost in sleep-walking gear.

I wished I had not seen them. Nothing conclusive came of it. Most apparitions wear long white nun-like robes. All I had done was indulge a donnish proclivity for useless research, complicating my vague fears in the process, compounding the sense of threat that hung over the woman I had decided to forget.

Once in the States, I settled down more seriously to forgetting her. I started by looking up an old girl friend in New York. She was smart, sweet, bitchy and independent – a good antidote to Nemo, I thought. But as soon as term had started at Princeton and I was absorbed into my new routine, I felt no urge to go to New York for weekends, and even less to bring her down to stay. There was metal more attractive at hand.

American academic society is, for the European visitor at least, almost Utopian. The infrastructure may be brutally pyramidal, in-fighting ruthless, the need to publish grotesquely important, and tenure hard to come by. But the visiting don can move freely and with privilege through all the strata. He can eat royally off a cafeteria tray with students and junior lecturers, dine heavily and at length at the clubs and lodges of the élite; he is invited to the homes of the big backers, the enlightened millionaires behind the foundations, as well as to intimate mind-bending seminars where the frontiers of knowledge are treated as so much elastic by some international astronomer or bio-chemist. At every level there is both mental alacrity (bred of insecurity?) that perhaps sets too much store by new ideas – but how exciting, how refreshing! – and the courtly foreign grace (they *are* foreigners) that automatically opens their very homes to you: in this they are quite different from Europeans, British included. So I met not only female academics, but the wives and families of academics, and I swear that in that three months I did not meet one woman who was not at least interesting. It may be – must be – different in other cross sections, other societies, but these women were never merely their husbands' wives, or their subjects' specialists, as I have found so often here, and especially in the older universities.

More particularly, and apart from friends, I had a brief and delightful tangle with a woman older than myself, who had at one time advised Jackie Kennedy on art treasures for the White House, and was in Princeton for two weeks overseeing the acquisition of pictures for a new museum. She was tall, immaculate, witty, big-hearted, and in no way beautiful, except in bed, where she was a glorious paradox, a submissive Amazon. It was uncomplicated pleasure, for we neither of us wanted to get involved; she was in the process of a rapprochement with a former husband.

Then, halfway through the semester, a lovely postgraduate student declared she was in love with me; and spring in New England will always be intricately connected with that interlude, an American Idyll. The hepaticas were coming out between patches of snow in the woods, the sudden hot sunshine striking down through bare boughs on the well-ordered picnic sites to which we carried our steaks and charcoal and flagons of Californian Mountain Barbera. She had the most beautiful hair and the whitest teeth I have ever seen; and she did wear white socks, she did have big breasts – and heavy periods and fantasies about Leonard Cohen and a marvellous openness about it all. She was highly intelligent, sweet-natured and deeply in love, and she *demanded* involvement. For an idyllic month I believe I gave it her; but, like the excellent local wines, I knew she would not travel. I tried to tell her she did not know what I was really like, what Oxford was like, what North Oxford and being a don's wife was like. She could not understand, but she was proud enough to see I was not as serious as she; and she it was who said good-bye, smiling like an angel, and went back before the Easter break to nurse her heart on her big white Californian ranch in the big white bosom of her family.

Here I need a tame PR man with a low sincere voice to say there is no element of self-advertisement in the preceding passage. My story is about Nemo, and all this was a background to my incurable love for her. Distance did not help; no day, no quarter of a day passed without my thinking of her. It was hardly thinking, for I simply carried my obsession with her everywhere I went. It would be unfair to my passing loves to declare to my unchanging one: 'Cynara, the night was thine'; but the subconscious surely was. I dreamt of Nemo repeatedly: she was part of my dreams. Sometimes she was simply there, my companion, leaning on a gate (in Devon?) looking out over patchwork fields, walking through a foreign market-place (North Africa?) to choose a rug for our house; sometimes it was erotic, and in detail, though I had never done more than kiss her cheek; but most often it was fraught with anxiety: I was looking for Nemo in a crowded underground, or in a wood, or following her on a wide seashore, unable to catch up with her – and always knowing she was in danger and that she was unaware of it.

I kept a diary during those three months: I thought it would be good discipline at the time and perhaps interesting later on. But I destroyed it all a few weeks ago; it had very quickly degenerated into a sort of conversation with Nemo – things I saw and did that I wanted to share with her. And at the end of my idyllic month-long affair with my lovely post-graduate, I broke down and addressed Nemo directly in my diary, telling her everything, blaming her for spoiling my life. 'Don't you see?' I said – 'This girl thought I was unable to commit myself – thought that she could see through all my talk about it not working in England, to the congenital, unsavable bachelor in me, and the vital privacy I could not give up. She might have been right a year ago, and the affair would have ended just the same way. But alas, I have lost that tough innocence, that instinct for preservation. I was complete before. I have often been in love but I have never needed anyone. And now I have allowed a neurotic middle-aged married woman to spoil my perfect wholeness. I am committed: I need you, Nemo, to be complete.' That sort of thing. It burnt well.

I actually wrote to Nemo twice from America, or, rather, sent off two of the many letters I tried to write, all in a friendly inquiring vein. I wanted news; for I was genuinely anxious about her, fears that were the worse for being so undefined. Once, I remember, I opened my heart to one of my fellow academics, early one morning towards the end of a bottle of Jack Daniels: he explained laboriously, steadying himself the while by my lapel, that I was projecting a security deficiency on to her in order to provide myself with a stability-demand situation. And I cross-questioned myself as I wandered back under the big frosty stars: was I creating a custom-built threat to fit my darling? Had it any real foundation? And during Sir Galahad's sabbatical, would not her lawfully-wedded husband keep an eye on her?

Nemo did not write to me: still I had no news. Instead

she sent me a beautiful ornate genuine Victorian Valentine, signed simply 'Love from no one'. It was a charming, whimsical, wanton thing to do, stirring up so casually my painful school-boy crush, that I almost hated her for a day. She was a mere Bathsheba Everdene, childishly unconscious of the real feelings of those about her. I buried my face in the breasts of my friendly Amazon – and managed to dismiss her for a while. But later I thought, could it be? Might she possibly – secretly – have some feelings for me? Be encouraging me? I saw her leaving the brutish insensitive James and flying into my arms – an Oxford scandal – exile on a small Greek island – a triumphant return to academic life – all the world loving the lovers – a cottage in the Cotswolds I would come home to in the evenings – all those long vacations suddenly making sense: 'you with your stained glass, me with my poetry', as the old Pont caption put it – even children maybe, fine-boned and golden-eyed, stroking the nose of the pony through the paddock gate . . .

The day before I left Princeton I met an incoming don from Oxford. He was one of the jet-and-telly set, only over for two lectures, but he brought me fresh news of the old country – mostly gossip about my colleagues and friends. He said:

'You remember the Boyces?' – Yes, I remembered the Boyces – 'They had a bit of a nastiness a few weeks ago. A workman was killed falling off one of their roofs, fixing tiles or something. Very upsetting really – Nemo? Well, she has these migraines, you know – up and down all the time – and I don't suppose a disaster on one's doorstep is designed to improve a nervous disease like migraine. I think James was in Brussels at the time – came straight back of course –'

I had been invited by some friends in Paris to stay for a long weekend 'on the way home'; I had already booked my flight to London, so I cabled them I would come straight on by the next flight. Now I wished I could get back to

Oxford in between, if only for a day, and see Nemo. When I arrived at Heathrow and inquired about planes to Paris, I found I had just missed one; there was another in about three hours' time.

'Can I hire a car here?' I asked on an impulse. I was directed to the Hertz desk, and half an hour later was driving along the tiny motorway on the wrong side of the road, in a heavy April shower, heading towards Windsor, Maidenhead, Henley, Dorchester, Sutton Hamden.

In a traffic jam in Henley I suddenly wondered what the hell I was doing. I had to be back to check in in less than two hours, I had not eaten, I had not telephoned. I pulled on to the side when I saw a phone box, found I had no English change, lit a cigarette and meditated, looking out at the rain. I began to realize I was giving in to a silly boyish whim. Why should I assume I would be welcome – tired, hungry and crumpled at three o'clock on a Thursday afternoon? They might be away; or Nemo might be down with a headache; and I would have half an hour there at the most, judging by the traffic.

I consulted my watch yet again – and now the pubs would just be closing. I managed to get a hot Cornish pasty and bottle of beer, and took them back to the car. As I watched the sun winning against the rain – the drama of an English spring – I told myself to grow up, eat my excellent pasty slowly, enjoy the warm fruity British beer and the light on the river; then turn round and drive back to Heathrow and get on with my own life. Nemo was only four days away – and even then, well or ill, she was not mine.

I drove gently, with a detour through Marlow and a long meander in the sparkling wet lanes, conscientiously savouring it as an outing, a fun thing to do between planes, and to recommend to my friends. No, I said to myself. Just try *not* telling your friends – it would be too like James. It's your own life you're concerned with, remember: this is a secret trip to England, yours and yours alone. And as I headed towards the motorway, I felt something like the independence of heart with which I had first enjoyed the Dower House, and that I had not felt since Nemo had walked into the dusty sunlight of the drawing room and fried me with her eyes.

IO

Paris in April upheld my euphoria; and my friends, a large
affluent family comprising three generations of charming,
bi-lingual individuals, filled every moment of the days, and
most of the nights, with diversions. There were outings,
ranging from food-shopping to the *Opéra* – both treated
equally seriously; bicycle rides, a picnic, two parties, and a
'concert' given by the children of the house. Regularly, and
of chief importance, there were long slow marvellous
meals, and talk.

The contrast with Princeton was total, apart from the
pleasure I took in both. The emphasis was on different
values; and in the big untidy house in Paris, my essential
European-ness hit me forcibly. Here cleanliness was nowhere near Godliness, except that God was all around: there
was Providence in the fall of an artichoke, and He was
thanked before and after eating it. In the States I had admired
and enjoyed the absolute democracy within the family:
children inhabited and had an equal say in the adult world –
though not actually the casting vote – and this made them
marvellously precocious. In that big French family, twelve
under one roof, there was a strict hierarchy, a sense of
protocol and the paramount importance of manners; and
this rigid structure, with *grand-mère* at the top and the infant
at the bottom, brought a sense of perfect security – what
Chaucer and the Elizabethans knew as Order, and related to
the Music of the Spheres.

Here the children had their own world, a rich brew of
Perrault and ponies and cello practice and football and fantasy. It was not a miniature adult world, such as that en-

joyed by their peers in Princeton or Stanford. But regular meetings over the Great Meals ensured they never lost touch with their seniors, and I saw fewer drop-out teenagers there and among their friends than I had in America. They remained secure and obedient until they earned themselves a higher place, or were pushed a rung up the ladder of creation by the arrival of lower forms of life – a new baby or even a dog – for which they would have to take some responsibility.

It seemed to work; and I, an only child and a bachelor, found it both fascinating and delightful. This, I thought, was the sort of family I would like to have – to have had – to produce. And inevitably I projected it on to the Dower House, filling every room with life and activity, and the cellar with wine and music rooms, and saw that it was good. I put Nemo at the centre of it, and it suited her.

If anything marred my long weekend in Paris it was my passionate wish that such a life could be hers. All her inspired practicality would be stretched to its full use in the service of a lively demanding family, instead of just a big beautiful empty house. She would be appreciated, teased, loved, exhausted, satisfied. There would be no time for idle superstition. Her blurred sense of identity would solidify into strong graceful lines; for so many others would be rubbing up against hers, looking to *her* for food, sticking plaster, reassurance, discipline, admiration, bicycle pumps, lavatory paper, advice, crayons, brief-cases, comfort . . .

But her lot, an enviable vocation to many, I suppose, was to give her blood to James and the Dower House – excluding, I trusted, old Sarah Moore. After all, she had a quality of toughness, perhaps simply a Quality: she came of good stock; her very feminine pliability was that of fine steel; and under the fey charm was a tart humour that is the stuff of endurance. If she endured, and did it well, was a successful hostess, and filled her time with house-pride, good deeds and art classes, she could look forward to being a professsor's wife with a nice town house and undergraduates as a surrogate-family. Then she would be over the hump. But I could not help feeling that this first year at the house was a watershed: from here she could either flow out to that wide sunlit professorial sea, or be turned back on herself into some dark unpeopled peak district, and be lost in a still green lake of unknown depth.

The first evening I was back I telephoned James, and he asked me to come out for 'pot luck'.

'Nemo's shopping in London,' he said – so much for my fears, my cold lost lakeland: I felt both foolish and comforted. 'She'll be back later on. Come on – it's roast hare and smells fantastic.'

I was there in time to look round the garden before the light failed, to admire the statues in the long walk and the new row of lime trees he had planted. The walled garden had been ploughed, and sown with grass, springing up like long soft new hair after the April rains. It was drizzling gently as we walked round, and we were drinking whisky and drying ourselves in front of the Aga, when we heard the car.

Nemo came into the room like a firebrand. She was brown already with the spring sun, and dressed in a red and blue and yellow quilted paisley suit like some slender Indian prince from a Golden Fairy Book illustration. She was wearing lipstick, I remember – I had never seen her do so before – a clear flame-like slash of colour that showed off the small rather pointed teeth, and her golden eyes were emphasized with kohl, or some Western substitute – points I only properly observed later. The immediate impression was a brilliant blur; she burst in and rushed to kiss me on both cheeks; and my emotion and her smell and colour and taste and warmth, together, were more like an explosion, or a sudden visit from the angel Gabriel.

'Well,' I said when I got my breath back, 'you look all right, Nemo.' My heart was thudding as if I had narrowly missed an accident.

'Like it? It's new!' She whirled round with her arms outstretched, then strutted like a Chinese pheasant over to James and pecked him on the cheek. 'Like it?' She spun round again. '*I'm* all right. I've just had a lovely day, that's what I've had. Yes, whisky, please – how's the hare?'

She threw off her jacket and tied on an apron to protect her finery. As she bent over the stove, chattering of the friends she had seen and the things she had bought, James looked across at me and rolled his eyes up, shrugging his shoulders in Gallic despair; but he was grinning with a sort of indulgent pride. For my part, I was entranced: I had seen flashes of Nemo's high spirits – indeed, had not my last glimpse of her, three months ago, been by the light of the sparklers stuck into her wig? Now there was a blazing vitality that was altogether new, a little frenetic, but quite marvellous to me, clearing away with a blow-torch three months of cobweb fears.

'But, Nemo,' I said when at last she sat down at the head of the mahogany table – and even in repose she seemed to glitter, to vibrate; even when listening, her eyes were bright, as if she were remembering. 'But, Nemo, what's all this I hear of migraines?'

'Oh, that's for tomorrow,' said James.

'Oh, James – *poor* James! Not always, surely. You make me sound so draggy and grim when you say that –'

'My sweet Mo, you don't – luckily – remember what they're like, when you don't have them. And when you're on top of the world you don't even believe in them.'

But Nemo was up again, lighting the candles, getting out table napkins. 'Come on, James,' she wheedled, tucking his napkin into his shirt front, 'don't be a bore now. Have you taken Harry round the garden?' She came up close to me to tuck in my napkin, and I breathed in her musky scent and felt her lightly but deliberately stroke my neck before she moved away, sending a shiver through me like an electric charge.

James was saying: 'Yes, and he approves of the Long Walk. He hasn't seen round the house yet.'

Suddenly, in the midst of my shooting sparks and over-loaded circuits, I remembered.

'I say, I'm terribly sorry about the accident, the workman who was killed. It must have been dreadful.'

'Oh it was, Harry,' she said, all at once intensely serious, looking into her whisky with only a line of glitter showing under the heavy mascaraed lashes. 'He was so young and lovely, too –'

'And what was more relevant, he had a wife and kids, I gather,' said James heavily. 'Yes, it was a most unfortunate business. He shouldn't really have been on the job alone.'

'He fell from the roof, did he?'

'Yes, on the north side – three storeys – died instantly they said. I was away and Mo had to cope – I came back of course. Wretched business – police, reporters – and poor old Mo had a grandaddy of a migraine, as you can imagine, after that. God, we even had Radio Oxford breathing down our necks. Publicity of that sort is very unpleasant stuff when you come up against it, I can tell you – Anyway, no more workmen now; all finished for the time being. Come on, I'll give you a quick tour while Mo serves up – oh all right, afterwards, then – and we'll have a go at the ivories.'

'New piano?'

'No, dear boy – billiards. Full-size reconditioned with brass knobs on –'

The roast saddle of hare was marvellous.

So was Nemo. I could hardly take my eyes off her; and

I got the distinct impression, not entirely wishful thinking, that she was leading me on, bestowing on me as she did a sort of constant teasing subtle awareness. It was a tacit admission that she knew I was attracted to her, no more – yet so different from our last meeting, or ever before. When her eyes met mine she would let them linger brazenly, so that I lost the thread of my American narrative more than once, and James's voice would fade out of focus. For those lost seconds the small sphere of candlelight contained only Nemo and me.

But when James had taken me round the house and we returned for our coffee she had disappeared.

'She'll have turned in, I expect,' said James. 'She knows it helps if she anticipates a headache: a well-timed Migril and an early night can actually deflect them. But it's often difficult to make her see sense when she's high.'

'What do you mean, high?'

'Well, like tonight: on the crest of the wave. You saw her. Absolutely typical – full of energy and the joys of life, then – wham! One doctor called it "cyclothymic", a series of elations and depressions – but hers are complicated by headaches as well. Elated today, headache tomorrow, followed by depression; then a fairly even keel, if you're lucky, until the next time.'

'Can anything be done about it?'

'Up to a point. It's a tricky question of balancing sedatives and anti-depressants, actually; I dare say it can be done, but she's so against drugs – says they dull her sensibilities and turn her into a vegetable. Understandable, I suppose: Mo sets a high premium on sensibility, as you know. I would gladly become more cabbage-like if it would save me a bit of pain. But reasoning with her gets you nowhere when she's up – and you can't very well bludgeon her with good advice when she's down –'

'I can see it must be wretched for you too.'

'Oh, I don't really see a lot of it, to be honest – I mean, I'm away so much of the day, and quite often longer. After all, there's nothing really one can do for her when she's got an attack: she doesn't need nursing – better left alone. Anyway, I've got my own life, you know –'

We took our coffee back to the splendid billiards room, which had been done up in the late Victorian manner, with Art Nouveau wallpaper and ornaments, and fringed Tiffany lights hanging over the green baize.

'I've got my own life and she's got hers, and they're both good but different. She's got her arty friends in London, and one or two in Oxford, and her amateur dramatics and, well, the house of course – we've both got that – and the garden: she's very taken up with the wood – spends hours down there tidying and planting –' (I thought of the tape, the insistent scratchy whisper giving its orders; the memory disturbed me, and I bungled an easy shot) – 'Oh, that's nice –' (James picked it off) '– And then she's started writing, too. She won't show me, of course, but if it keeps her happy –'

We had a leisurely game of billiards, only talking in snatches. He wanted to hear about my 'other life' in the States – what 'talent' I had found – anything serious? 'No? – Quite right, Harry old thing; don't get hooked –'

I must have disappointed him with my reserve. I felt he wanted some good male smoking-room talk, and that if I had played along he would have entertained me in turn with an account of his own affairs. For I had no doubt that affairs there were; and I realized I should have welcomed his confession, encouraged him and heard him out. The way would then be clear for me, emotionally and morally, to turn my full attentions on Nemo. But I held back. I was so shocked and repelled by the man I most envied that I could not bring myself to expose even my passing loves – however edited an account – in the cause of loosening his tongue, and exonerating my projected wooing of his wife. It might

82

be that he actually anticipated, was positively inviting, cuckoldry, in order to remove the burden of Nemo from round his neck and relieve his guilt. But I drew away in disgust.

And I felt no little disgust with myself as I drove home early, excusing myself from a second game: James might have served up the new, the even more delicious Nemo on a plate, and I had turned aside. A withdrawal symptom? Did I not want her once he had rejected her?

No. To be fair, the thing that most distressed me was simply that Nemo had not troubled to say good night to me. I felt, however superficially – well, physically – at supper, that I had more than a slender chance with her. I suppose in an old-fashioned way I wanted to win her, not to have her turn to me for comfort: yet I knew even then that I would have her on any terms at all. But in my own time – not in James's. And I think I began to realize that something was amiss with Nemo. That did not repel me: I wanted to protect her, look after her, in all her moods. The woman I loved – magnetic princeling, or grey mummy wrapped in pain – simply needed the right treatment. Me.

11

Now, of course, I wanted to see Nemo alone and, if possible, on what James called an even keel. However, term was due to start in two days' time, and I had an accumulated mass of correspondence, time-tables and College business to attend to. I was not lecturing, but I was examining: for the best part of two weeks in mid term I would be involved in invigilating in the Examination Schools, then marking papers, conferring with my fellows in judgement and holding Vivas over the next month. Meanwhile I had to arrange the farming out of my own pupils to other tutors. It was not the ideal moment to be caught up in extra-mural complications. But Love and Destiny consult no time-tables, and quite distinct from the importunate dictates of my heart, I had a vague notion of urgency where Nemo was concerned, as if good sense and a decent delay might prove regrettable. I had no idea till later what real urgency was: that yesterday was already too late.

At the time I was actually comforted when I looked back over the evening at the Dower House. Even the disturbing elements were open to explanation, now I had seen her: her headaches, her moods, her unhealthy concern with the wood – if, at worst, she were still under the influence of the mysterious tape-recording – were all a result of the life she was leading. Outwardly idyllic, a life of leisure in a little paradise, it was a lonely and fairly pointless existence, when seen in terms of Nemo's potential. Add to this the fact that her marriage was a failure, where she was reduced to the role of housekeeper, hostess and social asset, and there seemed reason enough for her to develop the symptoms of the repressed and isolated housewife, whether the *mise-en-scène* was a stately home or a high-rise flat.

First, I thought, she needed to realize what was happening; she was quite intelligent enough to appreciate it. Then perhaps, with increased confidence and some sense of purpose, she might be shown a way out of it. That way might not lead to my cottage in the Cotswolds; indeed, it might be the way of acceptance rather than of escape. After all, she had a lot to lose; and the state of her marriage was no worse than average – at least in the jaundiced eyes of a bachelor like myself. Her prison was no matter of mere bricks and mortar: it was a house and garden of quite exceptional beauty – her love, her brain-child, her obsession. And now, with April soon turning to May, each week of the unfolding seasons of that first year must be something like the first days of creation; how could she give it up? 'If ever I should leave you,' says the sweet schmaltzy song, 'it wouldn't be in springtime.'

All this I thought, but it was an afterthought. I simply wanted to see her again, now, today. By James's prediction, she might be unable to see anyone; at least I had the excuse to telephone and inquire tenderly.

'Oh, Harry.' Her voice was faint and far away. 'How nice of you – Yes, I'm afraid I have – but I'm on the way up – I'll be better by teatime. Come and have some tea and view the ruin – I think there's a large hole where my right eye used to be. You might have some suggestions on how to turn it into one of those dear little oval windows, with a discreet arrangement of ivy – and swallows will come and nest – Yes, I'm full of pills. I'll be fine by then – All right, you bring something – I'll be awfully hungry – buns would be lovely – see you.'

Till one, I concerned myself with the pile of papers on my desk; I had a working lunch with the other English tutor, Hendry, and wrote on till four. Then I went out into the warm wet air like a school-boy when the bell rings, stopping only at a small bakery in the Iffley Road to choose Nemo some worthy buns. I realized as I drove out towards Sutton Hamden that this was the first time I had gone deliberately to see Nemo on her own; and it is some measure of my famous bachelor detachment that through the whole of the autumn term I had only visited the Dower House at James's invitation. Now I wish I had let my resistance give way long before that; but, in the same way as Nemo, I too had had a lot to lose. Now I celebrated my defeat, and it felt like a victory.

Nemo was pale with dark rings under her eyes, and when she reached up and kissed my cheek her mouth was cold and she smelt of eau-de-Cologne. I lit a fire and sat her by it while I got tea.

'I don't usually let people see me like this,' she said. 'You're very privileged, you realize.'

'Oh, I do. And it's quite a treat to have the upper hand,' I said.

'Dear me, am I going to be chastised, then? Suddenly I see you as some terrible butch welfare officer, come to deal in one fell swoop with nits and night-starvation. Don't bully me, Harry – I know it's not a pretty sight – I feel as if even the skeletons in my cupboards must be in bad condition.'

'I won't bully,' I said, 'but let me cosset you and worry over you a little. Tea first –' I handed her a mug '– then squashy buns and sympathy.'

'It's not like me, you know,' she said after her second bun and her third mugful.

'What, swilling down unhealthy carbohydrates with Earl Grey and talking with your mouth full? For myself, I am deeply disillusioned.'

'Then it's your first tottering step towards adulthood,' she said tartly: I was glad to see her spirits were returning. 'But this is *the* cure when one's all dried up and hollowed out –

with just a handful of poisonous pain-killers rattling around inside. It's lovely, Harry. Thank you – you are a pal.' (I nearly interrupted rudely at that, but I remembered I must bide my time.) 'No – these headaches. Never a day's illness, then struck down. A semi-invalid, as James says.'

'Quite suddenly? And when did it start?'

'Oh, in the New Year. You must have been away.'

'No, Nemo, it was New Year's night. Your party.'

'Oh, yes; I suppose that could have been the first of them. The depression's the worst bit of it, actually. James can't take it. Oh dear – it's all such a mess, Harry. I mean, let's face it, James and I haven't been getting on for ages. I thought the house would Bring Us Together, as they say in those lovely hopeful magazine stories – the classic child-substitute –'

'Why don't you have children, in fact? Is there something wrong?'

She was gazing into the fire and didn't answer.

'Look,' I said, 'it's not raining now; the sun's out. Come and sit on the bench outside, and I'll wrap you up.' I took a rug and some cushions, and she let me settle her in a sheltered corner by the morning room, where the wistaria they had planted in the autumn was coming into flower, like bunches of tiny white grapes against the dull gold wall. Nemo sat shrunken and huddled in sunglasses, looking down the garden at the multicoloured foliage of spring.

'How fast it's all growing!' she said; 'it makes me feel quite breathless, as if one will never catch up – No . . . There's nothing *wrong*, Harry. We didn't talk much about children before we got married – it was a matter of one step at a time. I was still a bit windy about the whole thing after my first failure, and James played it very cool – you know, demanding nothing, offering me a way out all the time right up to the Registry door. He was incredibly patient with me, rather as if I was some rare wild animal he was trapping.

87

Now he only mentions the question of children in anger as it were – "what you need my girl is a houseful of kids to knock some sense into you". And when I called his bluff once and asked if that was what *he* needed, he said he wasn't sure he could face another tie – and anyway he was away so much more these days that it was really up to me. I suppose *I've* always felt that our marriage wasn't secure enough to risk bringing children into it. I think I've never quite committed myself, having seen how things can break up – not just my first go – but so many people one knows –'

Her voice trailed away, her eyes inscrutable behind the glasses, her fingers ceaselessly shredding a frond of wild sweet peas that hung beside her. I put my hand over both of hers, and my other arm round her and pulled her close to me. She tucked her head into the angle of my neck, and we sat there like Darby and Joan on our hill, looking out through the evergreens to the bright new aspens catching the breeze on the low outcrop known as Ice-house Hill, beyond the wood. The river, still visible through the stipple of young leaves, was a pale blue ribbon today, and a bright launch moved slowly up towards the lock.

'Anyway,' she said after a little, 'there's not much chance of the patter of little feet, the way things are. James's attentions are otherwise engaged.'

I turned her round to face me and tilted the sunglasses up above her forehead.

'And what about yours?'

'Oh, I'll be all right.' She turned back to the view. 'You needn't worry about *me*.'

Suddenly I thought of her as she had been when she got back from London the evening before, all alight and shedding sparks as she moved. I remembered how the swarming golden insects that formed her irises seemed to have been stirred up into feverish activity, and I thought: of course – she had been with a lover. I had been too ensnared and bewitched by them at the time to ask myself 'why?' The otherwhere look when listening to James or me, the restless energy, the sudden withdrawal of her company: she had wanted to be alone and remember. All at once I realized the male simple-mindedness of assuming I was alone in the field; and I was passionately jealous.

But she sat looking out at the dappled sunshine, her eyelids narrowed against the light that came and went with the scudding clouds. Today those Protean eyes had a drugged heaviness, like those of a gorged reptile. She went on:

'I suppose that if I did have affairs, it would be quick casual stuff, no involvement – nothing intense. I would prefer people I had never met before and would never see again –' while I thought to myself, subjunctives are for concealment. 'I could never see,' she said turning to me with a smile, 'why people go to bed with their friends' husbands. It's all so messy and complicated, when they are sentenced by society to go on dining out with them for the rest of their natural lives.'

'But, Nemo,' I blurted – it was not in the script – 'what about me?'

'Why, Harry, how gallant! I do believe you've got some sort of picture of me as a lonely unsatisfied woman, with her "megrims" and her petty obsessions.' She was painfully near the mark, and again I realized, not for the first time, that I had over-simplified her in my busy petty diagnoses. I had underestimated her. 'Why,' she said sweetly, 'do you think I'm unattractive – except of course to you who – quote – "understand" me?' I started to answer, but the question was rhetorical and she went smoothly on:

'So you'd like to help me, would you? You too? Did James suggest it? I can manage very well without James. I think I might be capable of organizing my own sex therapy.'

I got up and walked to the edge of the slope. Perhaps I hoped she would follow me and nurse my wounds. She didn't; and I pulled myself together. I had lost the upper hand – and with it the thread of my purpose in coming. I turned back and stood quite close, looking down at her. She raised her head to speak, but it was my turn.

'Nemo, maybe you are, and maybe casual encounters with strangers are what you would prefer. But it's not good enough. I've got something better to offer you. I'm in love with you, and I demand a serious affair. If I make you happy, I am going to take you away from James, and we'll have children and live happily ever after and –'

'Stop it, Harry.'

Her head was down and she did not move; but her voice was suddenly hard and quick, and it halted me. She sat quite still, looking only at her clenched hands in her lap, and the big bulging sunglasses on her crown glinted back at me like a second pair of eyes.

'Harry,' she said at last, 'take it from me: an affair would be fatal.'

'Fatal? Oh, come on now – be independent if you like, but don't make yourself out to be some sort of Black Widow spider. It's just too melodramatic.' Then I tried to be gentle, crouching in front of her and taking her hands. I could feel them tingling with her tenseness, and when I looked up into her face her eyes were tightly shut, like a child at the dentist. 'Nemo?' I said. I sat beside her and put my arm round her, longing to regain the Darby and Joan mood I had so rashly destroyed.

For a while we sat without speaking; then she said, 'You see, Harry' – with a sort of weary patience – 'I know you love me, and I think if I could have loved anyone it might have been you –'

'That's nonsense – it's not in the past: it's all in the future. Look here, I've sprung all this on you when you were low – I should have waited. I meant to, but I couldn't bear seeing you like that. I really came out to try and make you see *why*

you're in a mess, not to compound it with indecent pro-
posals. Poor sweet – just don't take on so. I can't help telling
you I'm in love with you – but there's nothing *fatal* about
that –'

'Oh, Harry – *please* don't get mixed up in this.' She
turned suddenly and gripped my arms with a painful
urgency. She gazed into my eyes intently, as if looking for
something there, then shook her head and leant back, limp
and peaky, pulling the dark glasses down over her eyes. 'I
just don't want to see you hurt,' she said in a flat monotone.

'Leave that to me,' I said, getting up. I could see there was
no reasoning with her in this mood, this depression that
sucked down even the stoutest lifeline. 'I've got to get back
to College now for a meeting, but I'm going to come out
again soon and get on with the gardening for you. What
about some digging and weeding? Or planting out those
nicotiana?'

She walked with me slowly towards the car and seemed
happy to talk of practical things. 'Everything's growing up
so fast,' she said again. 'All the nettles and willow herb –
down there in the clearing it's all getting out of hand –'

'Yes. About the clearing, Nemo. You're not still going by
the instructions on the tape-recording, are you?'

'Oh, *that*. Well, it faded out, you know – either that or I
imagined it. I tried to play it to James in a rash confiding
moment, but it had gone – just provided a bit more material
for his "dotty dossier" on me. He may be right. I'm not sure
now it ever existed.'

'But I heard it too – well, I heard something –'

'Yes, but only at my suggestion, Harry, you see. When
two people are as much in sympathy as we are, don't you
think one could make the other think something by a sort
of hypnosis? I've often wondered about it.'

'Well, it's certainly one explanation,' I said. I was pleased
that she should see it this way – flattered, I suppose – and felt

some relief that I did not have to take a stand on the question of the reality or otherwise of the ghostly voice.

'Of course I'll help you get the nettles up – or anything else.' I kissed her quickly and drove away.

When I sat down at the back of the Faculty Meeting, late and quietly, the Bursar leaned across and muttered a greeting. 'Did you see the *Mail*? Didn't you know Robert Maclean?'

'No – yes – why?'

'He's gone missing, apparently. Over a week. Thought you knew him – science-fiction chappie –'

I got the paper from the Lodge after the meeting. It was on the front page, with a picture of him, a rather flattering studio portrait probably off the back of one of his books. Apparently he had set out from home, just over a week ago, for an international science-fiction conference in Amsterdam and hadn't been heard of since. He had never arrived, though his car was found at the station. I rang James's College, and just caught him between getting back from London and dining in Hall. He had seen something about it in the *Evening Standard* and telephoned Bob's wife Sylvia; now he expanded on the newspaper story for my benefit.

Bob Maclean had left for a conference, to be followed by a series of lectures in the Netherlands, on Monday, eight days ago. Sylvia did not expect to hear from him, but the Dutch branch of the society had contacted her, after some delay, through his publishers and his agent, to see if he had got his dates wrong, for he was notoriously vague. They said he had not arrived. Taken by surprise, she covered up, said that he was unwell, apologized: for Bob was also notoriously promiscuous, and she suspected he had gone off on a stolen holiday with some girl, and it would only be embarrassing to start a hue and cry. She hung on for three more days, and then finally told the police. They found his car at Oxford Station, with the keys inside, and his suitcase. Now they were treating him as a Missing Person – 'Obviously,' said James, 'it's the abandoned luggage that's put the wind up them – passport, papers, everything – right down to a crisp new packet of French letters, according to Sylvie – "abandoned" in more ways than one, as I said – she's taking it very well: it won't be the first time.' Now the police had published his photograph and a description, and started inquiries as to who had seen him last, where, when, etcetera. Their only conclusion was that he had not left the country, but otherwise they had drawn a blank.

James seemed to me very hearty and dismissive about the whole thing. 'Old Sylvie shouldn't have panicked,' he said. 'I think she's rather regretting it now. I'm quite sure, myself, that Bob's shacked up with some blonde – and quite probably drinking himself into a stupor – doesn't even know what day it is, I dare say. Now all this has blown up, well – I would expect him to lie low until it's dropped out of the headlines: he's a bit of a coward, old Bob, hates scenes and fuss – not likely to step forward at this point and say "Hey, here I am!" I think he's gone a bit far this time – though I can't help feeling a touch envious: nice work if you can get it, eh? I've got this sweet little thing in London, Harry, talking of blondes – I must say, I could do with a lost week or whatever – Yes, I'm going up again tomorrow – business as usual –'

Already I had forgotten Bob Maclean. Tomorrow I would get pâté and bread and wine, like the old days, and go out to the Dower House for lunch and the afternoon with Nemo. Nemo off her guard: I would not even telephone first. James was welcome to his blondes.

12

There were spring gales that night. I was working late to make way for the time I proposed to take off next day. For I was quite determined to go: I could at least get on with the gardening. There would be branches down after this wind; I would make a bonfire, and dig in the vegetable garden. At most, moving from the humble to the sublime, I could make love to Nemo: playing the part of a pal – her word – and comforter had been sorely trying; for, subdued and diminished as she was by pain, she had still been to me painfully attractive. I did not fancy being a mixed-up male nurse for long.

Hendry came in for a late drink; I knew he had been worrying about one of our most promising second-year undergraduates, but it had been difficult to talk about it at dinner. He had a glass of brandy and stretched out his long legs by the fire; and, while the gale roared round the quadrangle, shaking the windows of my high room, he told me about Bertie.

Bertie Bull, our *enfant terrible*, was rather a joke at first – the world was his china shop. He was a brilliant, unstable, immensely likeable young man, whose greatest fault was that he excelled at too many things: he dropped rugger to star in an OUDS production of *The Revenger's Tragedy*; he was president of the Poetry Society, and was writing a slender book on orchids. I think he may have been a homosexual when he came up to Oxford, but even with a shortage of women he was swiftly converted to the other persuasion. In fact he was a very attractive spoilt young man, who, by the middle of his second year, had, he felt, done everything, and now, Hendry told me, was threatening to drop it all and become a monk. I was his Moral Tutor, and I had been away when this *crise* came at the end of the Hilary term. Hendry had coped, had reasoned with him for hours, and sent him away on a walking holiday with a long reading list, after securing his promise that he would at least come back at the start of the summer term and talk to me.

He arrived next morning, when I was finishing my breakfast, and heated up the remains of the coffee. I found him reasonable and much more balanced than I had expected from Hendry's report. Now he seemed happy to see the summer term out; and I let well alone and talked instead of his vacation, his family and mutual friends. It made his life at Oxford at once easier and more complicated having a professor for a father – albeit in another subject – and he often met his academic superiors socially. I remembered a dinner party at which he had met the Boyces, and asked him if he had seen them again.

'No,' he said, 'not properly. I was meant to go to their New Year party but was otherwise engaged. But Dr Boyce says I can come out and look for orchids in their wood. It's freaky sort of soil round those parts – about a hundred acres that's basically acid – hence the famous rhododendrons. But, of course, you know all that.'

'Yes, I do: it's an odd wood; you might find something quite unusual in the way of orchids, I should think, possibly imported, but no less interesting if they've taken to it.'

'Mrs Boyce is fascinating, isn't she?'

'Why, yes,' I said.

'Not at all the usual run of dons' wives, really. Good vibrations there – maybe more.'

'Well at least you don't talk like a monk yet,' I said, getting up and bringing the session to an end. Jealousy stirred under my ribs like an unwanted child. I did not like myself feeling possessive about Nemo any more than I liked the thought of the beautiful eccentric Bertie Bull going out to forage in our wood for orchids. I hurried off to an examiner's meeting, immersed myself in minutiae and dismissed him from my mind: as far as I could see, Bertie was once more a normal healthy boy.

I did not get out for the Dower House until two: a second meeting had dragged on, and I only had time to pick up some bread and cheese on the way out of town. Nemo would have eaten by now; but I knew she would be on her own: the woman who came to clean was only there in the mornings, I gathered; the gardener worked on Saturdays under James's supervision; and James himself was in London with his blonde.

I parked my car behind the hedge by the garage. Her little Fiat was there, but Nemo herself was nowhere to be seen. She was not in the kitchen or anywhere downstairs, and I walked round the garden and the wood without finding her. I did not call under her window: I thought she must be resting; I would wait.

Meanwhile there was a lot to do: fallen twigs and branches to clear up, as I had anticipated – but it was too wet, I thought, to get a fire going. So, when I had eaten my bread and cheese, and tidied up the lawns, I planted out the seed boxes of little tobacco flowers in the border and the two tubs at the entrance to the walled garden; then I went down to the end of the orchard where a vegetable patch was being made, and started digging. The sun came out and I took off my jacket, rolled up my sleeves and worked on. Once I went up to the kitchen for a drink of water. There was still no Nemo, but an empty wineglass stood on the big table – the only sign of life.

I took some matches and a box of old newspapers back down to the orchard: the wind was dropping now, coming and going in gusts, the sun was warm – good drying weather – and I thought that I could make a start on the bonfire. I tucked a nest of crumpled paper under the pyre, lit it, and soon the sweet-smelling smoke of burning twigs was billowing all around me, fanned by the fitful wind, stinging my eyes. And now, as I dug, I tossed the weeds on to it, tidying as I went. I had seen a pile of holly trimmings by the entrance to the drive, and collected them in the wheelbarrow. I knew they were resinous and would burn well; and, sure enough, the fire that had grown sullen with my weeds started to crackle and blaze again.

I suppose it was the crackle of the flaming holly that hid the sound of footsteps, and the veering smoke that blinded me. Nemo appeared suddenly through a great cloud, like a *dea ex machina*. She was dressed outlandishly in a small laced bodice and a billowing orange skirt – a sort of operetta milk-maid – with the diaphanous shawls and scarves round her bare shoulders caught up and streaming out on the wind like wild pennons and flags of war.

It was the most marvellous apparition. I dropped my fork and spread my arms to tell her so, when she threw herself into them and stopped my mouth with her own.

I had endured a sense of suppressed excitement, of a growing confident anticipation all through the hour or so I had worked, acutely aware of her resting so near me, waking perhaps and seeing me from a window, coming down to thank me – but I had not dreamed of this. Her kisses were deep and passionate; there was no question of pausing, of hoping, of catching breath. She drew me down where we stood, a few feet from the fire, among the weeds and earth and long grass. I don't remember fumbling with fastenings – perhaps she did, but it was all part of the most gloriously blatant streamlined seduction that ever featured in a hot-house fantasy. I do remember she had no underwear on at all: I pulled at the dangling laces of her bodice and her bare breasts came free – and the buttons were torn off my shirt as she wrenched it open and pressed against me, hot and sweet and fierce. I felt the young nettles and thistles burning my back, her marvellous warm weight moving and seething on top of me, her face, her veils, her hair and the great flounces of her tucked-up skirt blotting out the sky. It was total rape of the senses, too swift, too brutal, too devastating to be called making love. In moments it was over. I lay back panting and regaining consciousness.

As the ecstasy slowly withdrew and my other senses came back, I opened my eyes and looked up past her wild hair and her orange skirt to the eddying smoke in the apple boughs, and I felt bruised and shattered and complete. I began to take in what had happened: it was what I had always longed for, yet never in my dreams could I have constructed such an encounter with Nemo. I felt desperately moved once I could think again: she was mine, she had wanted me as much as I had wanted her, we were one flesh, at peace in a tangle on the wet grass.

'Nemo,' I said softly, stroking her hair. I realized with a shock it was the first time either of us had spoken.

She lay a full minute longer, inert, barely breathing. Then she gasped in the air with a great sob, sighed it out and slid off me. I bent over her and smoothed the hair from her face. Her heavy make-up was smeared like a clown, but she looked luscious and tousled, lying there with her gorgeous gaudy clothes still up round her waist and her breasts bare and tasting of wood-smoke.

She pushed me off suddenly, rolled away and got to her feet.

'That will do,' she said acidly with her back to me, lacing up her bodice. She brushed the grass from her skirt, but did not look round.

'But Nemo, darling,' I said, 'don't rush off like that. Come here and let me wipe the mud off your shoulder.'

I held the hem of her skirt and tugged gently, but she twitched it away from me and then very deliberately, and smiling for the first time, she stepped on my hand. It was a hard, hurtful crunch with the full force of her high heel – she was wearing very short laced boots that I had never seen before – then she turned and walked away.

This was too much. I got to my feet and followed her, belting and buttoning my trousers as I went. I caught her shoulder and swung her round, holding her firmly.

I had seen Nemo blazing like a brand on her return from London. I knew what James meant by 'high'. She was high today, sizzling with energy and conscious sexual attraction. I had not seen her high and angry, though. The sheer force of the revulsion in her face took my words away. With burning eyes, burning cheeks and the coldest voice she said:

'Don't imagine you have some special privilege. I suggest you leave without more ado.' She was looking straight at me, and I had the strange feeling for a moment that she did not recognize me.

'But, Nemo, Nemo darling – it's me, Harry – I love you, remember? Oh, I love you *so* –' At that moment I felt so overwhelmingly protective and grateful for her mad generous love-making, and desperate at her strange humour, I sank down and hugged her to me, burying my face in the folds about her thighs. 'Nemo, don't be like this – it's only the beginning. Don't you feel that? Don't you love me a little?'

She stood like a statue.

'Who said anything about love?' she said. 'When you are through with the high-flown sentiments, be so good as to let me go and leave me to myself.'

At this I did let go of her and stood back. Nemo drew herself up, shook out her skirt and arranged her shawls round her. She gave me one last smouldering scornful look and turned towards the house. I watched her walk away, rumpled, proud, adorable, remote.

'I shall come back,' I called, 'and we shall make love again. I'll teach you what love is –' She swept through the front door and it closed behind her.

I was alone once more in the garden. Like a robot I walked stiffly back to the bonfire and raked it together with automatic precision. I tucked the ends in and watched it blaze up again. The whole extraordinary episode had taken somewhat less than ten minutes. I stood gazing into the spitting flames, and I wondered if it *had* simply been a fantasy. But there was my torn shirt and scratches on my chest; there was a bright scarf trodden into the soft loam. I still had that physical exhilaration, the sense of having been caught up in a divine storm: but now, instead of peace, I felt only loss. Tossed off and tossed aside – no communion of souls, not even a real communion of bodies. It had been an experience of the most indescribable sensual bliss followed by the rudest awakening.

I stuck the fork into the ground viciously, picked up my coat and wandered down into the wood. I was in a turmoil; I wanted to sort out my muddled emotions, to make some sense of Nemo's behaviour. For the length of two cigarettes I sat on her log in the clearing, staring blindly at the azaleas, now in their dazzling prime; and the only sense that I could make of it all was that something was at an end. I felt, sitting there, that I was saying good-bye to the clearing, and as I walked back up the paths, I was leaving it for good. Ritually, I visited the Long Walk, the fig trees, full of hard green fruit, the walled garden and last of all the west lawn with its view of the distant river.

I did not look up at Nemo's room, but as I was turning to go, I stepped in through the french windows, and impulsively called to her. Suppose she had changed, had softened, wanted me back, was waiting for me to come and take her in my arms. I called again from the foot of the stairs. There was no answer, no sound of movement other than the ticking of the carriage clock in the big drawing room. I went back through the morning room. On the oval table in the corner there lay an elegant marbled notebook, with pen and inkstand. I opened it and recognized Nemo's hand: I wondered if this was the writing James had spoken of, and whether it held the secrets of her heart and of her strange behaviour. No flutter of conscience troubled me as I picked it up and folded it inside my jacket. I considered that I was due some explanation: if it did no more than show the working of her mind, I held a claim to it – or so I felt. I had a right to take something; she had taken everything from me, for she had taken my hopes.

I went out across the gravel drive and the grass circle where the yellow roses were already in bud. Soon I would have known the house a year. I had loved it so; now, how every precious detail hurt me, all that was unchanging, and all that Nemo had changed. Even the delicate red-tinged storksbill sprouting in the high wall by the garage that had been precisely there last June; and now the tubs of nicotiana that one brief hour ago I had planted out so snugly – all mocked at me: not just a rejected lover. A lover taken – how taken! – then rejected.

As I drove out I looked back in the driving mirror as I always did, and saw, as I had seen the first time, the rose tree against the pink brick growing smaller, fading away into past time. Then the plunge into the dark holly tunnel, and suddenly I was out in the lane; the house had gone.

The drive to the main road is flat and winding; I met no cars on it, passed no pedestrians. I drove slowly and, turning out into the highway, with good visibility both ways, I did not even have to pause: rush-hour had not yet started – so much for my day with Nemo. I headed towards Oxford and picked up speed. On the first long slope after the village

I caught up with a learner driver creeping along close to the edge of the road. I would have passed him, but a large lorry was coming the other way; so I pulled over behind him and braked. Nothing happened.

I just had time to change down before I hit the car in front of me; it jerked forward on the impact, then I saw the man in the passenger seat throw himself across and grab the wheel. As he turned the car into the verge and stepped on the brake, I hit it again; then I too came to a halt. The L-driver had stopped my headlong progress and very probably saved my life.

A red-faced man ripped open my near-side door and roared at me before I could move.

'What the hell do you think you're doing?'

Another car honked and swerved round us.

'I'm sorry – my brakes failed. I'm most terribly sorry –'

I left it in gear, though we were now on the level, switched off and got out to see the damage. My ribs were sore where the steering wheel had hit me; I was severely shaken, but even more so was the driver of the other car. He sat numbly, still strapped into his seat-belt, saying:

'What should I have *done*? I should have known what to *do* –'

My headlights were gone and the front bumper stove in. His boot and bumper were badly buckled. I could only apologize, and say I was entirely to blame. The red-faced man took my name and address, and made me write out and sign a statement to the effect that I accepted total responsibility for the accident. As he was getting back, this time into the driver's seat, he unbent so far as to say:

'If it really was your brakes, you should give hell to whoever MOT'd that car. How are you going to get back?'

'Oh, I'll manage. You go on,' I said.

They drew away slowly, and disappeared round the bend in the road.

Then I opened the bonnet and peered in to check the brake fluid; but then I saw the glint of bare new metal. It was the casing of the brake pipes where they had been clipped clean through.

13

I crept back to Oxford in bottom gear, and at last turned in to a garage on the outskirts. I left the car round at the back on the piece of waste land they used as a parking lot and dump, and told the attendant busy at the pumps that I had had an accident and just wanted to keep it there until I had recovered and sorted things out.

'Don't touch it,' I said. 'I'll telephone you about further arrangements.'

He seemed perfectly agreeable, even sympathetic.

'What happened, then?' he asked. 'Looked a proper mess – ran into something, did you?'

'Yes,' I said. 'I don't remember all that much about it.'

'You probably got a bit of a knock yourself – you ought to take it easy. Delayed reaction and all that. Want to call a radio-taxi? The phone's just in there.'

'I'll be fine on a bus,' I said.

I waited ten minutes in the bus shelter, grateful for the bench. But that, and the slow stately ride into the city centre, gave me time to think – the last thing I wanted. Anyway, I kept telling myself, the car was locked, I had the keys, they couldn't open the bonnet from the outside. Someone would have to know eventually, when the damage was repaired; the insurance people as well, I realized. There could be no hushing it up. The brake pipes had been cut. Would they feel obliged to report it to the police? Or could I satisfy them with some tale of a practical joke, or a ham-handed attempt at do-it-yourself repairs? I thought not; but at least I had a breathing space.

There was only one person who could have done it, and that was Nemo. What is more, she was perfectly capable of it. There were tools in the garage, a few feet from where I had parked it, and she knew her way round the engine of a car as well as I did: James was so often not there that she had learned to cope with minor problems of upkeep – oil and water, drying out the distributor cap or fixing a new fan belt. It would have been a matter of moments to release the catch under the dashboard, open up the bonnet, find and clip through the pipes with a heavy pair of pliers and cover her tracks. I must have given her nearly half an hour – I had tidied my bonfire, and wandered round the garden, spending perhaps as much as fifteen minutes in the clearing, well out of earshot. And there was no one else who could have done it. It had to be Nemo. But why? Was she mad? Did she hate me so much she wanted to see me dead? I thought again and again of the revulsion on her face.

I was back in my room about half past five. Two of my third-year pupils were coming to see me at six; there was time for a hot bath, and I took some aspirins. I threw my bedraggled shirt in the wastepaper basket: I neither wanted to get it mended nor wear it ever again. For the next hour I almost managed to put Nemo out of my mind; these were two of my finalists, and though, being both their tutor and their examiner, I had to stick to generalities, I did my best to advise them on their last few weeks of cramming, and boost their confidence. They were both hard workers, and I could tell them truthfully I had high hopes for them. Privately I suspected that exam conditions might quite undo one of them, while they could well fire in the other the spark of genius that I suspected was hidden under his bushels of careful notes.

When they left I felt drained of energy. My ribs ached and inside them so did my heart – or whatever it is that seems to contain one's spirit at roughly the centre of the body. I could not face dining with my colleagues, though I knew it would appear strange and invite comment after my recent and prolonged absence. What I needed was a good drink. I had a stiff whisky, then suddenly hated sitting there with my glass alone. I went out to the nearest pub. It was raining again, and the bar was full of hearty steaming undergraduates, the earnest gang who come back a day early to organize themselves and be ready to organize others. I drank deep and moved on. The next was off the main university stamping ground; here real men talked quietly about sumps and greyhound racing, and there were good solid sandwiches and sausage rolls, and a choice of mac. cheese or shepherd's pie if you were prepared to wait. I drank steadily. I had been raped and nearly murdered, and I needed it.

The third pub I went to filled up with the theatre crowd just before closing time. I sat in a corner with a newspaper I found there and stared at the cricket results and Oxford United's white hopes for next season. On the front page that fell forward across my glass, I saw Bob Maclean looking at me upside down. I turned it over, smoothed it carefully on my knee, and read 'Maclean Still Missing'. They're a bit out of date, aren't they? I thought – and what about Burgess? I was the last to leave when they closed the doors. I didn't like what was waiting for me. On my desk in College lay Nemo's marbled notebook. I recoiled from the mind of my beloved as from a snakepit.

All too soon I found myself at the Lodge gates, where the small inset door was still open. Two undergraduates were talking outside, and I saw the Chaplain, another bachelor living in College, nod to them and duck in through the door. There, I thought, is what I need: the love of God, and a wise and holy man to listen to my troubles; an understanding friend. And lest he should recognize and hail me, I crossed over to the other pavement and walked on.

What could I tell him, or anyone? 'It's like this, Chaplain. I went out to this don's house to seduce his wife and she raped me and then cut through my brake pipes – what do you advise me to do? Give up sex? Give up driving?'

I realized now I was very drunk. I kept walking heading toward the parks, up St Cross Road and past 'Jurisprudence'. What answer would the lawyers have for me? 'If you can prove malice aforethought, we suggest you sue Mrs – er – Boyce; but naturally you lay yourself open to the charge of adultery. Perhaps it would be wiser to settle out of court?'

The science area, as usual, was blazing with lights. Time matters not to them, I thought. Perhaps I should tell it all to a scientist. I did not know where the Department of Psychology was – not that it mattered: biochemist? Physicist? Nothing would surprise them. They'll listen expressionlessly and with complete concentration, I thought, feed all the data into a computer and hand me the answer in neat intergalactic type – letters with thickened legs, distorted into variations on a square for a blind machine to run its sensors over. I reached the park gates and they were locked.

Of course they'd be locked. But Port Meadow won't be locked, I thought; they can't lock Port Meadow away for the night. I set off across the residential hinterland of North Oxford, past the spacious smug Victorian houses, brick bastions of respectability. Here behind thick curtains, dinner parties would be just beginning to come apart, leaving behind in the tall rooms a thin and rarified iono- sphere of wit just above the cigar smoke; and in the chilly quarry-tiled kitchen, a pile of washing up. Perhaps if I knocked and went in, and perched on a Habitat stool, drink- ing the dregs of the coffee while she did the dishes, some kindly sensitive mother of six, flushed from her triumph (' – and the Provost actually commented on my cummin and cucumber soup'), would sort out my troubles. 'My dear, of *course* she needs a lover,' she would say, scraping the bones of the *ossobucco* into the Tidibin. And the brakes? 'She was just asserting herself, poor sweet. I suspect it was simply a rather extreme attention-seeking device – you should go back and tell her you understand . . . '

Smaller, sadder streets, *Mon Repos* and *Kenmarge* – I canna ken marge frae butter – Mon Débris and the black canal. Beyond it the playground; I had a go on a swing, but it was a mistake. Here, away from the streetlights, I noticed the sky was clearing: the same gusty wind that had fanned my holly cuttings to a crackling inferno was sweeping away the last rain clouds, and a misshapen moon came through. Port Meadow stretched before me, acres of bare scuffed common ground, looped by the same river, or part of it, that flowed through the water-colourist's view from the west lawn of the Dower House, into the highest branches of the further trees, past Ferry Cottage and disappeared round the ice-house hill on its way to London and the sea.

A message in a bottle now. I walked on slowly; I was tired, and the pain of my bruised ribs seemed to have spread all over me. When I came to the edge of the dark flowing river I sat down on the bank, and pulled out the quarter-bottle of whisky I had bought as I left the bar. Carefully I unscrewed the top and tilted it up to the moon and drank. I thought of the day I had toasted my newly discovered house. I sat and wondered. Then I took out my diary and tore off a page. By the light of the moon I wrote laboriously, in neat capitals, 'Nemo, I love you. Why do you want to kill me?' I folded it up to fit into the neck of the bottle, then realized there was still some whisky in it. I drank some more, and poured a solemn libation on to the little gravel shore at my feet. Then I put in my message, screwed the top on, stood up and tossed it out well into midstream. It was a slender chance, very slender, I told myself, that Nemo would be walking the dog down by the river when my bottle floated by. Then I remembered the dog was dead. Still I felt I had taken some positive action appropriate to my stranded loneliness, a gesture that she, who was clearly as mad as I was surely drunk, would appreciate. I turned round and set out for home.

It was a long long way, and all the way I thought about Nemo: how she had materialized through the smoke in her fantastic clothes – full sail, with silken scarves for spinnakers, bearing down on me. The suddenness of it, and her voracious passion, consuming me. That was what kept sticking in my gorge – harder to take than her attempt to kill me. A fate worse than death. For Nemo had raped me. I had used the word glibly to myself at first, but now I admitted to its awful accuracy. She had had the upper hand from start to finish in that encounter: she had even been on top of me. I had nothing against it as a position, and I had saved her from the worst of the nettles and thistles. But it had been deliberate, undisputed, a symbol of her domination, and carried through into her haughty dismissal. She had used me, nothing more.

And *how*. I had never known such a powerful sexual encounter. Now, in the wide open spaces of St Giles, I sat on a bollard, looking up at the lopsided moon, and let the detailed splendour of total recall, such as transfigured bodies hold on to for a few hours, hit me, like the wave of heat from an open furnace. Such a creature of air and fire – and the urgency of her two devouring mouths – and so little time.

I sat there randy and wretched as the memory faded, with only the streetlamp for company. It stood there dangling silly wire buckets of daffodils from stiff arms designed for lynchings. 'Severe overheating can cause accidents on the road,' I pronounced owlishly.

'You had an accident, sir?' inquired the policeman who gently moved me on. He was walking me towards my

College. 'You really should be lying down, sir. Delayed reaction. Did you report the accident, sir?'

Suddenly I felt very sober.

'Don't worry, officer,' I said. 'I'm fine really. Just a bump – you know, a bit shaken up. I'll get it all sorted out in the morning.'

'You do that, sir. You should always report an accident in case anyone turns out to have suffered injuries – '

A mere bagatelle, officer. I did not say it out loud, just muttered it to the moon as I crossed the quad to my staircase. Just a little case of severed brake pipes and heart strings. The autopsy showed that the heart strings had been severed with a strong pair of pliers – then I opened my door and saw the marbled book lying on my desk under the glare of the reading lamp.

I felt as wide awake as if I had had a bucket of cold water emptied over me. I made some strong black coffee, took it back to the desk, swallowed two more aspirins and opened Nemo's notebook.

14

It started with a poem, or what looked like a poem: as soon as I started reading I realized it was a neat ordered transcript of part of the tape-recording I had heard – or believed I had heard – and of which she had made some scribbled notes. It was rather pleasing, laid out on the page, and I could see why it had occurred to her to treat it so, particularly as she had now rejected any significance she might originally have found in it. Now it was a 'donnée', fresh and unworked on, sprung complete into her mind as some poems do; and, as poetry, it made sense.

> *I am the only candle*
> *Alight in the wood*
> *And I am burning low*
> *Winter coming apace*
> *I am going to need*
> *A new coat*
> *Fur is warm.*
> *Flesh is warmer.*
>
> *I cannot feel the holly*
> *When I go cautiously barefoot.*
> *The house was frightening*
> *At first*
> *So changed*
> *But I have found a looking-glass*
> *That knows me.*
> *I have not changed.*

That was all, though as I remembered it, there had been a lot more. It could have been a nice judgement that kept it so, but the rest of the page was blank; I think she meant to finish it.

Then she started something like a journal, a factual account, in some detail, of the state of the house when they bought it, improvements they had made and further projects for the cellar and garden. There were lots of corrections and insertions; she seemed to think it important to get things in the right order. But there was no attempt at 'style': it was a record and no more. She even noted at length the proportions of the mixtures of emulsion paint they had used, and the makers of tiles, and sinks, and louvred doors. It was Nemo at her most practical, and did not bore me, even with its lists, for both the writer and the subject were dear to me. When she dealt in projects for the future, her special loves stood out clearly: the morning room, the Long Walk, the clearing in the wood. She even sketched a little folly in the form of a rococo temple, for the centre of her magic circle.

'One will be able to see it glimmering white from the bedroom and even from the west lawn', she noted. 'Steps down to it, brick if stone is too expensive. It should all mellow quite quickly with moss and ivy down in that damp hollow. Clematis? or a Kiftsgate rose? climbing over it. There was a sort of rustic folly before, by the gate. Two gates, of course, and two driveways: one for the tradesmen. The Long Walk a rich border, the wistaria stretching behind it along the crinkle-crankle wall for a hundred feet, the gravel path, raked daily, that leads up to the bright blue iron gate in the box hedge. I love box – another evergreen, but in fact almost blue at times with the bloom of the new growth, and here by the little gate clipped so neatly on either side into the shape of two urns – a nice fancy. Enough vegetables and soft fruit in the acre of kitchen garden to serve the whole household through the year; the little standard apples in an avenue down the centre are pruned back, purely decorative, or they would cast too much shade to the north (and the orchard provides all the necessary fruit). Grapes do well here; they say in the village that long ago it was a vineyard. Herbs grow in the north-west corner, convenient for the kitchen; and bunches of them hang to dry from the great beam. The big bread oven draws well. The ceiling is very low and black from the smoke – best so for the hams to mature. They boil the big copper for the clothes in its own range down below stairs – so at least no clouds of steam. They keep the fish kettles and the cooking pans well polished, glinting in the firelight, as do the rows of knives and cleavers. But dark in winter and oppressive in summer – with what relief I return to the bright little sitting room overlooking the evergreen garden, green even when all else is bare and grey; a pleasant walk through all its leafy paths, leading to the still centre, my magic circle.'

And the description had come full circle, too, I realized. Back to the wood. It was the old pattern: everything began and ended there.

But in the process the 'before' and 'after' of Nemo's record seemed to have been reversed. From plans projected into the future, she had slipped back smoothly into the past; and this time it was not the immediate past, the house as they had found it, but the distant past, as the house might have been in its grand old days, its earlier incarnation, long before it was requisitioned during the war years, and then rented by a series of uncaring tenants. I glanced ahead to see if she would describe the main rooms: I found that the painted ceiling of the 'bow room' was there; and she described in passing the delicate French furniture, the great Adam fireplace where whole logs were burnt – now occupied by the smaller Victorian grate, and its surround of patterned tiles. She described the view out across the formal arrangement of many-coloured rhododendron bushes. Now I knew they had all grown gigantically and reverted to the semi-wild mauve: Nemo and James had planted a large number of new shrubs to restore the various colours that must have been there once.

There was nothing strange about Nemo's careful reconstruction, only the manner of her doing it. She was so precise about details, so ambiguous about time. Was she pretending to be living in the past, or projecting herself into an ideal future? If the latter, did she anticipate a life of candles and fires in every room, and the servants to tend them, to boil clothes in the copper 'below stairs', work the acre of kitchen garden, rake the gravel paths? I could not see her wanting this; and there was an insistent whining note that intruded whenever the old wing, the working part of the house, was mentioned.

Suddenly she seemed to lose interest – or to be taken with a different notion. At the bottom of one page she ended in mid-sentence, left the verso blank, then started afresh, in a firm clear hand. Looking back, I noticed that the writing had been deteriorating – slanting more and more downhill, more fluent but less controlled – over the last two pages. With the new start, it was Nemo's more upright hand, very deliberate; it seemed to be the opening of a story.

'It was a warm day in autumn, a ripe windless day when the trees, still heavy with turning leaves, caught and held the afternoon sun. The young woman had taken her apple-peeling out on to the stone steps. From here she could look down the garden, with its beeches, birches, chestnuts, in all their brief September glory. From here too she looked down on the wood, that dark, unaltering evergreen of laurels and rhododendrons the sun could not pierce. Down there –'

She broke off, and started an unconnected paragraph about the house itself; again it took one obsessively from room to room. At first it was no more than a fictional and idealized version of her 'progress report' a few pages back.

And again she executed a time-slip, as it became clear that it was the house, not as it was now, but as it might have been in its heyday. Then it drew one along endless passages to poky storerooms lined with dully gleaming varnished cupboards, to the huge dark kitchen with its complex of arches and ovens and hooks in the ceiling, the hams and cleavers and drying herbs and rows of heavy crocks on the towering brown-painted dresser. Here, it seemed, the windows were shuttered and the streaks of sunlight across the scrubbed table and the stone flags only increased the oppressive atmosphere, the brooding musty silence. It became apparent that she was searching for someone, and that the house was very quiet and empty – the servants' day off?

'He was not in the knife room, nor in the scullery. She would not call downstairs: he must come to *her*. As she passed back through the kitchen she thought how sad it was about the under gardener – he who was so good with the grapes. The smell of herbs, the heat in there with the sun on the closed shutters. Only the sound of an insect caught against the window, and that great heavy clock mincing the minutes – and so little time – '

The eye of the beholder, I realized, pulling myself out of the spell, had been entirely responsible: why in Nemo's story had the outlook of that nice wholesome three-dimensional girl peeling her apples given place, as she moved through the house, to that other, at once more jaundiced and more acute? As a story it did not hold together. She could not hold it together. Nemo's notebook was obsessed with the place almost as if she had wanted to write it out of her system. First the practical approach, the full progress report – then the time-slip. Then the attempt to write a story? a novel? Detached, anyway, into the third person; and again it got out of hand, back in time and with it the change from major to minor, that new, unNemolike whining tone – dissatisfied, pacing, restless, sick. And once more the writing had gone to pieces, sloping away down the page and petering out. Where was the apple-peeler now; or if it was she, for whom was she searching?

Four empty pages, then another fresh start. It was still Nemo's hand, but how more consciously sloped, more stylish and fast-flowing, unhesitating, neatly filling each page. Another story perhaps?

I heated the coffee and settled down to read.

15

. . . The young artisan who was sent to cure our leaking tank announced himself as 'Vic'. I preferred to call him Victor. He had Celtic eyes and thick black hair and a truly marvellous mouth – coarse in line but smooth in texture. Likewise the rough hands, I noticed, but the tender skin at the throat. He was vastly confident of his charm, with a tendency to stand closer than is customary.

When he had drained and soldered the tank, and was waiting for it to refill, I made him a cup of chocolate. It was exceedingly pleasant to sit and watch him as he elaborated on his many attributes, making it very clear that his skills in electrical work and building were as nothing to his ways with the ladies, who seemingly could not leave him alone. Encouraged by my attention – an enigmatic silence punctuated by small but delighted cries of outrage – he made bold to elaborate on his conquests, and the high class of lonely county dames for whom he had been the answer to an unbreathed prayer – though he did not put it so delicately.

Suddenly I wearied of his crowing.

'You are wasting your time and mine with this inflammatory talk, dear boy,' I said, rising. He looked very dashed, but I play by house rules only, and it was time to establish the upper hand. 'If you would be so good as to tell me why the study fire does not draw – as an encore, let us say, a mere trifle to a man of your many talents – you will please to follow me.'

While he peered up the chimney of the offending fireplace, and felt for and triumphantly slid back the iron plate in the flue (which I had closed in preparation for this exercise), I drew down the blinds and turned the key. He looked quite frightened for a moment – all his panache gone. He trembled as he stood with his back against the door and I unbuttoned his shirt. I tried to speak soothingly in spite of the fierceness that I felt rising in me.

'You see your references are irrelevant, my sweet. You were a marked man when you walked in at the door. As you would say, I "fancied" you. And now I am going to eat you alive – a new sensation perhaps, but one you are going to have to enjoy.'

He did. Once he had relinquished the whip hand he was accustomed to, he seemed not to know what had struck him down. He complied with all my requirements, surpassed all my expectations. He was a lovely young bullock; I did not look for subtlety, but savoured the contrast between his rough oil-streaked hands and his smooth body – I confess the beauty of his skin was a surprise to me. I may have hurt him somewhat – his mouth was bleeding a little. But I felt alive at last, intoxicated with the heat and violence, with the sweat, the taste of blood, the sense of power I have missed so long.

Then of course he would not go. He did not seem to realize when he was dismissed. He insisted that he would come back next day with his extending ladder (leering with the wit of it) and fix some loose slates on one of the roofs of which I had been complaining earlier over the chocolate, and which I now heartily regretted. But he was determined. A marked man indeed.

They used to say I could have been the most famous actress in the Kingdom if I had not so strongly resisted the whole conception of the Repeat Performance, the Long Run – and that it was the same case where lovers were concerned. Could not they comprehend my reluctance – nay, my repugnance? For, no matter how promiscuous a man may be, until he encounters Me he is virginal. Marvellously untrodden snow – unkindled tinder.

But alas, what can one do with ashes?

He returned late the next morning and set up his ladder against the tall north-facing side of the house. It proved a lengthy business – or he made it so. But no sooner had the cleaning woman left, nothing would serve but he must corner me with hot breath and hands – very full of yesterday's little business, as though for all the world he had made some conquest, and now confidently anticipated some sort of submission from me!

'But have you fixed all the tiles?' I said, evading him.

'Come up and see,' he said. 'You get a good view of them from that little room up there with the dormer window.' Very crafty and circumspect he thought he was! So be it, I thought.

He followed me closely up the stairs to the top of the house, grabbing clumsily the while at the forbidden fruit, and seemed merely encouraged by my hauteur. The little room was hot and stuffy and I threw open the window, much hampered by the great ox's ardent attentions.

'The tiles first,' I said, fobbing him off with the hint of promise. 'See those two below the chimney, all awry?'

'I could reach those from here with a little help – then maybe I can do something for *you* – ' the big wet mouth close to my ear.

I attempted to disguise my distaste, but by so doing, seemingly gave the impression that, as he prettily phrased it, I was feigning 'hard to get'. So I led him on, trusting that the roof under discussion would rid me of him.

He climbed out of the small dormer and was surprisingly sure-footed on the steep slope, the hammer between his teeth. He even looked not a little heroic, with the sun in his eyes, isolated by the huge drop and the valley – his admirable figure standing out very finely against a backcloth of distant blue hills.

I had noticed a long broom on the landing, and when he had some difficulty returning up the slope, I reached it out to him. He was already licking his chops over his anticipated reward, when, of a sudden, I pushed where before I had been pulling. For a moment I thought he would drag me with him, but at last, with a loud then dwindling cry, he went over the edge and disappeared. He fell about forty feet on to a glass roof, and by report he died instantly.

Spring is coming apace – hastening, it seems, it has continued so mild. The azaleas are budding out in the wood, even the new ones planted this year. The bluebells so thick now they make false distances amongst the taller trees; and the tawny, furry ferns are unwinding. We love it best alone in the evenings with no blustering masculine intruder trampling the young digitalis. And yet I think we will allow that charming author to visit it. He writes phantasies – albeit of other worlds – intricately descriptive. We find him profoundly sympathetic in conversation. He has a way with words, including many a shafted *double entendre*, and his lingering, his burning gaze makes abundantly clear which way advancement – and his intention – lies. He has long hands and exceedingly fine eyes, pale and mystical.

Down in the circle there was no breath of wind today, although it was sighing amorously in the distant tops of the cedar and the hollies. Down there it was all as still as a pool. As the marvellous Marvell says – and Henry, dear creature, soon to return, quoted it I remember, but unkindly – it is 'a fine and private place . . .'

My scout took one look at me and came back with a tray of breakfast. He pulled back the curtains and switched off the lights, clucking with disapproval. I got up stiffly and shaved, then sat down to eat, but I could only manage the coffee and some dry toast, leaving the kipper intact under its silver dome.

So that was how the workman had died. Of course I knew, and told myself repeatedly, it was another work of fiction, from perhaps a deeper layer of Nemo's mind – even a subconscious wish-fulfilment. The cool account of sex and of murder had a trancelike precision: the iron flue-cover, the tile below the chimney, the long-handled broom. Somehow it did not read like a work of fiction; but I told myself it could still be fevered imaginings triggered by some escape mechanism in the lonely housewife of my original diagnosis.

I found myself chain-smoking with my cold coffee and pacing in decreasing circles round my desk, postponing the next, the inevitable revelation: the disappearance of Bob Maclean, author of extra-terrestial 'phantasies' – yet all too aware that nothing in Heaven or Hell would stop me reading it now. I suppose I should have handed the notebook over to the police at the first suspicion, or at least contacted them when I discovered it contained a perfectly possible explanation of the young workman's death: there was the telephone on the desk beside the marbled book.

But as I waded yet deeper into the monstrous swamp that was the mind of my beloved, I had abandoned reason for complicity. I read on.

. . . Robert was as delightful as I had anticipated, though alas more difficult (I hope all is well). Although less simple and more problematical – but of course well worth the pains, as I do not doubt he would be the first to agree.

It was exceptionally romantic. He arrived unexpectedly – fortunately I was wearing my prettiest sprigged lawn day-dress – he came walking up through the wood – a good omen, I felt – and emerging like a satyr from between the dark laurels. He had left his car on the little track to the Ferry and 'approached the shrine on foot', as he said, to 'take the shy goddess by surprise'. He told me he was actually on his way to the Low Countries for a tour of lectures, but could not leave these shores without first sipping from the true fount of his inspiration. I was charmed and enflamed – we were so precisely in harmony – I felt all fire and air. Swiftly we made our way down into the wood, he carrying the rug and some chilled wine. It was perfectly delightful, and all as I had imagined.

Robert was a slight, goatish man, his dress as immaculate as his sensibility; and those pale fanatical eyes. A faintly evil mouth. His fine soft brown hair worn modishly long, albeit receding at the temples. He was as much of a sensualist as I had always suspected. As for his extreme dexterity with words, it was, I soon realized, compulsive: every separate sensation must perforce be expressed before he might extract the full savour. He whipped himself into a veritable frenzy of sexual passion with the most intricate obscenities. It was for a time both amusing and titillating – but soon I wearied of his little ritual. I bound my long scarf tightly round his mouth – even that he seemed to enjoy, groaning the superfluous and unguessed-at epithets through its folds – then I had things *my* way. I know I am too impatient and fierce – but there is so little time.

Afterwards we must have slept for a space. I awakened before him and looked down with a loathing unusually strong. The smell of corruption was powerful in my nostrils, and I rose up and set myself to search about under the laurels and see if any more deadmen's fingers were growing in the wood. Suddenly he was there, clawing at my skirts, still spewing words, wanting more of me. Fortunately the work on clearing the nettles from the circle was yet unfinished: the implements had been left there. I took up the big fork to ward him off.

'It is you that smell of death!' I cried.

The poor fool did not realize yet that the fatal act of intercourse with me had turned him into a hollowed rotting corpse. He kept pawing at me, spouting his phantasies – how beautiful I was with my starting hair and my raised weapon, like some Martian Queen. I could not abide his nightmarish touch and with two blows I felled the walking dead, and pinned his neck into the soft loam. That put an end once and for all to his obscene demands and importunate babblings, and it was peaceful again.

I put on the rough gardening gloves then, as I must needs touch him. It was not so difficult to lug him on to the wheelbarrow, he being small of stature, and seemed yet smaller now the wind had gone out of him. But I did not like the bloodied fork, and I went about the wood plunging it again and again into the earth until it smelled sweet and wholesome.

I certainly did not want him in the wood: his long fingers might grow through under the laurels. I wheeled the barrow out of the wicket gate and the rough undergrowth to the Ferry track. I knew dead bodies should be kept cool, and the old ice-house came to me as a happy thought. Tucking up my skirts like a serving wench, I went on down the Ferry road some little way to a spot where the hill sloped more gently, and made my way laboriously up through the brushwood to the spinney on top where the ice-house just showed its crumbling dome above the ground. Already nettles and brambles were growing around it in thick profusion, and it proved a considerable struggle to tip him in. I heard him fall and pulled the thorn brake back across the small opening.

Going downhill and returning through the wood to the circle was a simple task without that load of mortal flesh. I left the barrow there and went back through the wicket gate. Fatigued as I was, I was exhilarated by the pleasant prospect of a ride: it was discreet of poor Robert to conceal his car among the hazels while he enjoyed me, and it seemed only right to extend that discretion. The car should rightly be discovered at the railway station. So I drove it there, did some light shopping (for wisely, as it turned out, I had my purse in my pocket) and – feeling one of my wretched headaches coming on – I took a taxi home and went to bed.

Even in my pain, it was such a comfort to know there would be no pleading *revenant* appearing on the morrow, demanding more, like the unhappy Victor. Vastly unpleasing when the blood is chill. With Robert it was more of an extension of the act of love. But it would all be so much more pleasant, if only they could see that the Consuming – 'a consummation devoutly to be wished'? – is unrepeatable. For am I then to eat my vomit? They enjoy my deflowering them, burning them, slaying them – I know it, for they cry out their delight from the midst of their exquisite pain – even In Extremis. But soon they are done with. Am I then to take these dead spoilt creatures again into my arms?

Silly moths indeed that hope to be transfigured *twice* by the flame. . .

16

Fanciful or precise, my lovely Nemo was mad.

Yesterday (it felt like today – no night's sleep had inter-vened) we made love – more precisely, I had been had, but my male pride still resisted the concept. Then, when she realized I intended a serious affair with her, she had taken steps to kill me. Perhaps some old affection had prevented her taking up a chopper: I blessed that, or the cowardice, or the caution, that had made her simply clip through my brake pipes and leave me to kill myself.

But this gruesome notebook bore out the pattern. What was I to do now? If I told the police and Bob Maclean's body was found in the ice-house, then the 'journal' as evidence of a repressed housewife's wish-fulfilment, a theory that might have explained away the workman's death, would not stand a chance.

I knew that she ought to be certified and taken into care immediately, for, true or false, whoever had written that account was demented and possibly dangerous: supposing at best it was a deliberate work of fiction, it was still the product of a sick mind, as was the attempt on my life. But what grounds had I to press for this without actually pro-ducing evidence? The Nemo her friends and the world saw was the sanest person imaginable – highly strung, perhaps over-sensitive, but rational and tender-hearted – indeed, the sort of woman one goes to with one's troubles. I had troubles; but I could not take them to Nemo.

Nor to James – James who had been so entertained by my carefully unemotional account of the ghost. At least, on reflection, I did not fear any immediate danger to *him*: I assumed from all she had told me that they had not been sleeping together for some time – a fact which had renewed my hopes, reduced my guilt, moved me to action – and had almost brought about my untimely death. It meant that whatever part he played in her nightmare love-life it was not that of a potential victim.

But still I could not bring myself to tell him my suspicions; for, however detached he might be, and occupied elsewhere, my revelation involved his wife in two horrific sex-murders, as well as my own guilty implication in the third, attempted, murder. How do you tell a man, gently, that his wife is a homicidal nymphomaniac?

Meanwhile, even as I hesitated over a course of action, Nemo, with a terrible Blake-like innocence, was walking through a mine-field, protected only by the canniness of the mad – like the unnatural strength that supports them. It was, of course, the craft of the mind that possessed hers; for, if it turned out that her account was in fact a true one, I had to believe, against all my instincts as well as the dictates of reason, that she had quite literally been taken over by Sarah Moore. The style, in part, upheld this theory, though I still told myself that Nemo might be capable of constructing such a fiction in a sort of pastiche. Above all, nothing had been proved.

But though this was the central question – fact or fiction? – and like the circle in the wood, every alley I explored returned to it – I was unable to see for a moment how finding the answer could explain Nemo's behaviour. And yet, I argued, if Bob Maclean walked in tomorrow, the notebook would be clearly no more than a horrid pastime. Like trying to kill me?

Then I faced the truth about myself: I did not want to find the answer because I so deeply dreaded confirmation of my worst imaginings. It hung together too well; and the scepticism that had protected me so long was ripped away when exposed to what I had seen and heard, what I had vaguely feared for so long and what I had just read. If I was right, of course, my delay was even more grossly culpable; might not Nemo even now be rising, like some fabulous monster, from the deep sea languor, to repeat the cycle? She would have had a migraine after yesterday's 'elation'; but in a matter of hours, perhaps, she would be blazing like Lucifer, ready for the next victim. If that victim was a stranger on a train, or a passing van driver, he might survive the furnace; but if he lingered, or returned for more, the chances were that he would not.

It was a measure of my desperation that I telephoned Boris. He is the only psychiatrist I know – an eccentric, I believe I may say a 'kinky' man who, because of his own, specialized in disturbed childhoods, and in the process had developed a taste for almost anything sixteen. How far he indulged it I did not know, nor did I wish to know; and I was deeply reluctant to bring yet another bizarre element into a situation already over-rich in the unnatural. But at least I felt Nemo would be safe with him – and he, forewarned, with her. He would respect my confidences, and the secrets of the notebook. Above all, he could advise me where next to turn.

I contacted his clinic and asked to speak to him.

'I'm sorry: Dr Goodie' (originally Godowski, I think) 'is away until Monday. Could I put you on to one of the other partners?'

'No. No thank you.'

I needed more time to think. What could I have said to an unknown third party? 'I think this woman is dangerous and should be locked up – she tried to kill me after we had made love'? It would not do.

Meanwhile, would she not have missed the notebook? Would she trace the theft to me? If so, was she crafty enough in her madness to realize that if her deadly plan had worked, the notebook would not be in the hands of the law? And when she found it hadn't, would she then try to retrieve it? To kill me properly this time? Her motive – if so rational a word were appropriate – was now twofold.

I had not stopped loving her; I wanted to see her again, whatever she felt, for now I was sure that she needed my protection. At the same time I knew that until I had advice on what steps I should take, there was nothing in the world that I could do for her. It was the desperation of this impasse that prompted my next move.

I had been invited by friends to spend the last weekend of the vacation in the country. I passed the reins over to Hendry, locked the notebook in the drawer of my desk, and caught the afternoon train down to Wiltshire, after warning my hostess – it was only Thursday. I did not even contact the garage about the car: the severed pipes were evidence, and questions would be asked. I preferred to do without transport until I had some plan. And so, telling myself that Nemo's deeds of darkness, whether real or imagined, were a weekday preoccupation, that James, normality and the weekend were nearly there; and praying earnestly no foolish 'moth' would call on her in between, I fled the field.

That weekend I paid heavily for my cowardice and procrastination in terms of lost sleep; and daylight hours when I was hell to myself and not much better to those about me. I could not concentrate long enough to stay with a conversation, to count trumps or even keep a billiards score. My hosts blamed overwork, covered up for me indulgently. But it was made worse by the fact that they had provided female company for me, in fact an old girl friend – a highly decorative pillar of the rag trade, of whom I had seen a lot before Nemo came into my life; and it was a terribly conclusive proof of my continuing enslavement to that middle-aged, mad, married murderess that my former love moved me not at all.

Indeed, what gnawed into the small hours and my vitals was more than anything that Nemo was lost to me, not through honourable defeat by a better man, not even because of a rapprochement with James – spoilt blind wastrel, envied fool – but because she had changed, had gone. It was the first thing that got through to me when, after making love, she had so spurned me, and, being unable to say good-bye to her, I had made my formal adieux to the house and garden we had loved. For someone else had taken her place, wore her clothes, spoke with her voice. Someone who had tried to kill me.

The idea, seed of desperation, had taken root, that it *wasn't* her, that it was someone else who did the deeds Nemo had recorded in the first person. Or again, back to the possibility that it was all imagined. This turned the 'journal' into a ghoulish literary exercise, but I found myself clinging to the theory that the workman's death and the disappearance of the science-fiction writer had come together in her mind and she had spun them into a sado-sexual fantasy. It left me with a sick Nemo, but not a murderess.

Except where I was concerned. And that no one need ever know about. All I had to do was dump the car, remove its number plates and licence. It might be cannibalized for parts or scrap, but, with luck, not reported to the police, unless by the red-faced man or the garage. If it should be traced to me by reason of its engine number, surely my only crime would be against the litter laws. It was my car, and I had a right to dispose of it if its performance fell short of my requirements. Indeed, I was fairly certain they could not even demand an explanation of the severed pipes.

I realized that by this course of action I became involved in attempted murder, and an accessory after the fact. But how far could this be carried when the murder was my own, and I was the only witness?

Meanwhile, beneath all this speculation, like the drone that accompanies the nervous pluckings of a sitar, and constant amidst my doubts and inconsistencies, ran the knowledge of a sure way to the truth: the way to the ice-house.

Late on Saturday night, when the other company had gone to bed, my friends pinned me down with a night-cap and cross-questioned me. Raymond and Sue had always been close to me; I do them less than justice in giving them such a passing mention. My only excuse is that by now I was wholly engrossed, and they were irrelevant. I could not tell them: they could not help me.

'Are you in love?' Sue asked.

'Yes – I think so.'

'Well, how *super*, Harry! Can't you tell us about her?'

'I wish I could, Sue,' I said. 'You see, I think she's mad – you know, literally. Crazy. Round the bend. And that's what's eating me up. I'm sorry I'm such hell to have around – and thank you for giving me time and space to think. I know I'm just using you. I'll tell you more when it comes clear, but at the moment – look, I think I must leave tomorrow morning. Will you understand?'

Raymond did his silent British shoulder-grip and Sue pressed a sleeping pill on me; we drank our drams and went up to bed. I slept heavily that night, with just one dream from which I broke with a start, and saw the sunrise, and slept again. I dreamt that Nemo had smothered Boris with a rug and I was digging a hole just outside the wicket gate in the wood, so we could bury him. It was a round deepish hole, more suitable for planting a tree, and Nemo was insisting we should put compost at the bottom, and I was saying 'That will make it too shallow', when I woke up.

I was back in College by lunch-time and found a message in my pigeon-hole that I was to ring James. I walked up to my room like the doomed zombie of a Hammer film, gravid with its terrible secret. If Nemo had done some dreadful thing in my absence, I was the murderer.

I closed the door and locked it, then I sat down at my desk and rang James. An unfamiliar voice answered and fetched Dr Boyce to the telephone.

'Who was that?' I asked.

'Oh, that was our friendly neighbourhood policeman – ' James sounded slightly hysterical, and I went two degrees colder. 'You see,' he went on, 'the farmers had a pigeon shoot yesterday . . . Yes, yes – with dogs, of course. And one of the dogs set up a howl and fuss in the spinney – you know – at the top of the hill beyond our wood – '

So they had found Bob Maclean. No, I didn't say it, but only just. I closed my eyes and listened. He went on, and on.

'He wasn't killed by the fall, though it's quite deep, you know – well, *you* remember the old ice-house: you led us to it last autumn when the nettles had died down enough to get through. Poor old Bob – rather beastly: foul play and all that – apparently he had wounds in his neck. And of course they've been swarming all over the wood – ours is the nearest house – and asking endless questions, but we can't help at all. I think they're having a bit of trouble because with all the rain we've had, and the time of year – you see, it's nearly two weeks since he went missing – well, everything's grown up since then. They could hardly get through the spinney without cutting a path, and the ice-house itself is just a mound of brambles – ' Yes, and young untrodden nettles that had sprung up since Nemo – 'And various cars and lorries up and down the Ferry track. And what's more, the weekenders who live down there in that cottage were away that Monday when Bob left for Amsterdam – not that it's been established he died that same day – and *they* weren't back till Friday and can't help either – '

I broke in: 'How's Nemo taking it?'

'Oh, she's fine – taking it very well, In fact, amazingly detached about the whole thing. I used to think she rather fancied old Bob. Actually I think it would be easier in a way if she seemed more distressed, if you get me. It would be more, well, natural. Her attitude is rather "please do not walk on the digitalis" – foxgloves to us, I told the bobby.

'And then they came up with tracks through the wicket gate that fitted our wheelbarrow.

' "But there must be lots of those," says Mo, cool as a cucumber. "We found the remains of an old box hedge further down the Ferry track and I've been digging up bits and transplanting them. I don't think I'm really meant to – it's not our land – but I just hoped the farmer wouldn't miss them. After all, what use are they to him . . . " '

Yes – and there they would be, too: slightly wilting, filling a gap in one of Nemo's beloved box hedges. And the wheelbarrow would have been used a lot in two weeks, perhaps for fresh manure, and then been washed out. And the fork: there would be no traces on the fork by now. Sterilization of murder weapon by honest toil.

It was the perfect crime.

17

That was Sunday. It was on the nine o'clock news that evening; and next day the papers were full of it. It made the front page headlines in the popular Press. 'Maclean Found Murdered', 'Body in Ice-House', 'Ice-House Murder'; and the subtitles gave more room for word-play: 'Cool Reception for Body of Britain's Mr Sci-Fi', 'Mysterious Murderer Keeps His Cool'. One had photographs not only of Bob, but of the Dower House, angled up from halfway down the slope to the wood – turning it into a sinister pile, and taking in the blasted acacia as a sort of maimed accomplice. 'Tragedy Dogs Dower House' it proclaimed, and exploited the dreadful half-pun, since it was a farmer's dog that had led them to the body. They retold the tale of the workman's death and linked it with Bob Maclean's by implication, simply because it was the nearest building to the ice-house on its little hill. 'For the second time in less than three months, police cars are parked in front of the elegant old Oxfordshire house, the home of Dr and Mrs James Boyce, etc. . . . The autopsy showed death from neck wounds. . . . Time of death between seven and fourteen days previously. . . . Greater exactitude impossible due to unusual conditions. The ice-house in which it was concealed was a device used by the gentry in past time to preserve game and even ice-cream – a prehistoric refrigerator!' Confusion with a game larder, and some vagueness as to the definition of 'pre-history', combined to increase rather than diminish the desired dramatic effect – a piece of purest *Grand Guignol* in which Bob Maclean hung head down, like a rabbit, among the stalactites of some dank cave.

The ice-house was in fact, a beautifully constructed brick egg, about twenty feet high, and all except the dome of the big end was sunken into the hill. The deep pointed section would have been filled with ice cut in winter from the near-by river, and remain well into the summer months. I had seen it marked on the Ordinance Survey Map last summer when I was finding out all I could about the house and neighbour-hood, and had fought my way through to it and identified it – just an outcrop of brambles to the inquisitive. Only by wading through the deep nettles and cutting back the briars could one get nearer; I turned back, satisfied that I had located it, for I got close enough to see that there was mossy brick under the tangle of stems. I took Nemo and James there in early December, one day when I went out to help them with tree-planting. By then the nettles had died down, and we were able to crouch and look down into the ice-house, and see the perfect egg arching above and curving down in the gloom until the 'little end' was lost in rubble, some from its own decaying roof and more that looked like bottles and shards, as if it had been used as a dump. But by its very isolation it had been saved from further vandalism; so it had been neglected and allowed to crumble and so also had it become the perfect spot to dispose of a body.

There was a sort of mad genius in Nemo's choice: not only might it well have gone undetected for months, until the shooting season (it was only by chance that three or four farmers had decided to unite in an April pigeon slaughter). But having been detected, it was impossible to determine the day of the murder: the body had, as the newspapers gleefully reiterated, been 'artificially chilled'.

I had slept little, risen early and walked down to the station to meet the incoming papers. There was plenty of time for wild speculation and endless theorizing while I breakfasted at a stall in the market and walked back to College. By nine o'clock I had read all the papers I had bought. I pushed them aside, took up the telephone and rang Boris's clinic. He had not arrived yet: would I try again at ten? I saw my nine o'clock pupils and gave them some sort of tutorial. At ten I telephoned again.

'Dr Goodie is here now. I'll put you through.'

When Boris heard the distinct sounds of desperation he arranged to come to my rooms in an hour. I had no engagements from eleven till one; he postponed his, and bounded up the stairs soon after my second pair of pupils had left. He always looked absurdly well preserved and tanned and healthy, with special regard for his pale thick wavy hair. Boris made a fetish of fitness, all bound up in his mania for youth and the young. He was four years older than I. He might have been skiing with the jet set and got back yesterday, to judge by his looks, and his deliberately casual cashmere, and the soft suede jacket. He had in fact returned from a long weekend with a young friend in Bournemouth. His year-round wall-to-wall tan was from a sun-lamp, his fitness the result of a swift trot round the parks in running shorts and a cold bath every morning.

To this extent, and perhaps more, he was always the expatriate con-man; but he had a passion for people, and I did not think it was simply an infinite curiosity. I realized that the circumstances were curious (with knobs on, as James would say) and that I would have to endure some measure of morbid fascination in anyone to whom I disclosed them. But my choice was small. Boris might not be the ideal – the wise, sympathetic, authoritative, well-balanced god we all look for in a doctor; but sometimes one has to go into the back streets for a special kind of help. Boris would not shop me: of that, and of his full attention, I was sure.

I related the events to him, in order and with minimal comment, starting with the incident of the music box, and concluding with the morning's newspapers. I showed him the most important parts of the notebook, and told him the gist of the rest. We speculated on the unexplained phenomena, and the possibility of a supernatural; of the unnatural, of the dead actually interfering with the living. After all, was a ghost contrary to Nature?

'If we take "natural" to mean normal or habitual in Nature,' said Boris, 'we would say that it was "natural" to lie in a grave and decay – while the spirit, perhaps, would return to some reservoir for similar recycling.'

'Yes, and that only in *un*natural or peculiar circumstances would the troubled essence return. It's like a track on a tape that normally death "wipes", but some disturbance in the mechanism trips the wrong switch, so that the tape is replayed instead, endlessly, and regardless of subsequent recordings.'

'Well, my friend, most of us – even the more sceptical – would admit that the ether may be thronging with sounds and patterns of past happenings – we simply have not yet invented the delicate machine that will pick them up. Of course, there are some people who can: we call them psychic.'

'But these manifestations,' I said, 'such as they are, seem to move only along clearly defined railway-lines – their actions in life: the same place, the same gestures, the same tragic scenario. So how – ?'

'Aha!' Boris was warming to his subject. 'But it is always *unnatural* circumstances that are portrayed, no? Violent death, cancerous greed – or blighted love – or the need for revenge. This is the point: life not properly ended, you see, something still to be done. Otherwise they would lie still.'

'But how could a ghost perform a new action – not included in its original track?' I asked.

'Possibly it is only by taking over the body of a living person, my friend.' And I remembered the high scratchy voice, like a twig against a window-pane: Rest – no – one more little life, then rest.

Boris got out a notebook and proceeded to question me closely, picking on odd small points. He was interested in the handwriting; he asked me whether Nemo had had a headache after hearing the music box, or discovering the looking-glass. I did not know, but said that by her own report they had started 'in the New Year', and that when I pinpointed New Year's night as the occasion of the first, she had said vaguely 'she supposed so'. Then he asked me if, when we made love – 'All right, Harry,' he said when I interrupted him, 'although I suspect an element of self-punishment that could be self-indulgence – So, when she raped you, did she have an orgasm?'

I was completely taken aback. I found myself echoing her vagueness.

'I suppose so. After all, that's what it was all about, surely.'

'Oh, you *men!*' said Boris tetchily, looking down with pity as from some hermaphrodite eminence. 'Yes indeed, my friend,' (patiently now, massaging his heavy eyelids; then fixing me abruptly with those intense brown eyes, burning with all the age-old knowledge and sadness of *mittel*-Europe). 'Yes, as you say yourself, that may well be what it is all about. That may be what your Sarah Moore is coming back for: satisfaction, completion. As you remarked earlier about the nature of hauntings, something still to be done. Had it really not occurred to you? Someone, after all, from the slender evidence we have, who could not form a normal relationship, a nymphomaniac who could not bear a "repeat performance" – right? A nymphomaniac perhaps *because* she could not bear it, could not accept the submission and tenderness that a full relationship might involve. So – a vicious circle: literally vicious in this case, powered by unsatisfied lust, turning to murder as a sort of orgasm substitute – surely enough to meet your "unquiet grave" theory. And perhaps the ghost of Sarah Moore can only be laid by being laid – if you will pardon a crude English pun.

And how could she achieve that? Only by inhabiting another body and using it. Not any body: one that crossed her "railway-line", as you put it, was sensitive, had a receptive – perhaps a negative – personality (I find the name "Nemo" *deeply significant*, by the way) and was also attractive enough for her vile purposes. But I should not say "vile" – that is a value judgement, and I am not here to judge, only to try to understand, and to explain.'

I broke out of the claustrophobia spun by his web of words. I went and opened the window and breathed deeply to clear my head of psychiatric jargon.

'Look, Boris,' I said, 'your diagnosis makes a pleasing rounded whole – I can see you are delighted with it. No. Listen to me. What can we *do*? I don't want to know any more than that: you are moving too fast for me – in strange unexplored country – and leaping happily to conclusions. Let us just forget the supernatural, and simplify. Nemo is mad, and, I think, dangerous. What do we *do*?'

'All right. You want her certified and de-fused. We could sedate her thoroughly and interrupt the cycle, the cyclothymic pattern, by a period of long sleep. If then she showed signs of reverting to it – and as it manifests itself it almost amounts to schizophrenia – we could try shock treatment; I think it might be highly effective. Bell, book and candle is altogether too dramatic in my opinion, although that too might work: there is ample evidence that it does.

'But both of these courses, as you have already realized, involve revelations that may not stop at the psychiatric couch. The secrets of that couch, as of the confessional, are sacrosanct; but suppose *she* confides in a nurse – or rapes an intern? It would be almost impossible to be sure we could keep her secret contained between the three of us. In fact it would be four: her husband would have to agree to it. We might be able to convince him that she needed treatment for her headaches without telling him the full story, and that a period of complete rest and sedation might break the pattern; from the way you describe his attitude, he may well be only too pleased to have it taken out of his hands. I could – possibly – and at some cost of course – arrange for her to go into a small nursing home, and during the course of sedation she would be harmless and I alone need to see her. But if we had to use shock treatment, other specialists would be involved.

'On the other hand, we could wait and see if she effects her own cure. Once the need that drives her is met, she may return to normal. I would prefer to say "once Sarah Moore's lust is sated", but you don't like that. Yet you yourself may have given her that satisfaction, Harry. Any woman, possessed or not, is far more likely to have good sex with a man who loves her. After all her casual physical encounters – how many we do not know – to come up against real love like yours must make some impression – be different, be special.'

'It didn't stop her from trying to kill me, did it?'

'Harry, Sarah Moore cut your car brakes: perhaps it was her last act. Maybe already she has gone. Why not telephone Nemo and see what sort of state she is in? She needs friends, not isolation. Do not arrive suddenly, as you did, un-announced; do not threaten her with sex; and, if she agrees to see you, ask if you can bring a friend to meet her. I should very much like to observe her in a normal social situation, no?'

'But, Boris, every hour may be precious! We must – '

'Must what? Short of kidnapping her, what can we do? Be sensible, Harry. We have a plan now; we must make haste slowly. First see her, talk to her, find out how much she knows of her condition. If she is clearly better, let well alone; if not, talk to James, get her into a nursing home, sedate her and see if we can break the cycle. You cannot act faster than this, my friend – only the police can, and you do not want them to arrest her, do you?'

The force of his argument, underlined by the guttural emphases and precise, expressive hands, found a way through to me and calmed me. In fact, I felt not calm, but numb: he confirmed what I feared – that we could do nothing immediately. Dully I picked up the telephone and dialled the Boyces' number. It rang and rang. No reply.

'Ring later,' Boris said. 'Now you must eat, and perhaps get some sleep.'

I looked at my watch: it was a quarter past one, and I was late for a lunch appointment. I leapt up, sorted out some papers and got my jacket on.

'Listen, my friend – ' Boris took me by the lapels and turned his beam full on. 'We are going to do all we can. I will return at five after my last patient. You try meanwhile to see your Nemo, if possible today. As for me, I will stay a little longer, if I may, to read through the notebook. It is very interesting . . .'

I left him to it.

I had to lunch with the English fellow of another College, to whom I was sending some of my second-year pupils. It was mainly a courtesy call, and one I could well have done without; but I was able to tell him more about them and their work than he had in writing. I excused myself at two; I had an important meeting I must attend at three, and my eyelids were as heavy as shutters.

First I rang the Dower House again. This time the phone was picked up, then put firmly back, and I was left with the empty burring. I did not try again. I shut my mind to all the possible interpretations that might be put on this; I lay down on my bed, set my alarm and slept.

There was no time to ring again before the examiners' meeting. When we got back, soon after five, Boris was already there; he was standing by the kettle waiting for it to boil, the notebook in one hand.

'I thought we both could do with some tea,' he said. 'Did you manage to contact her?'

I started to tell him of my two attempts. But I got no further. There was a clatter on the stairs. The door was banged open without so much as a knock, and Bertie Bull staggered into the room. He had blood on his face and neck, his eyes were wild, and there were wood shavings among his tangled hair.

'For Christ's sake, Harry,' he babbled, 'tell me I'm not going mad. I don't believe it, you see – I swear I'm not on acid or *anything*, Harry – tell me I'm not hallucinating – I still don't believe it really happened – but that Boyce woman – she just tried to kill me – '

18

I got him to sit down and gave him some brandy. Boris brought a wet towel; he mopped Bertie's brow and wiped away the blood on his face. There was a long shallow scratch down one cheek, and more on his neck and chest. I felt suddenly faint. I found myself sitting with my head between my knees and Boris had taken charge.

'Now both of you sit quite still and calm yourselves. Let us begin at the beginning, no? Who are you, young man?'

'Who are *you*?' asked Bertie, couchant but still wild-eyed and now suddenly suspicious.

'It's all right, Bertie,' I said. 'He's a friend and you can tell us everything. Bertie Bull, Boris Goodie.'

'But for Chrissake – you don't seem to realize – that woman tried to kill me, I tell you – you don't even seem *surprised* – '

'Look, Bertie: you just tell us what happened. I'm a psychiatrist. Nothing surprises me.'

'Well – Jesus – I mean, all we need is a priest and some boiling water and we're ready for anything – ' He was laughing weakly, on the edge of hysteria, but Boris's even voice went on.

'We have the boiling water – see? I'm making you some tea – OK? Strong, sweet tea for shock, right? You probably learnt that in the Boy Scouts. Now, just keep that towel against your cheek – it is still bleeding a little – and tell us all about it, eh?'

'Well, I'll be – !'

'You may well be. But we want facts now, young man, not hopes or promises. Did Mrs Boyce ask you to visit her or did you just pay her an unexpected call?'

'I had a sort of standing invitation, see, to go out and look for orchids – in their wood – and I was nearby and just dropped in on the off chance – and got quite a shock, the way things worked out. I'm afraid this'll be something of a surprise for you, Harry. Or maybe not – maybe you've had the pleasure? Look – for Chrissake don't pull rank on me, Harry – this is my business – I'm not swapping smut. I want to know. Is Mrs Boyce perhaps a notoriously easy lay, and I've just joined the ranks?'

I couldn't answer him straight.

'I'm not pulling rank, Bertie. What I think about Mrs Boyce's morals is simply not relevant. I gathered from our chat the other day you found her attractive. So – did you make a pass at her?'

'Not really – I didn't have a chance.'

I got up and stood with my back to Bertie, looking down into the quad, pretending to sip the tea Boris gave me. I did not want to expose my face.

'You see, when I drove up, there was no sign of her or anyone – except there was a police car halfway down the lane. I suppose they're still hunting for clues in that Maclean business, are they? Well, I knocked and called but no one was there. So I went down into the wood and hunted about for orchids. I heard voices in the distance – the police again, I reckoned – I think they had dogs with them. And then there was a rustling near at hand, in the wood itself. I called out again – but no answer – so I carried on hunting. Then I saw what I thought at first was a peacock moving about and rustling beyond some laurels – something very brightly coloured, passing behind, moving up towards the house. I tried to follow it – I couldn't get through the thicket at that point – but I kept getting glimpses of this brilliant blue – by now it was on the slope above. I went quickly up a back way, thinking I'd cut it off – and when I came out into the open on the hillside below that little dairy place – you know, beyond the kitchen – I saw a woman all got up in fancy dress: she even had an enormous hat, and she was disappearing up those old brick steps. She turned round at the top. It was Mrs Boyce – and she smiled at me. Didn't say anything. So I ran up after her and saw her going into the dairy. I called out, "Hey, Mrs Boyce – you look gorgeous – I thought you were a peacock" – or something like that – and I went up to the dairy door. It seemed very dark: I was dazzled coming out of the sun. And then she – well, sprang on me like a tigress. It was like some sort of children's game until then – only she didn't say "boo!" Then it quickly turned into anything but.'

He shook his head as if to dispel a bad dream, and sawdust from James's workbench floated down on to my carpet.

'She was so – I don't know – fierce – voracious. A real man-eater. It was fantastic, actually. She ripped off her peacock dress and my shirt and – there were lots of shavings and wood wool and stuff on the floor: it's kitted up as a sort of workshop – and for storing apples; I'll never forget the smell. . . . It was all over so quickly. Extraordinary seeing her lying there among the shavings in just her boots and her hat – a bit askew but still pinned on. I was quite knackered afterwards – but she was so fantastically attractive – well, in a little while I felt it was time for pudding, as they say – oh *God*! – at which point she came alive again, but not quite as I expected. She suddenly started putting on her dress, but I pulled it away from her. Then she scratched my face – well, I reckoned a bit of aggro turned her on, so I persisted. But she got away, grabbed up a big coal chisel and hammer from the bench, and she positively came at me. "Oh, all right," I said – "*Pax*. End of game." But I must have lost my balance backing away, and she swung at me with the hammer and I found myself back on the floor – and my *God* – she was *taking aim*!

'What a *sight*! She'd got the hammer raised and the damn

coal chisel held up in front of her, one eye closed and she was looking down the chisel at me – standing there naked except for her long boots and this crazy hat – I tell you, it was like a nightmare by Buñuel – just his thing – but I managed to jerk sideways. She brought it down so hard the sparks flew up from the stone floor – I'm not mad – I could show you the mark – d'you believe me, Harry? I swear – '

'Yes, yes – we believe you,' said Boris. 'And then?'

'Well, before she could recover – I mean she put so much force – so much *venom* – into it – I got up and out of the door and into the car and didn't stop till I was near the main road. And then I did up my flies – I'd left my shirt – but I had this old jersey in the boot – I was shivering, man – shivering and shaking and bleeding and scared – and I came here. . . . '

It was like the messenger's speech in a Greek tragedy: as the words tumbled out he lived through it all again, and by the end he was pacing and trembling, sobbing out the last syllables.

'What happened, for God's sake? One minute it was so marvellous and mad and great and then suddenly the violence was vicious – she looked at me as if I was a toad or a – snake or something *vile* – that had to be destroyed – God – it was horrible – ' He sat down and put his head in his hands.

Boris soothed him like a nanny, picking the wood wool out of his tangled hair, and making him lean back and drink his tea.

'You say marvellous, and mad, and great; and I think – don't you? – you have hit on the word? We think Mrs Boyce may indeed be mad, Bertie: we have been talking about it. It is something that has been concerning us greatly, and your story has now confirmed it. Don't worry, we are taking action. But we must be very careful and tactful, because we suspect not even Dr Boyce knows about these extraordinary moods she has.'

'You mean she's done this before? Harry, did you – ?'
Boris cut in smoothly again.

'Look, you have had a bad experience. You are very
shaken up, no? You must –'

'Hell, man, she's a potential *killer*!' He stood up abruptly,
spilling his tea. His face was white. 'Did she kill Bob
Maclean? My *God* – she could have, you know. . . . You do
know something. You've got to –'

'Oh come, my dear boy,' said Boris. 'Be calm. How
could she murder a man and dispose of the body –'

'But she was strong – and how! No – it's one hell of a
coincidence.' He looked sharply at me. 'Harry, what's up?
How did Maclean die? Do you know?'

'I know no more than the newspapers tell me,' I said. 'It is
being simplistic to jump to conclusions – I consider we're
letting the matter get out of hand even talking about it.'

'But there you have a potential murderess – and we've
got to tell the police.'

'What we have, Bertie,' I said, 'is a possible case of
schizophrenia which is going to be treated. Turning her
over to the police as a suspect isn't going to help her get
better. Meanwhile they have their tracker dogs and their
clues; with what conclusions – if any – we aren't in a
position to know. If they decide to arrest her, let it be on
evidence, not because she happens to be mentally disturbed
and also happens to live nearby. After all, it isn't as if she's
likely to flee the country, is it?'

'And you want me to keep *quiet*?'

'Well – who else do you want to tell, Bertie? It would be
less than gallant to tell your friends; and it would only shock
your father.'

'Hell, man – and what do I say about these?' He pointed
to his wounds.

'You've had a passionate encounter – that's all – with an
amazing woman who shall be nameless. No need to lie.

146

Won't that do to intrigue and satisfy your interrogators? –
and a touch of antiseptic, Bertie, for good measure.'

He did not smile.

'Look, Harry. Don't think you can fob me off – I'm part
of this now – and your tame psychiatrist and your soothing
words just don't cover this situation. Can't you see, Harry,
man – ' He came up close to confront me, cutting me off
from Boris, forcing an independent reaction. For an awful
moment I fancied I could smell Nemo's warm musk still on
him. I stared at the welts raised by Sarah Moore's nails. Then
I met his eyes, as the words came to me.

'All I can do is swear, on my honour, that the murderer of
Bob Maclean is dead.'

'Now, Harry – ' Boris tried to break in.

'No. Listen, Bertie. I can't tell you any more, but that I
can say, if it reassures you.'

'Dead? You *know*?' He looked across at Boris, who
nodded. 'And are you letting the police in on this?'

'It's not quite as simple as that,' I said. 'We've got to be
able to prove it. Meanwhile, Mrs Boyce must be protected,
you see – certified if necessary, from what you've said. We
need a couple of days to sort things out. But you'll just have
to trust us, Bertie.'

'You'll keep me in touch? You'll tell me what happened?'

'I'll explain it all, and just as soon as I can.'

'OK. Yeah. Well, all right then, I suppose. OK – I'll be
back.' He lifted his hand in a sort of weary salute, the
walking wounded – ignoring Boris – and left.

Boris sat down with a long sigh as if he had been holding
his breath.

'Thank you,' I said. 'I'm afraid I feel directly responsible
for all this – '

'Oh come, come, my friend – '

'No – you see, I even knew that James had asked him out
to look for his precious orchids – I should have anticipated –

I let it slip my mind, and oh, Lord – when I think how nearly – ' I tried to reassemble myself. 'And I'm sorry I nearly passed out, Boris. All in all, I wasn't much help.'

'Oh yes, Harry: it was to you, basically, that he told his story – I only calmed him and set him going. And what a story. Poor Harry: it must be hard to listen to such things about the woman you love. It was not so much the horror of blood as the horror of jealousy that made you weak, I think.'

'I suppose so. A sort of wave of blinding nausea, when I saw those scratches on his chest, like mine. My uppermost thought was: It should have been me, I wish it had been me. As strong as the pull of a cliff edge. Do you know what I mean?'

'The overwhelming desire to be killed by the loved one, if no other contact is possible. Yes; and for your own health of mind you must see it for what it is: the ultimate in masochism. Pull yourself out of it. Think in practical terms.' He was up again and was stacking and clearing the teacups briskly. 'You must try to contact her again.'

'But she will be in the migraine stage now – probably at its worst.'

'Try at least. We must not delay.'

I was grateful that I had cancelled my six o'clock tutorial in the hopes of going out to the Dower House with Boris. Now it was nearly six-thirty. I went to the telephone. As I put my hand on it, it rang.

I was still so jumpy, it made me step back a pace. Then I picked it up. It was Nemo.

'Hullo, Nemo,' I said a little shakily, and looked across at Boris, who nodded encouragingly. 'You're right about our telepathic contact,' I said, determined to get back on to the footing of the last time we were together, and close, and sane. 'I was just going to ring you.'

'Oh, Harry – how nice. Sorry if I sound a bit woozy, but

I've been asleep with a real bone-crusher of a headache – I'm not rid of it yet. But I woke up and remembered I didn't say anything about our Recital.'

'Recital? Tell me more.'

'It's just an excuse for a party really – nothing big – rather short notice, so I've been telephoning people: you were away at the weekend, weren't you? A bit of the amateur dramatics, and a tame violinist, and the odd folk-singer – you know the sort of thing. And soup and sausages and wine. I'm determined those boring policemen won't stop us – and I'm sure old Bob wouldn't have wanted us to cancel everything. We were hoping to hold it down in the circle if it's fine – to catch the azaleas before they're finished. Oh, on Saturday, as ever is. You can? Oh, good, wonderful. Well – '

'Nemo, can't I come out and see you before then? Perhaps do some gardening? I've got a friend I want you to meet, and show him the place – '

'Well, I don't know what James is doing – '

'Never mind about James; we'd love to see you on your own. What about tomorrow?'

'Oh, Harry – there's so much to do before Saturday: I have to go up to London one day, possibly tomorrow – I really can't think straight now – you know how I am with these beastly heads – '

'Don't worry. I'll ring again.'

'Sorry to be so feeble – look, bring him to the party anyway – OK? See you then – ' She rang off.

I put down the receiver and turned to Boris. 'In the middle of a headache now and then too busy with a party on Saturday – to which you are invited. So that's it. Not much good, I'm afraid.'

'No, no – busy is good. If she has too much to do and maybe James around helping, and a trip to London, I think she may stay on the level. The danger lies in those times when she is basically purposeless, feels beautiful and unused –

dresses up and paces about. Imagine the restlessness of being physically and emotionally "high" and no one to see or know or be dazzled. Then superimpose this Sarah Moore, coiled in her subconscious like a hungry snake. Enter a desirable man, and – '

His talking hands, never still, now became a darting cobra striking a rabbit: horribly precise, the way the struck hand went limp and fell into his lap. Then he spread them both and shrugged. 'A dangerous combination, no? Whether you bring in Sarah Moore or not.'

'So you think we should wait till Saturday?'

'I think we have a breathing space. But I seriously consider we should attempt to talk to Dr Boyce.' And I seriously considered it was time for a drink.

'But, Boris,' I said, getting the glasses, 'how much do you propose to tell him? I'm not prepared to lay bare my soul except as a last resort.'

'We tell him the minimum, my friend. You introduce me as a migraine specialist, with my sedation treatment, which has indeed been effective where migraine is not congenital. Tell him – '

As I passed the window, I looked down into the quad and saw two men heading for my staircase.

'Boris,' I interrupted, 'I think I may have visitors. Can I telephone you about this later on?' Heavy steps on the stairs. 'Will you be at home? – Yes, I've got to dine in Hall. Good.' Heavy knock on the door, much louder than necessary. 'Come in,' I called. There was a pause, so I went over and opened it. Two tall, serious, highly respectable men stood there. They both wore sensible macintoshes and a patient, respectful look.

'Can I help you?' I said.

'We're police officers, sir. Looking for Mr Henry Harris.'

'I'm Henry Harris. Please come in. Dr Goodie is just leaving. So I'll ring you, Boris. Thanks for everything.'

Boris took up his coat, patted my shoulder, nodded to the Law and went out. I know he would have liked to stay, but only as a fly on the wall. He certainly did not want to be questioned at this juncture: we were both of us busy withholding evidence for dear life – Nemo's – and had not been prepared for this. He smiled benignly as I closed the door on him, laying one finger across his lips as he did so.

'Well, what can I do for you gentlemen?' I asked. My deep handsome voice sounded full of confidence and sincerity, as John Ridd's would have done.

'I am Detective Inspector Blunt and this is Sergeant Pearce. We understand you were acquainted with Mr Robert Maclean, and we want to ask you a few questions.'

'I only met him three or four times, actually, but I'll tell you all I can. Excuse me,' I said to the Sergeant, 'but haven't I seen you somewhere before – perhaps in uniform?'

'Yes indeed, sir. Less than a week ago. I walked with you from St Giles to this College, sir. You were feeling somewhat shaky after an accident, I believe.'

'Of course, Sergeant.' (What else had I said to him? I wondered.) 'And I had had a few drinks too, I remember, in an excess of medicinal zeal.'

'Some excess, sir, yes.'

'Not, I hope, to the point of unpleasantness.'

'Oh no, sir. Very pleasant and talkative you were, sir.' (God, what *had* I said?)

'Good, good. Now, your questions, Inspector. Do sit down. Can I offer you a drink?'

'Thank you, but no. But don't let us stop you, Mr Harris. Now, you know all about this unfortunate business, I'm sure.'

'Yes – what I've seen in the papers and heard from Dr Boyce, whose house is nearby.'

'Ah yes. You talked to Dr Boyce on the telephone yesterday. Is that right?'

'Yes – ' I was surprised. 'Nothing wrong in that, I hope?' My relaxed laugh came out rather too high, and I cleared my throat and sipped my whisky.

'No indeed. Perfectly natural in the event. We may as well come straight to the point, Mr Harris. During that telephone conversation it seems you said something rather interesting from our point of view.'

'Why – were you listening in? I didn't think it was customary for – '

'No. I said "it seems" – we only heard Dr Boyce's words. They went as follows, according to my notes at the time. Now he said, in explanation of the strange voice that had taken the call: "Our friendly neighbourhood policeman. You see, the farmers had a pigeon shoot yesterday in the wood beyond ours."' Pause. ' "Yes, yes, with dogs of course. And one of the dogs set up a howl and fuss in the spinney, you know, at the top of the hill there," etcetera, etcetera.'

'Well?' I asked, and now my nerves were like bowstrings, just as was intended, no doubt. His direction was still unclear to me; as far as I could recall, I had simply responded to James with the usual encouraging noises. The Inspector's flat, measured tones as he read from his notes had been deliberate, almost as if he were timing himself.

'Well, what did I say that was interesting?'

'I'm trying to read as he said it, Mr Harris. You will have noted the pause: that was when you spoke.'

'But I can't remember what I said, Inspector,' I retorted, getting up and going over to the sideboard. 'Perhaps you can refresh my memory, as they say in the court-room dramas.'

'We have no record of *your* words, Mr Harris. But from his answer – ' he consulted his notes again – ' "Yes, yes, with dogs, of course" – well, Mr Harris, from that we can only assume you said "Did they have dogs with them?" or something to that effect.' I stood very still at the sideboard, while the Teacher's label burned its image irrelevantly and indelibly on my brain, and my thoughts raced.

'Why did you interrupt Dr Boyce to ask if the farmers had dogs with them? Could it be that you were afraid of what they might find?'

19

I poured out a drink slowly and carried it, very carefully, back to my chair.

'Yes,' I said. 'I can see what you mean. It sounds as if I already knew Bob Maclean's body was there, in the ice-house. And all I can reply is that I didn't know. I certainly don't remember saying it, but I agree: if that is what he replied, one must assume I asked some such question. I simply have no explanation. I did not know the body was there. I telephoned Dr Boyce at his request when I got back to College, and I remember him telling me about the shoot and the dogs and one of them leading the farmers to the ice-house. That was positively the first I heard of it, Inspector. Any more questions?'

'Yes, Mr Harris, there are. Do you know what sort of relationship Dr and Mrs Boyce had with the deceased?'

'Very friendly, so far as I could see – and I only saw them together twice, I think. He and Dr Boyce seemed to get on very well indeed – enjoyed each other's company.'

'And Mrs Boyce?'

'I think she found him amusing.' (The words of the notebook – 'that charming author . . . profoundly sympathetic in conversation . . . we were so precisely in harmony –' kept coming back to me like an actor's script: but the play had gone wrong and I was forced to *ad lib*. That is one of my recurring nightmares.) 'He was more her husband's friend, I think.'

'Did you ever suspect that Mrs Boyce's relations with him might be more intimate? That she might be having an affair with him?'

'It didn't occur to me. I certainly saw no sign of it.'

'And your relations with Mrs Boyce: how close were they?'

'I think "just good friends" is accurate in this case, Inspector. We were – we still are.'

'I see. When did you first meet Mrs Boyce?'

Again, I could not see the direction of his questions, unless it was to establish some motive for *my* killing Bob Maclean – in which case I was not merely parrying an implied charge of complicity, but of murder. What did they know that I did not know? I could only stick to a story that protected both Nemo and myself. I knew my assumed question to James on the telephone could convict me of nothing. But might they have some evidence more damning that they were keeping under covers, and leading me towards it, question by question? I must be accurate where I could, and lie convincingly where I had to, for both our sakes.

I told them how I had met the Boyces, of our interest in the house, of my visits there in the autumn and early winter – I had spent the night there on two occasions – and of the party. The Sergeant – he to whom I had babbled gnomically of overheating and accidents and I knew not what else – took it all down, while Detective Inspector Blunt watched me over the church steeple of his long bony hands, glancing down only to refer to the notes on his knee. I had sat down – defensively? – behind my desk, and they were in my two tutorial chairs. But it was I who was the guilty pupil, concealing my misdeeds and the neglect of my duties. Already, I was well aware, I had fallen short in failing to report the accident, even after the Sergeant's earnest admonitions.

'Then, of course, I was away in America for three months. I only returned to England a week ago,' I said, and thought, almost smugly: and that takes care of my alibi, so there.

But I left it to them to work that one out; I must not be too eager or too well informed. Instead, I must be innocent and ignorant.

'Yes, just so. We will come to that,' said the Inspector. 'I must ask you again, in your relationship with Mrs Boyce, was it the same on both sides? Or did you perhaps feel more for her than she did for you – a great deal more?'

They must know something. What had James said? What had *Nemo* said, for God's sake? Clearly I would have to give a little and hope to get a little from them in return.

'Well, Inspector, I always found her very, well, attractive and sympathetic, from the start; and I think that I developed a sort of school-boy crush on her in those first months. It is not unusual for a bachelor don at times to envy his married colleagues – the whole set-up really – and especially where such an attractive wife and lovely house are involved. I'm sure in this case the house played a large part in it: I told you how very much I, well, fell for it,' (light laugh) 'and Mrs Boyce was somehow part of that. But I realized very quickly how foolish it was and deliberately set myself to get over it. And I did. My time in America completed the cure.'

'So you never at any time had intimate relations with Mrs Boyce?'

'No, Inspector, though naturally there was a time when I wished I could. As I say, she is a very attractive woman, as I think you'd agree.'

'Certainly, and with such vitality. But I think you should know that Mrs Boyce told us you were very much in love with her and wanted to have an affair with her. What have you got to say?'

'Well, she may have guessed my feelings and assumed, with justification, that I would at least contemplate –'

'She says, in fact, that you declared your feelings for her. We were questioning her this morning.'

What was Nemo up to? How did this fit into a murder inquiry?

'I suppose on one occasion I did let myself get somewhat carried away – but that's all over, Inspector. I don't see what relevance –'

'She said that this was after you came back from America, Mr Harris. Not before.'

There was just time for a pin to drop. Then I said:

'In that case, I really can't defend myself without laying myself open to an accusation of ungallantry.' I must be consistent, I decided.

'The accusation may be more serious than that, Mr Harris. Did you or did you not make such a declaration to Mrs Boyce since you returned from America?'

'No, I did not. Mrs Boyce has either muddled her dates, indulged in wishful thinking or told a lie. I find it very distasteful having to insist on this, but it all comes down to my word against hers.'

Now I waded in deep and could not go back. If I was consistent and stuck to my story, I could not see how they might fault it. Unless there was something else I did not know. But what could there be? Except emotionally, I was not involved. I was only concealing evidence – the notebook – to protect Nemo: altruistically, as, for myself, I *was* innocent. How ironical, then, if she were trying to set me up as chief suspect. But there was never time to think. The Inspector was speaking again.

'As you say, Mr Harris, it is your word against hers so far, and it is our business to sort that out. But you do admit, do you not, that you have been to the Dower House more than once since your return?'

'Oh, certainly. It was, let me see –' No point in lying: there would be ample witnesses in the village to my comings and goings – 'it was three times. I had supper there the evening I got back, at Dr Boyce's invitation. I went to tea with Mrs Boyce next day: I made tea for her – she was not well. She was recovering from one of her recurrent migraines.'

'And she was well enough to come downstairs, or did you take it to her room?'

'No, we had tea in the kitchen. She was at the convalescent stage, I would say.'

'And then?'

'And then I went out again next day.'

'That would be Wednesday, sir?' The Sergeant spoke this time.

'Er, yes, Wednesday. That's right.'

He turned to Blunt. 'It was late that night, in fact at one-thirty a.m. that I encountered Mr Harris in St Giles, sir.'

'Thank you, Sergeant. So you went out to see Mrs Boyce on three consecutive days?'

'Yes. On Wednesday I did quite a lot of gardening for her. I had said I would when I saw how unwell she was. I did some digging and made a bonfire and – '

'About how long would you say you spent at the Dower House on that occasion?'

'About two hours, Inspector, from two to four – in the garden, not in the house.'

'And you saw Mrs Boyce?'

Quick decision.

'No, I think she was resting. I imagined she was still suffering from the after-effects of the migraine.'

'So you did not enter the house on that occasion?'

'Yes, I went into the kitchen and called, but got no answer. And then later on I went in for a drink of water. Into the kitchen. I was thirsty. But, Inspector – ' (I felt it was time to show a little spirit, as the innocent do under cross-questioning: after all, I was missing my dinner at their convenience) 'I don't see what this has to do with Mr

Maclean's murder. I gathered, both from the newspapers and from Dr Boyce himself, that he had been killed two weeks ago. How can my visits to the Dower House last week throw any light on your investigations?'

'I think you can leave that to us, Mr Harris. We have to establish a pattern, identify and eliminate where we can a multitude of clues and prints and footmarks and wheeltracks in order to narrow things down. You must appreciate that where a crime has been committed and there has been, as you point out, a considerable lapse of time, every day within that period has multiplied our problems.'

'I do see that, Inspector, and I hope I've been of some help.' I got up in my most conclusive manner, as I had ended many an argumentative tutorial – a brave gesture, at least, that I was in command and on my own ground. But Detective Inspector Blunt had not finished and the tone of his voice shifted my target from the door, which I would have opened for them graciously and firmly, to the sideboard on which stood my Dutch courage.

'There's another point, Mr Harris.'

'Now, if we return to the week in question, the week in which the murder took place.' I poured myself a short sharp dose and returned to my desk with an air of stretched patience designed to cover the layer of stretched nerves just beneath. Now what? My alibi was already established; yet they seemed to expect more. Was I imagining a new element of controlled anticipation, almost of suppressed excitement, in the two big, quiet men, sitting there so upright – straight-faced and feet together – in my pupils' chairs, like a pair of Quakers at a prayer meeting? No: I was probably projecting my own. But I felt sure that they were deliberately with-holding something, something – and this was what mystified me – that they knew *I* knew. But what?

'Yes, Inspector?' I'm innocent, I told myself, and have an alibi to prove it.

He flipped through his notes and settled on the relevant page. From where I sat it looked like a typed report, stapled on to his longhand jottings.

'Can you account for your movements during that week?'

'Yes, I think I can.' I sipped and took my time. 'I was in Princeton on Sunday, Monday and Tuesday.' I took out my diary and consulted it. 'I spent Wednesday, and Wednesday night in New York, and flew to Paris on Thursday, via Heathrow. I spent Thursday night, Friday, Saturday and Sunday with friends in Paris – would you like their address?'

'Thank you, Mr Harris, but we have it.'

I felt very cold. You do when you find you are not supplying information, merely confirming it.

'Then you will know I flew back on Monday and returned by train to Oxford. Is that the week you are concerned with, Inspector?'

'That's right. From the post-mortem, and taking into account that the deceased's body was found in an old ice-house, the murder could have taken place any time between the Monday when Mr Maclean left his home and the Sunday, seven days later. The body was examined the following Sunday, and, according to the forensic report, the time of death was determined to be not less than seven days and, of course, not more than would be consistent with the time at which he was last seen alive.'

So I was still in the clear. I felt almost helpful.

'What about the car, Inspector? I gather it was found at the station. Did no one notice it there? I mean, wouldn't that help narrow the gap in time?'

'Yes – but unfortunately not. Of course, we put out a search for it and found it, as soon as we were notified that Mr Maclean was missing. If Mrs Maclean had not delayed, we would have been on to it that much sooner, and, as you say, narrowed the time gap to perhaps a couple of days.

After all, he could have driven straight to the station from his home: it may have been there in the car park from Monday on, for all we know. Naturally we are following up that line of inquiry; but commuters are notoriously unobservant – late for their trains in the morning, late for their supper in the evening – you know how it is – ' and we joined in a general shaking of heads over the habits of commuters. It was almost cosy. 'No help in that quarter,' he concluded.

There was a small hiatus, and I filled it, feeling the need to preserve the new atmosphere, even by actually making conversation. For the questions seemed to be over – and why not? I had been away that whole week.

'But I gather all his luggage was left in the car – even his papers and so on,' I said. 'I suppose that suggests he may already have been killed, and the car put there by someone else, perhaps his murderer.'

'That seems more probable, on the whole. One thing we are sure of is that that car was driven and parked down the Ferry road beyond the grounds of the Dower House, whether by Mr Maclean or by whoever killed him, we don't know, but we suspect the latter: someone who knew of the old ice-house and drove the body there to dump it.' (Even his vocabulary, I noted, was more relaxed. Ten minutes ago it would have been 'dispose of'.) 'We also found crumbs of mud on the steering wheel and more on the floor. And of course in the treads. It's fairly easy soil to identify, that is. There's just a patch of it in that area, very acid, I understand – which is how they manage to grow those azaleas and rhododendrons. There's not a lot of them around Oxfordshire. But, of course, you know the place, Mr Harris – better than I do, I dare say, though I've seen a lot of it and those woods in the past couple of days.'

'Yes, indeed. And now, Inspector, if you'll forgive me – '

'Certainly, Mr Harris. I'm afraid you've missed your

dinner. Just one more thing we'd like to clear up. You said you flew via Heathrow. Why was that?'

'Yes, I did. I could have flown direct, New York/Paris, but I had already booked my flight home when I received this invitation from my French friends. So, rather than cancel it, I flew over and then took a plane on. It didn't take all that much longer.'

'How much longer, Mr Harris. I mean, when did you arrive in Paris?'

'About six o'clock, I think.'

'And you arrived at Heathrow about one?'

'Yes – or a bit later.'

'So there wasn't an immediate connection?'

'No – just missed one unfortunately: delay over Customs, the usual thing.'

'So you had to wait for the five o'clock plane?'

'Well, I had to check in at four, as one does – it didn't leave till five.' I was not cold now: I was solid ice – my lips so stiff with it they could barely move.

'What did you do while you were waiting, Mr Harris, to kill the time?'

They were both looking at me now. I realized I had paused too long.

'I hired a car and went for a drive,' I said. 'There seemed no point in hanging around the airport.' And no point in lying. They had obviously checked with Hertz. 'It turned into a lovely afternoon, as I remember – ' (babble for time) 'I drove as far as Henley and back.'

'In two and half, nearly three hours, you drove to Henley and back.'

'I took it gently – traffic was bad. In Henley I gave up and had some lunch and came back slowly through Marlow.'

'You gave up *what*?'

'Oh, I don't know, Inspector,' I said finishing my whisky. 'The unequal struggle, if you like. I simply wanted to take my time and enjoy it. So I had my lunch and then followed the smaller roads to see the countryside.'

'Or did you drive on through Dorchester to Sutton Hamden? Find Mr Maclean with Mrs Boyce, kill him in a fit of jealousy, put the body in the ice-house and drive back to Heathrow? You had three full hours to do it in – you did not actually check in until nearly half past four – three full hours unaccounted for during the very period when it is considered most likely that the murder took place. You had the opportunity, the time, the motive, the cover up – that too perfect alibi – and you apparently told no one about your secret visit, your excursion into the English country-side, during the course of that vital week. I suggest you had good reason for your secrecy.'

'But I *couldn't* have done it! Bob Maclean was killed on Monday – '

'I see. You seem to be very sure of the fact, Mr Harris. Perhaps you could tell us why.'

20

The reflex action of self-preservation is one of Nature's sleights of hand. My finger was on the ejector button before my thought processes had begun to catch up with the secondary question: where my unpiloted plane, abandoned in a flaming nose-drive, would land. But as I came to, and my mind's eye opened once more, I had an image as clear as a TV news flash, swift and unforgettable as a subliminal implant, of a blazing wreck plunging into the evergreen wood like a comet; I knew that Nemo was there – or was she the plane? – and I saw the dark resinous hollow explode into a nest of flame. For that second it was no mere metaphor it was as sharp, and as certain, as second sight.

But the Law was impatient for an answer. Perhaps I had never been a suspect; they may have played a hunch: I was concealing something and they had bluffed me into saving myself with at least part of the truth. As the room settled back into place, I focussed on them as clearly as I could through the scarlet mist of rising anger, and I vowed that the words I had been tripped into uttering would never find their way into a sworn statement. Let them draw what implications they liked from my panic reaction, I would retract it, and I would stand by my denial if it meant perjury and prison. They would not get Nemo that way.

'Mr Harris? *Why* did you say Mr Maclean was killed on the Monday?'

'I don't know – I suppose I've always assumed it.'

'I think not. You spoke with complete certainty, and knowing too that it would put you in the clear. How did you know?'

'I repeat, I've always assumed it, Inspector. After all, no one had come forward to say they saw Mr Maclean at any time after he left home that Monday. His wife was the last person to see him alive, right? Well – he couldn't just disappear. He would have to see people, simply to buy food – possibly a razor – how many days' growth of beard was on the body? The papers mention none. If all his belongings were in the car, and no one saw him, even buying a hamburger or going into a barber's shop, I would assume that he was dead before he could need either, and the murderer probably parked the car at the station unnoticed on Monday. Isn't that a fairly logical deduction for someone in possession of only the published facts? *You* may, of course, know a lot more – and you may use your knowledge as tripwires for the unwary –'

'Mr Harris, are you saying that you are not in fact withholding information? Something that prompted you to say' – (a glance at the Sergeant's notes) – ' "But I couldn't have done it. Bob Maclean was killed on Monday"?'

'Yes, it was an assumption only. I was taken by surprise when you virtually accused me –'

'I suggested it was possible: the timing, the opportunity and, according to Mrs Boyce and your own partial admission, the motive, were right. The pseudo alibi and the secrecy it involved, as you must see yourself, make you a natural suspect. And if you persist in denying that your immediate reaction to this implication sprang from some knowledge that you have decided, on second thoughts, to withhold, then you must assume the full weight of your chosen role: that of chief suspect in a murder case. No, we are not going to charge you. But we must ask you not to leave Oxford, and we may find it necessary to keep some account of your movements.'

'Have me followed, you mean?'

'Yes, Mr Harris. I think that will be all for now. If you

change your mind, and wish to come forward with any information that might help either to clear yourself or lead us to the real murderer, you only have to telephone me. And of course I shall probably need to question you again when we have cleared up one or two points that we are investigating at present. There are several unexplained factors that may or may not be relevant – how your brake pipes were cut, why you did not report the ensuing accident, how Mr Maclean's car was taken to the station – all points you could no doubt throw some light on. But I feel we have talked enough about it for the time being. We will make no further progress at present. Thank you, Mr Harris; we will see ourselves out.'

They took up their coats and their papers very quickly and quietly; everything seemed to fold squarely and fit into a pocket, a brief-case or at right angles over a stiff arm. I stood up, but they were at the door ahead of me; I did not look at their faces, just nodded at their chests. And then they were gone. (So, someone *had* reported the accident.)

Now, I thought, I must get it all clear. What did they really suspect, and how much proof had they? What could I assume about their line of thinking from the little they had said?

If they had some other reason for putting the time of Bob's death on Thursday – or even if they were content for the present with the 'secret murder dash' theory (as the newspapers would put it, I knew with a shudder), then I must assume that in their books Nemo was my accomplice: for she would have had to drive the car to the station – something I knew they could not prove, because it was on Monday not on Thursday that she had done just that, and they would be looking for witnesses for the wrong day. On the other hand, could I conceivably have done the whole thing? If I had made good time to Sutton Hamden, say just under the hour, killed Bob on my arrival, dumped the body in the ice-house (twenty minutes?), driven in to the station, parked the car and hitched a ride back on the London road – not too difficult – to Sutton Hamden, walked down the lane, got into my hire car and driven back to Heathrow, I might still have been able to clock in at four twenty-five. It was just possible, I worked out, but I would have been running an enormous risk of ruining my alibi by making the trip into Oxford, and especially by getting a lift out. Would they now start a nation-wide appeal: Who gave this man a lift? and photographs of me?

How was the role of chief suspect going to affect me, even if they did not go so far as this? The Press was hungry for facts and faces: would I be thrown to it? And was I to be followed to examiners' meetings, on walks in the parks, to dinner parties, by a big man with flat feet and a folded newspaper? I felt hunted, hounded for something I had not done. I was suspected of the murder I knew Nemo had committed, and I was not prepared to absolve myself at the asking price. There was no way to turn; I was trapped, and rapidly growing panicky.

And that was just what Detective Inspector Blunt had intended. I was busy stewing in my own juice, spiced with a pinch of his own Ingredient X, and left to simmer. And, I remembered, I had even missed dinner.

I realized I had to calm down and think clearly. I would eat, then begin to sort myself out. I must telephone Boris, and we could examine the whole situation in its new, even more colourful, aspect. Boris would be good at that. I rang the kitchens and pleaded my cause, without enlarging on my reasons for missing Hall: no doubt the two tall serious men asking their way to my rooms would duly have been noted and the news flashed round the lower echelons of the College. I was not going to add any free information. They sent me up some soup, an omelette and greens, and a spare Queen of Puddings. Meanwhile I contacted Boris and arranged to meet him at a quiet pub near his flat. I still had no car, but I felt I might be the better for a walk.

For I still had not thought through the other course of inquiry. Taking my Big Line 'But I couldn't have done it. Bob Maclean was killed on Monday', and my immediate retraction, as a starting point, and seriously – as I had seen they did – where did the investigation lead from there? First of all, I must assume for good measure that they had some other information that pinpointed that Monday, the day Bob left home, as the day of his murder. It might be something as simple and classic as a stopped date watch, or as complicated as the evidence of a passer-by. But it appeared to be inconclusive: that my confirmation of the date was important, and the source of my certainty absolutely central to the whole case. This way they were faced with not a chief suspect, but a chief witness who turned out to be both hostile, and clearly willing to take the whole guilt rather than give away the true murderer.

As I walked down Longwall and over Magdalen Bridge, I looked round two or three times, but could identify no 'Tail'; the solitary male pedestrian I chose for the part was joined by a woman, and then both disappeared. Perhaps they already knew I was going to see Boris. When a bus halted almost beside me at the Plain, I boarded it for two stops, just for good measure, got out at the top of Headington Hill and walked on. And as I walked I wondered how much of a case they had against Nemo.

Motive, opportunity, timing – how did she rate as a murderer? My blurted and retracted self-defence had done her more harm than anything, since she herself had made so much of my passion for her: if I was trying to protect anyone, it would obviously be her. The most uncomfortable gap in my knowledge was what she had said to the police; but I had to assume from the little they told me that she had taken trouble to implicate *me*. I wondered what sort of mood she had been in when they questioned her; and I could not help feeling that whatever arc of her cyclic pattern she had been passing through at the time, the thing that Boris called 'Sarah Moore coiled like a snake in her subconscious' would have guarded her, made her wilier than Nemo on her own knew how. And Sarah Moore was determined to nail me as an accomplice – at worst. At best she might rely on my besotted devotion to assume all the blame.

It was so difficult to see into the workings of that double mind. In between her bouts of criminal insanity, Nemo, I was sure, knew nothing of her crimes. Her telephone call earlier in the evening had confirmed this: she had spoken to me as if that sublime, grotesque sexual encounter had never taken place; as if the last time she had seen me was Tuesday, when I had brought her fresh buns from the bakery, and we sat on the garden bench and were close. So close indeed that she had confided her troubles, and I had confessed my love. But some dark memory of her other self had disturbed her, had made her warn me against having an affair with her. How melodramatic it had seemed that day sitting with my arm round her in the spring sunlight that came and went; I had been so certain then that it was typically part of her depression. Yet at about that same stage of convalescence she had telephoned me this very evening, and I had no feeling she was speaking to a man she had tried to murder in the interim: she remembered nothing. So what had been her attitude to me when questioned by Detective Inspector Blunt? If she knew, as Nemo, she was innocent, why was she so ready to tell him of my love for her, unless it was to involve me in Sarah Moore's crime?

Boris was waiting for me at the pub in Old Marston that he most favoured. He seemed to have an arrangement – a private corner, discreet but regular service – and I wondered how much he used it as a more casual extension of the clinic couch. He listened to my account of the policemen's visit, and was as surprised as I – though I was still smarting over my own stupidity – when I came to the incident of my excursion from Heathrow; and I realized I had not told even him.

'So they trapped you into defending yourself? Did you say you could not have done it – and why?'

'Yes, Boris, that's exactly what I did. And then I realized I had probably put the whole pack of them on to Nemo, I dug my feet in – a little late, I fear – swore I had only assumed it was on the Monday that Bob had been killed, with the very natural result that they designated me chief suspect, and asked me not to leave town. So here I am, a wanted man, probably being followed – and now you're involved too. I'm sorry, Boris, but I couldn't say anything on the telephones. The porter or someone else on the switchboard could have been listening; and, as you can imagine, my position in College, once the law had paid me a prolonged visit, is delicate – and liable to be scandalous, if they really put a Tail on me. I didn't want to say anything more on the telephone – '

'Of course, my friend. Forget it. They will already be making a file on me, no doubt. It is embarrassing: there are always so many little things in the past one would not really want to have subjected to full excavation, now one is respectable and established. But I do not think they will see me in anything but an advisory role, and they will know before they start that questioning me about my patients' secrets is, as you say, a non-starter. For this purpose you are a patient, Harry: I shall probably have to send you a bill.'

He did not seem unduly ruffled. He ordered another drink for us both and we turned to the problem of Nemo's double-think. We went through the whole question of how much she knew, half-knew, knew subconsciously, and suspected; whether it was likely that she had told the police of having sex with Bob or me or both, and how much such information would affect their view of the case. Boris cited instances of dual nature; but as far as I could see, the necessary element that virtually defined the condition was the total separation of the two halves. By this ruling, Dr Jekyll, for example, was not strictly truly a split personality, because he was aware that he had an *alter ego* that was potentially criminal – though he had no knowledge of what those crimes might be.

'In the same way, but to a lesser degree,' Boris said, 'Nemo seems aware of her own danger to others, or she would not have said an affair with her would be "fatal". What we do not know is the extent to which her *alter ego* can influence her when not completely in charge. Like Jekyll, Nemo is not truly "split," because there is clearly some give and take between her two natures. At least she retains some sense of her potential threat when she is on an even keel. That is good. What is bad is that Sarah Moore or whatever it is seems able to influence her, perhaps increasingly. It is even possible that the evil half is taking over more and more of her daily life: the gaps between headaches, or cycles, seem to be getting shorter.'

'But you thought she might be all right this week, being so busy preparing for the party.'

'Yes, but I did not anticipate the pressure of the Law on Nemo, and I cannot judge its effect on the delicate balance of these dual personalities. You see, it is both a threat and a challenge, and the nervous excitement is more likely to tip the scales towards the dangerous side: for the threat is to the criminal in her, and may summon up all the reserves of electric energy – which you have observed now on two occasions.'

'Yes. That is probably the mood in which she encountered Blunt. I have been trying to imagine what her attitude would have been. I remember James saying on Sunday, when he first told me about it all, that Nemo seemed rather detached: I think he found it a little embarrassing. He said it would have been more normal if she had seemed upset – instead of asking the Fuzz not to walk on the foxgloves. But when they questioned her closely – and that was this morning, I understand – I can imagine that it was more like the Nemo I first saw last week. And I'm sure that then it was not just that I had not seen her for so long. She *was* different: she arrived back from London positively blazing with vitality. And I remember Blunt used that very word when forced to agree that she was attractive. I can see her pacing up and down in front of the Law, fairly sizzling with animation, telling them about all the troublesome men who fancied her – in that sort of mood she would – and they would be charmed and diverted however hard they stared at their shorthand.'

'I think that's right, Harry. Their questioning would have alerted her and tripped off that almost manic adrenalin charge that I call Sarah Moore. And then, of course, our unfortunate Bertie Bull drops in during the afternoon and finds her alone but still high and thirsting for action. Through him she as it were earths the electric storm, and in the evening is found to be in the middle of the migraine reaction.'

'And all in one day. My God, Boris, I fear for the investigators themselves at this rate. She'll tackle any policeman or forensic expert that strays away from the herd – all we need now is a raped and murdered bobby to give an already interesting case the real way-out Bring-back-capital-punishment appeal –' The laugh I heard was disconcertingly wild, and it was my own.

'Yes, Harry, just so. Come, my friend – you are the one who needs the tranquillizer now –'

We were out on the pavement now: Boris had not even paid the bill. (He's got an account, I deduced, with Watsonian speed – and liquid assets.) He just waved to mine host and led me out.

'I'm going to drive you home and give you a pill to take when you go to bed, and another for if you should wake up in the night. I want to talk to you again. What we have got to face up to is that you are going to tell the police everything, and we are going to get Nemo certified. I can see the pressure is too much – too much perhaps for both of you in different ways – '

All the way home he spoke soothingly about the special treatment she would receive from the police; of the ins and outs of pleading guilty but insane; of the possibilities of getting her into some particular nursing home. Of course I agreed with everything he said: I had to reassure him. But telling the police was the last thing I intended. I felt that he was taking it out of my hands; but at the same time, I knew that Boris had become irrelevant now. I sat hunched with my arms folded tightly across my chest as he drove. I was only half listening: I was imagining as precisely as I could the feeling of a strait-jacket – so successfully that I had some difficulty, when we parked outside College, in believing I could get my arms untied and my hand out to take the tablets from him. Perhaps he sensed my withdrawal: he seemed anxious about my silence, tried to get me to talk again. But I did not want to talk. Boris was no longer on my side.

I smiled and thanked and reassured him, and left him quickly. I could feel him watching me as I crossed the street and I made my hands swing loosely. As I ducked in through the small door I heard him start up the engine, and I wrapped up my arms again and bowed my head and trudged up the long staircase to my rooms.

Now my mind was clear. For the first time I found myself beginning to see in real terms what had happened. I realized that through endless words and speculation we had escaped from the true issues, as academics so often can and do. We had regarded it as a sort of jigsaw puzzle, or crossword – had fiddled around with possible police theories and probable criminal states of mind as if they were anagrams. When I had heard myself speculating on the added complications of a murdered bobby, and my wild guffaw – I saw – I had lost touch with flesh and blood. Boris, like the well-trained psychiatric bloodhound he was, bayed a warning: 'signs of strain'. I flushed his pills down the lavatory and sat down with a big glass of barley water to flush away his whisky.

Boris had joined the Baddies. I must have no hard feelings: after all, Nemo was still only an interesting case to him; his main loyalty was to me – and, of course, to himself. He would have committed perjury, concealed evidence, walled up Nemo in his very private nursing home, as long as the circumstances justified it – according to his reasoning, and in the absence of any real moral code. But now the situation had changed. Instead of us and Nemo versus the police, it was Nemo against me. I suppose he was fond of me, and saw me as an innocent – and giving way under the pressure – set up by her to take her blame, serve her sentence. Moreover he was considering, I felt sure, the danger of his own involvement in a lost cause; and immediately Nemo became simply dangerously mad – ultimately curable, he might hope, but meanwhile meet sacrifice to the police investigators.

He was reckoning without me. I could destroy the notebook, and he would have no ground from which to save me. I wondered if he had copied extracts and whether they would be valid in a court of law. I did not think that, without exhibit A, he could prove anything against Nemo.

I lit the neatly laid fire in my grate, unlocked the desk drawer and took out the marbled notebook. I sat and read it through again. Deliberately I subjected myself, put myself into Nemo's struggling mind, as the power took it over, and the writing sloped wildly down the page. I mourned my lost peeler of apples, sitting on the south steps looking down the garden at the golden trees; then I let the encroaching evergreen wood enfold me. I paced through the deserted house and felt the oppression of the shuttered rooms and the sick hunger of the huntress.

I came to those fast-flowing pages, which I now thought of as the Journal – the seduction and death of the workman, of Bob Maclean. Repelled as I was, I forced myself to be involved – to feel both her urgency, and the horror of the fall from the slates; the white wine and the rug, the rape in the windless well of the magic circle, the fork through my neck – *and* the force I needed to drive that fork through the sinew and into the soft loam. I tried to sense how it had been, and to get far away from the words. Words were my living: they were also a sort of little death. I was trained to observe how things were described, not how they felt. Now I tried to get into the mind and flesh of Nemo, as Sarah Moore had done, and so understand them. It was not to any visible end – I had no plan, though I knew I must make one. I just wanted to get back to reality, however fantastic that reality might be; to know, to try to comprehend.

Suspending my disbelief and subordinating my will – it was as if I were being raped again. I lived through every page of mad Nemo's notebook; and then I burnt it on my fire.

21

That disposed of the most damning evidence. Now it was only Boris's word against mine; for I knew Nemo was on my side.

After that I went to bed and slept well. But soon it was light, and ordinary life pressed in on me. I had tutorials and meetings all day, and I decided there was no choice but to concentrate on my neglected duties. I had not yet dined in College, and the Dean telephoned me just before nine to ask if I was all right, and would they soon be having the pleasure of my company perhaps?

After the Master, the Dean was possibly the most important and busy man about the College; but not so important as he liked to think, nor more busy than the post itself demanded, by reason of some measure of academic failure in his prime. No doubt he thought of himself as an *éminence grise*, but the total impression was more that of an excellent nanny.

Of course, I said, I would be at dinner, and apologized for my shortcomings – family troubles, I said, and he made understanding noises, reminded me about the Senior Common Room meeting at two, and wished me well.

During the past week I had lunched twice in Hall and had seen almost all the Fellows at some point – crossing a quad, in the Lodge or the Common Room. Those nearest to me like Hendry had dropped in for a drink the first two days and welcomed me home: it was not as if I was out of touch or under a cloud. But I was well aware that, though I had only missed one College meeting (when I left early for my weekend in Wiltshire) and cancelled only two tutorials, which I would make up within the next week, my mind had not been on the job. I had allowed myself to become absorbed into a situation about which none of them knew or could begin to understand.

I made a point of having an early breakfast in the Buttery. As I anticipated, Hendry and others asked me about the progress of the Maclean business. They knew I had met him, and had heard that the police had been to see me the evening before. I told them what I could about the difficulties of the case, that the Law had divulged nothing, and I feared I had not been much help, contributing what little I knew of him, his way of life and his relationship with the Boyces. I did not inform my colleagues that I was chief suspect, in spite of the small mad inner voice that kept saying, 'Go on – shock them!' There was an even stronger desire to confess to someone, to get some sort of understanding or even approval of what I was intending to do. I wondered how they would take it when it all came out, and who would still be my friends. Who would come and see me in gaol.

My first tutorial was at ten, and from then on I hardly had time to think, except glancingly, of my lurid private life. But two things nagged me like a perpetual toothache and its reflected pain: what was Nemo doing? I prayed she had been well enough to go to London. And what was Boris up to? I had been expecting – with some misgivings – a call from him: his silence was even more disturbing.

By lunchtime I was feeling the lack of sleep, and filled up on black coffee to carry me through the two o'clock meeting. Between my five and six o'clock tutorials, I telephoned Boris's flat, but got no reply. Then, impulsively, I telephoned Nemo. I hoped most of all to get James – the assurance of the norm and company and party preparations. It rang and rang; I heard my pupils on the stairs; I would let it ring three more times. On the penultimate ring it was answered.

'Hello. This is the Dower House, Sutton Hamden – ' I put the phone down gently. The voice that answered was male, but it was not James's, and it certainly was not that of the friendly neighbourhood policeman. It was quite unmistakably Boris's.

Fortunately, one of my pupils had written a very long and convoluted essay which he enjoyed reading aloud; then his partner who had produced only excuses and a bunch of notes, proceeded to knock down the whole elaborate edifice with missiles from a ballista in the opposing school of thought. All I had to do was to halt the battle at intervals for a few well chosen slices of lemon, blow the final whistle and pick up the wounded – any recognition of injury time would have made us late for Hall. As it was we all made it, shrugging on our gowns as we crossed the quadrangle. The essay writer was still sniping from his ruined battlements when we parted at the Hall door.

Very good mackerel, and a friendly historian on my right. I tried to concentrate on both, but my mind kept slipping out of gear. What was Boris doing? Had he gone out to see Nemo alone? Or the police and Nemo? Had he taken it out of my hands completely? Was he setting up an independent investigation – the Magnificent One? Or did he no longer trust me with his strategy? Perhaps he simply could not resist the possibility of an encounter with Sarah Moore; and he believed I was telling all to the police: his time was short.

I could not leave until at least dessert was over. I made myself mix and talk. I paid my respects to the Master as well as the dear Dean, and I heard myself asking the right questions about families, friends, and small papers on early Persian politics. It came almost automatically; in turn, I told of the wonders of the United States – of the skiing, or the girls, of student unrest or microbiology, according to my interrogator. But the subject of the Ice-house Murder came up more than once. I was called upon to describe the brick egg, say a few words on Bob Maclean's qualities, both personal and literary – and so at last diverted the subject, with no little relief, on to fantasy in fiction. No one had read any Maclean, but the Chaplain had read C. S. Lewis, and even the Master had read Tolkien.

There was one dangerous moment when the port had lowered my guard and the Tempter – the same who had suggested I should shock the early breakfasters that morning – said, 'Go on – try your own true fantasy on them. Don't worry, they'd never believe it. Tell them of the beautiful mad actress, dead for a hundred and fifty years, making her entrance like a neon sign into a room full of jiving teeth and claws. Tell of her blazing in the wood like a Martian Queen with her bloody fork upraised, or materializing through a cloud of smoke and ripping the heart and jissom from a living man – or in a dark stone dairy, naked but for hat and boots, squinting down a chisel at a favourite pupil and member of this College –'

'Why are you shaking your head, Harry?' Hendry asked.

'Just thinking about the incredible and dismissing it,' I said. 'I must go: I've got to make a telephone call before ten.'

'Tomorrow's your London day, isn't it?'

'Lord yes, it is – thank you for reminding me. That means two telephone calls. So – see you Thursday.' And I excused myself.

I wanted to try Boris's number again. And then I would have to call Blunt – or whoever was on duty – and report my intended day in London. There was no answer from Boris's flat. When I rang the number the Inspector had given me, the policeman who took my message seemed quite unruffled by my rather tentative request.

'That will be quite in order, sir. Just so long as we know.'

I felt I had to speak to someone. On a sudden inspiration I rang James in his College.

'You've just missed him, sir: he dined in Hall and left for home about five minutes ago.'

I waited twenty minutes, then dialled the Boyce's number. I desperately wanted reassurance: that Nemo was all right, that James was there, and would be there on and off for the rest of the week, that the police had not –

James answered.

'Oh, Harry, old thing – so glad you can make the party on Saturday. No – Mo's asleep, I should think – left a note to say she had a headache. But I was just looking at the list. Yes, I just got back. Off to London tomorrow for a couple of nights. No, I don't think she'll need a lot of help: it's quite a simple little do, you know – sausages and wine and things – nothing like the last knees-up. Just a chance for some of her arty friends to dress up and act and strum their guitars. And there's someone special playing the violin, the real thing – you know – unaccompanied Bach and not much bite. What? Yes, I think she's fine, apart from these head-aches. Oh, the police – they haven't bothered us much. The usual questions: how well did you know Mr Maclean. Why should anyone want to kill him. Where were you on the morning of the sixteenth – actually one would need alibis for so many damn mornings that it's all rather ridicu-lous – and my alibis are usually rather compromising at best. They don't seem to have got any nearer to pinning down the day – except they seem to fancy that Monday, the day he left home. Plodding along, beginning at the beginning, I dare say. It's all an awful bore. Yes, they questioned Mo, of course. Same as me, I imagine. Oh yes, as good an alibi as they could hope for, considering. Oh, I don't know, Harry – well, she was here all morning in the house – didn't hear or see anything unusual. Some London friend passing through gave her a lift into Oxford in the afternoon – a bit silly as she had to get a taxi back – well, yes, from the St Giles taxi rank. What's all this fuss about, Harry? Honestly, Harry, my dear fellow – don't *worry*. Yes, they asked about you, so I imagined they might pay you a visit – leaving no rolling stone unturned. But they seem to be at rather a dead end from what I hear. No they haven't been back. It'll all simmer down – just rotten luck having a nastiness so near the old homestead. Good Lord, no – no policemen or anyone else watching the house. What for? They've been in the woods, I understand, looking for clues, but they've gone now, I reckon.

'No – Mo's *fine* – busy dressing up and rehearsing her recitation or whatever all day and then she'll be fussing about the cooking and the flowers – and I'll be back on Friday. Look, Harry – lovely hearing from you. See you on Saturday, OK? I must get an early night – the London life really takes it out of one, eh? The sort of girl one has to get into training for – strenuous stuff. Ah well, not that I'm complaining. Be seeing you – '

What had I got out of that, at the expense of making something of a fool of myself? That Nemo was going to be alone for the next two days: that was bad news. That she had an alibi of a sort for the vital Monday – at least for her trip into Oxford: that was the good news. And the police seemed to be at an impasse and were not in any way hounding Nemo, or even keeping an eye on her.

I could not help wondering about the 'London friend' who had been prepared to lie for her. He/she would have certainly been checked out by the police, and had clearly upheld the alibi. Nemo must have many such chums, young, liberated, all too ready to ally themselves with her against bobbies or husbands or whatever other establishment figure seemed to threaten freedom. How easy for her to have lovers and excuses to fit round them with friends like that; not that James would be difficult about a casual affair. He simply wouldn't want to know. He was, as Nemo said, otherwise engaged.

Before I went to bed, I rang Boris again. No answer. I wondered if his first encounter with Nemo could have proved 'fatal' – and, jealous and resentful as I was towards him, I felt sick at the thought...

I overslept badly: amid my fears and phone calls I had forgotten to set my alarm. There was no time for breakfast; I gathered up my papers, put my razor in my pocket and took a bus from Carfax to the station. On the train that I narrowly caught, I shaved in the lavatory, then went along to the dining car and had a noble British Rail breakfast, with all the extras, including sauté potatoes. I was not just hungry, I felt I must keep my strength up, as if some great ordeal lay ahead of me. I was right: as it turned out, it was to be the only square meal I had that day.

A man I had noticed on the platform was last on to the train behind me, in spite of having had time to buy a newspaper, and appeared in the dining car as I was starting on the orange juice. I wondered if he was sent to watch me. When I saw him sitting on a bench in Bedford Square as I came out of the publishers' meeting just after one, I was sure. But I had other worries. I found a telephone box and boldly reversed the charges to Boris's clinic: I could not waste time on getting the right change, and I was sure they would be used to it.

I was right. They accepted the call without a flutter.

'Dr Goodie is out to lunch. Would you telephone again at two? Good. I shall tell him to expect your call.'

So Boris was alive.

I went to the *chic* little French restaurant where I was meeting my agent, and found him queueing for a table.

'I should have booked,' he said. 'They're not usually as busy as this.'

By the time we had got a place, and a waiter, and ordered our meal it was ten to two. I had a glass of wine and half my soup, then I could bear it no longer.

'Look,' I said, 'I've got to make a call to Oxford. I'll be back by the time they've brought the next course –'

There was a telephone box on the upstairs landing outside the ladies' room. While I waited for a pretty girl to finish a call to her father, I saw my Tail walk slowly by on the pavement outside, glance in and move on. I hoped he had had a sandwich.

It was not an ideal place for the telephone conversation that followed. Fortunately I was for the greater part on the receiving end – and Boris, I am sure, had padded walls to his 'surgery'. I had to censor my reactions for the ladies who came and went; and afterwards I realized I said very little. I went down the steep stairs and straight out into the street, my agent and my *quenelles de brochet* forgotten. I had to get back to Nemo.

I hailed a taxi, told the driver to take me to Paddington and got in. Only as I slammed the door and leant back did I notice the flurry of activity in my wake: my agent flapping his hands at me through the plate-glass window of the restaurant, and the silent watcher dropping his paper bag and sprinting after another cab. I watched out of the back window: he caught one going the other way, and it was doing a three-point turn at some inconvenience to others in the narrow Soho street when I lost sight of it. I did not want to take him with me. When I was sure he was in sight of me again, I told my driver to turn right into Oxford Street: I had changed my mind. I got a fifty pence piece ready and waited until we were in a traffic jam near Tottenham Court Road. Then, without a word, I dropped the coin through the sliding panel on to the taxidriver's lap and slipped out of the right-hand door, between two buses, crossed to an under pass and went down it. I would think of an excuse for my eccentric behaviour all in good time; but I wanted to get to Sutton Hamden, and it would have to be by country bus from Victoria. It was slow, but it was direct.

It took nearly two and a half hours, in fact, and I had plenty of time to think about Boris and Nemo. Bertie Bull's account of passionate love-making had made me faint. Boris's had perhaps driven me mad.

'Harry, you must not allow so petty a thing as jealousy to come into this,' he said, repeatedly. 'Remember, it is not Nemo, it is Sarah Moore who does these things. Keep telling yourself that, and you will get it in its proper perspective. You must see I had to achieve an encounter with this creature. It was a question of research and proof positive, by controlled experiment, of the evidence in the notebook. I was the only person to do it – no? For I am a detached observer with the qualifications to make some balanced judgement on the case. You are far too *involved*, Harry, as your wild suggestion that you should assume her guilt only goes to prove. Yes – well, in her bedroom, in point of fact – Harry? Are you there? Ah – I thought we had been cut off. Of course you are right – she is a fantastic creature, so fiery – as you put it – so voracious. Not Nemo, Harry, remember: Sarah Moore. But what an *experience*, my friend – to be raped by a Regency actress – something you and I have both had now, no? So – and we are both adult: we can talk it through together, and see it for what it is. You must appreciate what this is for a scholar of the psyche like myself – a unique experience of a rare mania at *first hand*! I have made so many notes, Harry – even, would you believe it, some recording – but alas, she discovered the machine and smashed it in a fine frenzy. You should have seen those *eyes*. Well yes, of course you have – incredible, like a tiger's eyes . . .

'But the greatest thing – Harry, listen to this: this is *great news*, Harry – I believe she can be cured. Of course she must, as we decided, plead guilty but insane – what was that, Harry? You mean you have not told the police yet? So – you will do that today – right? But listen, my friend. I have formed an opinion, from this experience, this *research*, Harry, that a good lover may be able to cure her. An experienced man – if necessary myself. Well, yes, my friend, but I feel you may *at the moment* be too involved to – later, yes – of course; and you want to take her away from James and marry her – yes. But while this condition is rampant she needs, well – very special treatment. I am going out again today after clinic hours. No, Harry; you see, I am forewarned and so forearmed. And I know how to handle her. No, I must not wait – I have high hopes to make the break-through, so to speak, this evening. No, Harry. I *order* you, as a doctor – your doctor and hers. Leave it to me. Look, my friend, it is ridiculous to bring jealousy into it – yes, yes, you may fear for my well-being, of course, but when you look into yourself you will see it is chiefly this childish misguided envy of my – Listen, Harry: it is for you, ultimately, that I am doing this thing, is it not? You will be the beneficiary when I effect the cure – no? Try to look at it calmly and clearly: this is a sick woman, I am a doctor – I am not going to take her from you! I do not *want* Nemo, my friend – it is Sarah Moore I want – that is, that I am after – to, as it were, exorcise – Harry, will you be calm now? And sensible? And I will tell you all this evening – it is so difficult to talk to you like this – and I will tell you everything you ask, and whether your Nemo will be cured, perhaps. OK, Harry? – Harry, are you there? – Operator, I seem to have been – '

That was where I had put down the phone.

The countryside bumbled by at a sedate pace and I pressed my forehead against the cool glass and tried to think what I intended to do. Reaching the Dower House was my only idea at first, and seeing Nemo. Now I had time to think: why, and to do what? To get there before Boris and save her from him. Save Nemo – and what if I found Sarah Moore? Would she kill me this time? Whatever she might do, it was I who should be involved. I would be another moth.

Dark seemed to be coming early. It was only four-thirty as we crawled out of Maidenhead, but car headlights were on, and now they switched on the lights inside the bus, so that my reflection against the window was superimposed against the glass to blot out the glare, and saw again the thinning houses, and the heavy trees of May. I realized that the slate blue air was not that of evening but of a great gathering storm. The west was barred with muddy light where the sun still hung, but otherwise the whole of the sky right over to the east was solid with a stifling blanket of banked rain clouds. Once a shaft of sunlight found a gap in the shifting grey and picked out a clump of brilliant lime and russet trees in the middle distance – invisible till then, as if painted on a gauze curtain and suddenly spot-lighted. But that was the last flicker of day; in the east, bright enough to be visible beyond the passengers' reflections, there was distant lightning.

I got out one stop before Sutton Hamden – I did not want to walk through the village – and set off, across the fields and the great park of the Mansion, in the direction of the Dower House. It was breathlessly still and humid; the air itself seemed to cling to my skin like a thin plastic wrapping, and my haste made me feel hot, tangled and helpless, wading through thick gloom that dragged at my legs as in a terrible dream. I took off my tie and jacket and hurried on, ridiculous in white shirt, London suiting and thin shoes, and lumbered with a bulky brief-case. It was already five-forty-five: I did not know what time Boris normally left the clinic, or whether he would come straight out to keep his appointment with his newest patient. But I was sure he would have apprised himself of James's absence, and hoped, therefore, that he would be taking his time.

How passionately I regretted having told him about

Nemo. It had been such a relief at the time to share the impossible burden of my knowledge, once I had seen the notebook, and knew from the discovery of Bob Maclean's body that it was no mere fiction. Now everything was turned upside down. Not only was Boris determined that Nemo should be proved guilty and insane, but, meanwhile, in order to get that proof, and, incidentally – oh irony! – to initiate her cure, he had become her lover. Should I really have been delighted? Suppressed my 'childish' jealousy and trusted him?

No. Surely a 'child' would have seen through his excitement, even when he attempted to disguise it in the mystique of psychiatric flummery. It was all literally balls. He might be there already, his smart brown Porsche snugly parked in my gravel circle; would it be the bedroom again this time, shuttered against the gathering gloom, and softly lit under the houdah-like canopy that I had helped James to fix, while Nemo had sat directing us and sewing the silken drapery? I broke into a run.

Then, within sight of the tall trees, the long wall, the lighted windows of the upper floor of the house, I stopped. What was I doing? What did I expect, or hope, to find? What did I really intend to do about it? Was I, in fact, deeply afraid that Boris would succeed where I had failed? – that he might be returning to make love again and live to tell the tale – exorcise Sarah Moore, and find a tender and submissive Nemo in his arms? Is that what I most feared? If so, I was not merely jealous, but insanely selfish, to interfere.

Or did I foresee the inevitable pattern – four times repeated already, to my knowledge – of rape, revulsion and destruction? Why should not Boris be as repulsive to her now as I and the others had been, once the sexual act was over?

I walked slowly on towards the boundary fence where

our eucalyptus trees, like delicate silver mobiles, trembled in the still air. I stopped and leaned against an old pear tree on the very edge of the ploughed field. From here I could not see the house: the holly tunnel and the shrubbery nearby hid it from me. Already I might be too late, and Boris might be dead. Or perhaps there was time to save him. Still I did not move.

For I realized there was no hurry. I believed that Sarah Moore would kill Boris, for all his fine words and 'special treatment'. And, I realized, moreover, that this was what I really wanted.

22

I wanted to be there.

There was no hurry, but I knew that I must be there to protect Nemo from the consequences: I must not, after all that had happened, shield her successfully from one murder only for her to be accused of another. But I had to admit that my fondest hopes were that I should find Boris already dead. In my present mood I might be prepared to kill him myself: it would remove at a stroke all danger to Nemo's freedom. For he had quite convinced me on the telephone that he intended to use his evidence against her, and it would be far more damning that that of the notebook I had so triumphantly burned. Yes, I thought, I might have to kill him myself; but given time – and it was now nearly a quarter past six – Sarah Moore would do it for me.

I climbed over the boundary fence and cautiously approached the house, past the big flowering chestnut looming like a low-slung cumulus against the stormy sky, and through the spinney of nut trees that bordered the orchard. The damp leaves of last autumn made no sound underfoot. I came out into the walk and stepped softly through the longer grass at its edge, careful not to trip on the old edging-tiles that I knew still stuck up through the turf in places like worn molars. I knew the way so well I could have done it blindfold. Now I could see the lights of the upper windows again, but the box hedge that ringed the gravel circle still hid the drive from my view: I could see through towards the garage, and only Nemo's car was there. I ducked under the low boughs of the ornamental beech: here the drift of old leaves was so thick they whispered as I

moved, and the sound was loud in the silence. Now I was
close to the wall of box and only had to move a few paces
along it to find a gap, low down between the trunks, where
I could look through. I could see the front porch, and the
lighted window of the passage, but there was no car in view.
I crept along to the wide opening into the circle and stood
shielded by thin shrubs. The whole of the drive was visible
from here. Boris had not arrived – yet. So. I would wait.

I went back to the first opening and settled down on my
rolled-up jacket. I even lit a cigarette. From here, not only
could I see the porch, the study window and the passage,
but even if Boris drove up and past me through the opening
to the garage, I would be invisible, buried in a hollow of the
deep hedge.

As I waited I became aware again of the strange stillness
and of the almost Biblical darkness covering the land. No
birds sang, and the breathless blue gloom was only shivered
from time to time by the lightning in the eastern sky. But
looking straight up at the patch of sky above me, I could
see how the clouds raced and boiled in the upper air, and
now I heard a distant drum-roll of approaching thunder.
The next was sharper, a crack and a rumble. Somewhere the
storm had started. Meanwhile, an interloper on my own
well-known ground, I crouched among the cool blue-black
box leaves and watched my house – a killer without a
weapon, without a plan. A mad don in a chalk-stripe suit
waiting to help his haunted mistress murder a bent psychiatrist.

The house looked back at me out of its two big lighted
windows, the passage and the study with the heavy dark
nose of the porch between. It brooded, as patient as I. Its
golden plaster was a uniform charcoal against the grey
green of the garden and the slate grey of the clouds; the
growth of honeysuckle a black fungus spreading over one
cheek; and under the study window, the delicate fan of a

trained rose, like a broken vein. I could see the edge of the border and a glimmer of white where the nicotiana I had planted out last week was already flowering. That was the day Nemo had raped me. And beyond the shaggy lines of the border, the long low mass of the evergreens, just the iceberg tip of the deep wood, midnight black in a grey world.

As I gazed at its dark lizard shape lying crouched along the lawn, a movement in the house brought my eyes back and I saw Nemo. She moved across the lighted study, paused for a moment in front of the looking-glass, whose corner I could just make out above the mantelpiece, then passed back, disappeared and reappeared crossing the passage window. She was in fancy dress, and wearing a large hat with plumes, like the Garrick portrait. A minute later she returned, more slowly, bearing a small tray with a decanter. She carried it with panache, on the fingers of one hand, like an Italian waiter. Then she was back in the study. I saw her sip from a glass and place it on the mantelshelf, then address herself once more to her reflected image. She appeared to be talking and moving – rehearsing a speech, perhaps – with graceful gestures that, as I watched, seemed to pick up a rhythm and turn into a dance, and she began to sway and circle slowly, always coming back to the looking-glass. Suddenly she stopped, adjusted her hat, picked up her glass and moved out of sight.

For a moment I wondered if it was the real Nemo I had seen, practising her part for Saturday's revels – why not? But then I knew that it was Nemo possessed by Sarah Moore: for there was something extravagant, larger than life, in her least movement, even as she glided along the passage, or picked up a glass – and Nemo would never have carried a tray like that. Even at this distance, the keyed-up vitality of the creature was that of Sarah Moore; the true Nemo's economy of movement, her understatement, the aptness and simplicity of mien, were no longer there.

Brazen, flamboyant, this flitting, gesturing figure even held herself differently, carried herself consciously like a gaudy banner.

It was little more than a series of glimpses, but I had ample time to think it over as I sat waiting and watching. And now I was backing Sarah Moore against Boris in this encounter – that ancient evil against the newest science. Both were corrupt: for I considered that Boris was perverting psychiatry in the search for sensation. What turned him on, it seemed (and he had used the phrase), was the basic paradox of getting physical pleasure from a ghost. The more I reflected on it, the more I was sure that ghost would win.

I heard the beech leaves above me moving in a light breeze; it died away and was followed by noisy gusts that tossed about in the tall trees and rushed down through the wood – chill forerunners of the rain. And through the roaring and rustling I heard the sound of a car in the lane.

It came slowly – muffled through the holly tunnel – and on up the drive. Now I could see it had only sidelights, and that it was Boris's Porsche. It stopped at the front door with a soft crunch on the gravel, and Boris got out. He shone in the dark; he was wearing an ice-cream white summer suit. He must have gone home to change: white for the glamorous seducer? for the high-priest doctor-figure? for both? But my only thought was how it might show the blood.

Before he could ring or knock, the porch doors swung open and Nemo stood there in silhouette, except for the plumes in her hat and the gauzy wrap that rimmed her with light. I could not hear her words, but her fine gesture of dismissal was clear enough. Boris caught at her outflung hand and she recoiled, drawing her wide skirts round her, and now I could see, in the lighted porch, how every line spoke of repugnance. But Boris pressed forward, and the doors closed behind him.

Then Nemo was in the study again, standing by the mantelpiece, one arm up in a dramatic gesture of defence. Boris appeared with his back to me; he was offering no visible threat. Instead he sat down on the study sofa – the sofa where I had found myself after passing out at the party. The sofa, I assumed, on which the many-talented Vic had met his match.

I could only see Boris's head, and now and again those expressive hands as he gesticulated and talked. He seemed to be doing all the talking. Nemo stood with one hand on the mantelpiece and the other at her throat in a pretty gesture: the wood nymph at bay. And Boris was still alive: I had to know what it was that he was saying that seemed to mesmerize her so.

I put on my jacket: it would hide my glaring white shirt; and I was glad of it – the gusty rain-wind was cold. I came out of my hiding place and, hugging the hedge and then keeping close to the wall of the house, I made my way quickly round to the shelter of the porch. As I crept up under the window I saw Boris stand up and I ducked back into the shadow of the car. From there, I saw him reappear with a glass of something that looked like sherry, which he sipped and placed on the window-sill before he sat down again.

This time I got right under the window, partly masked by the long new growth on the climbing rose. Here I was very close to the protagonists, brightly lit in their proscenium arch. I felt I could almost put out my hand to touch Boris's glass, and his luxuriant waving hair was only inches beyond. I felt that Nemo, if she looked, must see me, but then I realized that in the lighted room, nothing would be visible on the other side of the panes except perhaps the tossing trees and the lightning. Meanwhile the wind in those trees filled my ears: I could hear the sound of talking, but I could not make out a single word.

Boris was still speaking at length, and though I could not

see his face, I could tell he was using his charm, by the way that he tilted his head, and tossed back his wavy hair, by the way his hands, even his little finger, worked together, like the hypersensitive conductor of a chamber orchestra – and a little too aware of the zoom-lenses of the encircling cameras.

By contrast, Nemo had not moved: from my hiding place in the shadow of the window ledge, I could see her immediately beyond him – often actually framed by his hands that seemed to caress, but never touched her. She stood with her back to the wall, still holding the edge of the mantelpiece, as she had when they entered the room – he must have poured his own drink. Her other hand responded speakingly to his movements, and so perhaps to his words, touching her hair, arranging her shawl between the open-armed blandishments, as I watched; flying to her throat or her breast when he pointed at her accusingly, relaxing again as he wagged the admonitory finger naughtily. She looked as if she were completely under his spell, trembling at his warnings, flattered by his praise, hypnotized by his eloquence.

But not completely under his spell. Less than three yards away from me, her eyes were now clearly visible, and they were alive and watchful. It was not just the restless coruscation that had so fascinated me on our very first encounter – that golden swarming motion, the separate particles of the iris that seethed like organisms under a microscope. It was the way they watched him ceaselessly but with their own thoughts, and though the lids flickered when he threatened and widened when he marvelled, the wildness behind them was never once cowed or soothed. Her hands, her posture, seemed to mime response, but her tiger eyes only watched.

What was Boris saying that so held her attention? Was he actually explaining her psychological problems to her? Or expatiating on his qualifications as a lover? Or accusing her of all her crimes, to blackmail her back into bed with him?

He might use any course, both for his pleasure and her good; he might use them all. Whatever he was saying, he had survived longer with her than any of his predecessors. Would he succeed where we had failed? I almost wished him well, almost admired his nerve; but I loathed him too much. So close, so confident, in his white suiting – and sipping delicately now at his Madeira – being appreciative, being boyish, being intense. Then he actually leaned forward and picked up the hem of her dress, tilting his head as he glanced archly up at her, fingering and admiring the rich braided border, giving it a playful tug, then dropping it and spreading his hands wide in expansive admiration. But she did not strike him down with the poker: she listened, her hand at her throat – and she watched.

Perhaps encouraged by her silence, interpreting it as the beginning of passive acceptance, Boris leaned back luxuriously, and opened his arms wide in a gesture of invitation – the sensitive conductor demanding a climactic *tutti*. Then his long hands, that seemed so to enclose her, began to beckon slowly, to wave her towards him with a mesmeric, rhythmic pull.

Sarah Moore smiled prettily, baring her small pointed teeth in the semblance of pleasure – and it reminded me of the moment, by the bonfire, when she had trodden on my hand. With a shiver I knew, and wondered if Boris knew, that all was not well. She slowly raised both hands to her hat, unpinned it and tossed it to the floor in a mime of ultimate surrender. She moved towards him and bent over him. His arms closed and caught her round her thighs, straining her closer. Now her face was only a few feet from mine: she wore the same fixed piquante look, and her eyes were golden slits in a smiling mask. She raised her two hands in symmetrical adoration like a high priestess, then slowly brought them down to cradle Boris's luxuriant head. In her right hand she still held one long hat-pin.

I saw it glint when she raised her hands; I saw it clearly as she brought it round in that slow swooping embrace. I stood up, and she caught sight of me across Boris's head in the light of the window. Her eyes met mine in one full swift look, and I saw into the mouth of Hell: such naked savagery was inhuman. They burned like flowing lava. Then she looked back at her prey and I saw her grip the hat-pin and drive it, with an awful strength and accuracy – that was most horribly Nemo's – right up to its silver knob in the waving hair. Her left arm flexed as her cradling hand steadied and forced the head on to it in a neat pincer movement. I was scrabbling at the glass and yelling something, but she did not even glance towards me. She dragged out the hat-pin with complete concentration, as I have seen her take the butcher's skewer from a boiling fowl in order to put in the stuffing; and she wiped it on a scrap of lace handkerchief tucked in her sleeve. Only after that did she turn to the window; graciously she motioned me to come in. Then she put across the shutters.

23

The study was warm and still and bright. Nemo stood by the fireplace; she sipped her Madeira and smoothed her hair, gazing at her reflection.

Boris lay back on the sofa where he had sat and talked. His head was limp on his chest, but there was no sign of blood. I laid him down and listened for his heart, but he was dead. I lifted the thick hair, and could find no wound below the edge of his skull. Then I saw a smear of blood on his ear, and more inside. The long pin had been driven through his eardrum and into his brain.

Nemo sipped from her long-stemmed glass and looked down at her handiwork.

'Please remove this foreign lout,' she said. 'He was pestering me – I was driven to these lengths to protect my virtue.' She turned back to the looking-glass and seemed once more absorbed in her reflection.

I did not remonstrate with her: she would not have understood. But all my own hot blood had drained away and I was horrified and numb. I only knew the most important thing now was to get Boris's body away as quickly as possible. So I wiped the blood off his ear; then I caught him up under his arms and pulled him off the sofa, out into the hall, through the porch doors to where the car stood. Heavy splashes of rain were giving way to gusty squalls, cold and drenching. I propped him against the car, opened the passenger door and eased him on to the seat, where he slumped forward against the dashboard. So I put his head down on to his knees and closed the door on him. I knew I should get in and drive away, but I had to see Nemo again. First I collected my brief-case from the box hedge and put it in the car. Then, huddled in my turned-up collar against the driving rain, I ran back into the porch.

Nemo was still in the study. She had tidied the cushions on the sofa and was carefully arranging her hair before the glass. With the same helpless fascination I had felt standing outside the window, I watched those capable brown fingers pick up the murder weapon from the mantelpiece where she had laid it and re-pin the great plumed hat in place, tuck in a wild lock and tease out her fringe. She turned half sideways, admiringly, and stroked a tousled feather smooth, ignoring me utterly.

She had good reason to admire what she saw. Never had she been more lovely, more violently alive. The Regency actress who inhabited her seemed positively recharged by another victim: the dead thriving on the dead. Colour was high in her cheeks. Her lids were heavy with makeup: the blackened lashes and smudgy shadow only emphasized the volcanic eyes, twin craters; and her thick brown hair had been twisted into glossy curls and ringlets, all framed by the slanting oval of the great hat.

But most of all my gaze was drawn to the big silver knob of the pin that secured it; I seemed mesmerized by it. Then, abruptly, it forced me back to the needs of the situation, as distinct from my own. I could not leave that pin here: even doubly wiped, on the handkerchief and on the fabric of the hat – and on Nemo's hair – it might carry traces of blood. And yet, I thought, would it not be safe enough, tucked into the hat and put away in the big white cupboard in her room? I would not trouble her about it, or disturb a second time the picture in the looking-glass that pleased her so.

But I picked up the handkerchief that still lay on the mantelpiece. It was strongly perfumed with the dark Eastern musk which, even during the day, always lingered about Nemo's clothes and hair; and suddenly I felt such

198

intense and painful love for her that I could no longer endure it: I must touch, must hold her, even if she killed me afterwards.

I know it was the pull of the cliff edge: what Boris had called the ultimate masochism. And Boris's blood on the handkerchief I so lovingly folded brought me up sharply – a little Morse Code of rusty red on the lace-trimmed lawn. If I loved Nemo, I must remove the signs of her crime, not involve her in yet another. So I gently took her hand, uncurled it and kissed the palm. I did not look at her face for fear of the abhorrence I might see there. Then I went out through the rain to the car.

I got into the driver's seat and found the light switches and the windscreen wipers. I had started the engine, and let in the clutch, when a wild figure appeared in the headlights. It was Nemo, and now she was at my door scrabbling at the window, as I had done.

'You must bury him deep, you see – ' she babbled against the streaming glass. 'He said he would be at my salon on Saturday night. Take him far away – I would not have him appear at my dramatic evening – not for all the world – '

It was horrible. I felt if I opened the window she would claw me to pieces. I flattened my hand against the glass to blot out the wet mad face and slid the car forward, till the image vanished, and I picked up speed and swung round the circle. I saw her again in the light of the open porch doors, her plumes and scarves flapping like witches' rags, then I was down the drive and past the tunnel of the holly trees.

Before I reached the village I drew to the side and stopped. I found Boris's soft leather coat on the back seat, and his wide-brimmed felt hat. I took off my wet jacket and spread it over the huddled figure in the passenger seat; I put on the hat and coat and drove slowly to the main road. The down-pour was steady now; I wondered as I drove if it would remove Nemo's fingerprints from the side window. Then

I thought of the twenty-four-hour car-wash. It was some distance away, on the other side of the city, but that was all to the good. I took the Ring Road by Cowley and Headington to the North, driving carefully through the blinding rain. As I remembered, the car-wash was beyond one of the big roundabouts, and I prayed I was right, and that the petrol station itself would be closed and deserted by now.

When I caught sight of it, it was so brightly lit that I approached it cautiously and stopped on the other side of the road. But the 'closed' sign was up and I could see no movement, so I turned in and circled round to the back, following the arrows. I decided on the more expensive 'Wash 'n Wax' and manoeuvred the Porsche into position.

For a few precious minutes I stopped and opened Boris's brief-case. There was only a plain file labelled 'N', and I glanced through it. It started with a dated report of his 'interview with H', and at the back, neatly stapled and annotated, were photocopied pages from the 'journal'. I did not wait to read further; I put the file in my own case. Next I took the car duster and rubbed the steering wheel, dashboard, and door handle and brief-case, counted out the right change into the duster and polished that too. I kept my eyes away from Boris, and got out. I slotted in the money and pressed the starting button, using the duster as a glove.

Only as I tossed it back into the car did I realize I was wearing Boris's coat and hat – and my jacket was still spread over him. The great jets and spinning brushes started up with a whine and a roar. I dragged off the leather coat and threw it into the back seat with the hat. The brushes were drumming on the bonnet, and two whirling green dervishes were moving up the front wings, as I tried to move the dead body into the driving seat. I did, but it was too stiff to prop up against the steering wheel; so I let it lie sideways, with the head on the passenger seat. Then I took my jacket and backed away, and the green dervish slammed the door shut for me.

I put on my wet jacket over my wet shirt, picked up the brief-case and started walking. There was a bus stop not far away on the other side of the roundabout; I wondered if I dared risk it, when a car pulled up beside me.

'Want a lift into town?' the driver asked with a strong Australian accent. I accepted, and sat hugging my case, glad of the powerful fan heater.

'Miserable night,' said the Good Samaritan.

'Filthy,' I replied. And that was the full extent of our conversation, until he dropped me in St Giles. Perhaps I should have found out whether he was a visitor passing through – or not – but I did not feel inclined to push my luck. I walked round to the side door of the College and hurried up to my room. I locked up the file, changed out of my wet clothes and lit a fire.

I felt exhausted and dazed; all I had done had been strangely automatic, one action leading to the next. I did not even wonder now how well I had covered my tracks: I did not much care. One more murder attributed to me would only divert the police more thoroughly from Nemo; and I dimly appreciated the madness that is its own best ally. The consummate skill with which Nemo had despatched Boris in such a way that at first sight he might even have died a natural death, had to some extent been passed on to me. I knew I had behaved crazily, that it was only a short-term remedy, that even if I was charged, sentenced and imprisoned, it would not stop Nemo from further horrors. I could see quite clearly the insane mess I had involved myself in and the hopelessness of it all. But I was strangely numb to horror; like Macbeth I had waded in so far I could only go on.

I had behaved in the last hours with a kind of natural guile. Yet the whole question of the police inquiry had seemed a mere irrelevance beside the drama played out between Nemo, Boris and me. At the moment when I might have prevented the murder, I had been helpless – how deliberately I did not know – as unheeded outside the window as the wind and rain itself. But now that it was over, and I was back in my own room, I felt little more than weariness, and surpassing relief that Boris was dead.

When I spread out the file on the desk, it revealed nothing that changed my feelings. I tried to read Boris's notes and managed to skim through those he had made after our first talk – mostly the facts as I had presented them, and a few revealing comments on myself. 'Not a reliable witness as most clearly under N's spell and believing himself in love with her. May not last the course' – at which I managed to smile grimly. Then he referred to the journal; and I realized with a shock that he had come on that first day with a small flash camera at the ready, and had photographed the relevant pages after I had gone off to my meeting.

I fed them, marginal commentary and all, into my fire, as I had the notebook itself. I looked back at the notes, and began to read compulsively of his first encounter with 'N/S.M.'; how she had come up out of the wood, very elaborately dressed, and when he introduced himself, asked him into the drawing room and brought him a glass of wine.

'A pleasant light hock. No time to finish it. N came behind me and started to stroke my hair as I drank, then my neck. Extremely stimulating. N appeared sexually aroused: lips moist, breathing rapid, eyes dilated (note v. remarkable irises). Startled by distant sounds (police and dogs?) in wood. N said: "Poor Robert (*sic*). He was so sensible (*sic*) and empassioned." On my demonstration that I was "empassioned" too she started out of the room and up the stairs, undressing as she went. I followed.' Then the report became so detailed, while still so coldly clinical, that I could not take any more of it. I burnt it all, including the manilla folder; and was happy to think of Boris, cold now, slumped across the passenger seat of his newly washed and polished Porsche.

There was no one now, I believed, who could prove Nemo's guilt; for, between us, she and I had disposed of the only person who had seen her as Sarah Moore and stayed alive, not merely to tell but to record the tale. Now he and his ghoulish report were done with, and there was no one else.

Of course I was wrong. There was someone I had forgotten.

I was celebrating our success – Nemo's and mine – when my crazy cosy world collapsed about my head. For that was when my favourite pupil, Bertie Bull, dropped in for a drink.

24

I did not want to kill Bertie, but (I supposed wearily) I would if I had to. I might (I feared) do the simplest thing, at that point: I could not bear his undoing all that I had so laboriously achieved.

The ethic of the 'favourite pupil' is a knotty one. For many lonely bachelor dons, or even married ones with unsatisfactory children, they are straightforward child-substitutes. I had enough young cousins, godchildren and outside interests, including the hard-dying hope that I would marry and have offspring of my own, to resist the pull. But every now and again a peculiarly sympathetic pupil comes one's way. One tries not to single them out, to look forward instead to the not-far-distant time when they will become equals and true friends – unless, of course, one never sees them again, which is statistically more probable.

But in Bertie's case he was already a friend when he came up, and the son of a friend. Indeed he chose to read English at my College in order to work with me. Naturally he was young and headstrong and often foolish; my exasperations with him were the more wearing because I knew him so well; misguidedness and waste are that much more distressing where one can see the enormous potential. But I suppose, all in all, he was very much like the sort of son I would hope to have: generous, imaginative, gifted, warm-hearted to a fault, and, of course, as handsome as one would wish one's child might be. Yet I sat there measuring him, as it were, for his bag of cement at the bottom of the river: that is what Nemo's madness had done to me. For Bertie Bull knew more than enough to spoil everything.

He looked as if he had not slept – heavy-eyed, white and on edge. He said:

'Harry, may I talk to you for a bit? You see, I can't get this Boyce woman out of my mind. Whatever you and the shrinks are fixing up for her, to make her safe, I feel I want to go out again and try to make some contact with her. I know she basically needs understanding and help – I might be able –'

'No – don't do that.' I roused myself. 'That would be foolish, Bertie, and do no good at all, believe me.'

'But what's going on? You say mysteriously that Bob Maclean's murderer is dead – but the police are still after someone. I mean, are you *sure* it couldn't have been her? And is your psychiatrist friend doing something about her? I feel she may go and do something terrible unless we help her. You can't just let it be, Harry – at least tell me what's happening.'

How could I prevaricate? Should I say that she could not have killed Bob Maclean, because, despite my sworn protestations, I had? That Boris had emigrated to Argentina? That she was cured? Would such fancies, short-lived as they might be, comfort and silence him for now? Would the truth be any better?

I poured brandies for both of us and made him sit down.

'Listen, Bertie. I could tell you something no one else alive knows, on condition that you keep it secret. Or I could tell you a whole lot of other things to satisfy your curiosity and you can go and tell whom you like. Which do you want?'

He was silent; then:

'You mean I can choose the truth –'

'And tell no one.'

'Or what is perhaps generally regarded as true –'

'Just that, Bertie – so you'd do no harm repeating it. Your call.'

'OK. Tell me the truth then. I swear –'

'You don't need to swear. And it'll be the short truth, not the whole story. For a start, I haven't got the energy left to go on for long. And I have other people's privacy to consider, whatever I do about my own.'

I sat opposite him, on the other side of the fireplace. He nodded and sipped his brandy. He looked almost scared, and I wondered if I was expecting too much of him. I suspected, moreover, my own motive. I had just killed, or rather, failed to avert the murder of my only *confidant*; was I simply setting up another, unable to bear the burden alone? But I could not turn back now. I had already said too much. I took a deep breath.

'The police suspect me of killing Bob Maclean,' I said. 'Motive: sexual jealousy. They can't prove it, because I didn't kill him – and the person who did was a dead Regency actress, using Nemo Boyce almost like a murder weapon. So, to all intents and purposes, Mrs Boyce is guilty. But I am trying to take the rap and get her off. I happen to be in love with her. My biggest problem is that I wasn't here the day he was killed, but I was on a day he might have been killed. I still don't know what sort of case they are making, but I'm afraid they will concentrate their investigations on her sooner or later, and that in her present state she won't stand up to much cross-questioning. She is mad, as you saw – taken over by this creature. And you can imagine what chance a story like that has with the Law. My only way to save her is to let them go on thinking it was me.'

'Poor Harry. My God.' He was silent, gazing into the fire. 'So you'd go to prison and lose everything. Isn't there any other way?'

'Not that I can see – but by now I may be a little mad as well. Or I wouldn't be telling you.'

'Just for the record,' he said, looking across at me, 'why did you?'

'I gave you the choice – '

'In such a way as you knew I couldn't refuse. Is it because I've seen her in her killer part? Was it all just in order to shut me up?' He observed my silence, then said: 'And how many people know, Harry? Are you going to fix all of them? What about your friend Boris? Didn't *he* know everything? Is *he* safe?'

'Yes. He's safe. He's dead,' I said wearily. 'She killed him this evening, and I removed the body.'

'*My God.*' He stood up. 'Am I the only other person then, Harry? Is that how it is?'

'Yes. You're the only other one who has got away. You, and me. Like you, I nearly didn't.'

'Does that mean you're going to kill me now? Tell me the whole story and then dispose of me too?'

'Well, Bertie, I considered killing you. Then I decided to give you the choice. I realized you were a danger to her with as much as you knew. But I also was perfectly certain, as you yourself pointed out, that you would choose to hear the rest and keep silent. You did; and I, for my part, am content. I don't need to kill you now, because I've bartered the truth for your peace of mind. But it's better, surely, to have a terrible secret than to be dead, Bertie. Don't you agree?'

Quite suddenly I felt very ill.

'I'm sorry,' I said, trying to get up, 'but I think I may be sickening for something. I really should – ' And then everything went blank.

There was a hissing in my ears, and I tried to decide whether it was the tape-recorder, or the rain on the windscreen, until I discovered it was only in my head. I was lying in my bedroom and Bertie was sitting by me. My face was wet from the flannel he was holding.

'Shall I get a doctor?' he asked.

'No – I'll be perfectly all right – really I will. I'm sorry about that, but I suppose that it's just the price for a peculiarly exhausting day. Come to think of it, what I need is food. Breakfast on the train was my last real meal, since when – '

'Don't talk now,' he said. 'I'm going to get you something to eat. You must stay where you are, Harry. I'm in charge now.'

An overwhelming feebleness lay on me like six feet of wet clay. I wanted neither to think nor to lift a hand. I made myself nod in agreement, and sank back into the mud.

I don't know how many minutes or hours went by or what time it was, but he returned with a 'takeaway' meal of soup and rolls and two cartons of chicken stew. I felt better after the bread and soup, and moved to my chair in front of the fire. I still felt that deep chill, and seemed quite to lack any resistance. Bertie fetched my overcoat and draped it awkwardly round me; he made up the fire, and reheated the chicken stew in my cocoa saucepan – the very phrase and my twinge of irritation at the misuse of the receptacle, made me suddenly aware what an old maid I had become, and how unaccustomed I was to being cared for by anyone except my scout. Nemo, of course, had looked after me, at the Dower House, so many times, and so capably. She was an excellent and thoughtful hostess. I could close my eyes and see those clever capable hands, tilting the heavy kettle, picking up a tray, snapping kindling, pushing the long hat-pin into Boris's skull. My eyelids jerked open and I found myself on the edge of my chair gripping the arms to stop my headlong fall.

'You've got the horrors,' said Bertie. 'Here, eat up.' He pulled up a table and a chair for himself and we ate the stew in silence, spooning it from the greasy cartons and sharing the last roll.

'I'm sorry to be so vaporish,' I said at last. 'That's the second time I've passed out cold in six months – and Sarah Moore was the cause of both.'

'Sarah Moore? The dead actress?'

I realized then how little I had told him: only the bare results of the accumulated horror. So I went back to the beginning and related the happenings; their order was very clear in my mind; I had gone through them so often – indeed, had just read Boris's account of them as I had reported it. Bertie Bull listened to it all intently and with hardly a word. Then he got to his feet. Suddenly I was afraid of him leaving.

'I'm just going to make some coffee,' he said.

He brought two big mugs of it, strong and black, and poured us a glass of brandy each without any question. He seemed to have aged a lot in the short time that had passed since he burst into my rooms three days ago. The harder lines of what would be his adult face had emerged through the puppyish charm; strain had pared him down, hollowed out the eye sockets and sharpened the cheekbones.

'You don't look too well yourself, Bertie,' I said.

'I haven't been sleeping,' he answered shortly. 'It's not just this business, though it's all related, I suppose. I was partly coming to tell you that I've finally decided about the monastery thing. I *am* going to be a monk, Harry. As soon as term is over – nothing dramatic. But I badly need sorting out.'

'Isn't that the wrong motive?'

He smiled. 'And would that be worse than doing the wrong thing for the right motive? That's what you're attempting, after all. But any motive, even simple weariness, according to George Herbert, is good enough for God. The right reasons will follow in time.'

'You make it sound like an arranged marriage. Surely love should come into it?' I said.

'Arranged marriages admit the possibility of human error. I don't think this is such a gamble – putting myself into the hands of God. And love takes so many forms, as you must know, Harry. Its strength can sometimes be measured by the stubbornness of one's resistance to it. You see, I don't think I'm just opting out. I want to submit to something so big that it absorbs all my energies and thoughts.'

'But a monk's life allows so much time for self-regard. I would have thought that serving others strenuously would be more absorbing – not endless hours of meditation.'

'A monk's life is as strenuous as an army training, they tell me, and twice as useful. I wish you could have such a life as they offer, Harry, in place of a prison sentence. But I see a parallel, and I think we may both be on the same track – in terms of submitting and finding ourselves. Can you see it like that?'

I had to admit I had not. But he went on, quietly enumerating the dry virtues of discipline and humility – there would be plenty of that – of living among fellow beings not of one's choice and learning patience and understanding, with no chance of avoidance or escape; of hard routines and hours of loneliness. And I began to see what helped Bertie to accept, for his own peculiar reasons, the mad course I was set on. Not once, after his initial reaction, did he question it; and that was strangely comforting.

'Why do you think,' I asked – the tutorial system temporarily inverted – 'that I'm doing the wrong thing then, from whatever motive? Morally wrong, do you mean?'

'No, just legally, I think. They've got you, legally, I suppose, even if they can't prove you responsible for the two murders. Man, you have witnessed, aided and abetted. Morally you are doing all you can to save someone you love, and that's a time-honoured justification for way-out actions. But as I see it, you are doing all you can only if you manage to get her cured or cared for – whatever else you do in order to protect her. That's a private responsibility you've taken on, and your time inside will drive you right round the bend if you're wondering how she's managing without you to protect her.'

'You're right: that's my chief worry, really.' (It was eerie sitting there at two o'clock in the morning, discussing murder with a pupil: I wondered if it was all a fever dream. But it was altogether too precise and rational. I did feel feverish and weak, but very clear.) 'There's a parallel also, surely, with suicide: the weak point in both our chosen courses is the well-being of those we leave behind. But it is difficult to see how I can involve James Boyce, and get Nemo's illness recognized, without endangering her.'

'It's how you present the case, isn't it?' said Bertie. 'A matter of selection. You see if you'd look at it from the outside – and even I find that quite an exercise – you could see the whole case *as* a case: nothing "supernatural" about it cannot be explained away as "suggestion", by someone who has not *seen* the ghost and *heard* the tape as you have. If you suppress the evidence of your own senses – which I for one (and the late Boris, it seems, for another) accept – the story is of an over-imaginative lonely attractive woman having a sort of nervous breakdown, right? Involving herself in a dead actress and, at the high points in this cycle she goes through, living the part. As far as you know they can't prove the murders, so it's only the moods you have to explain. Surely there is time before the police take some positive action to talk to Dr Boyce. Your next move is to work out a censored version for him and the doctors – that will convince them, and take it out of your hands – You have to, Harry,' he said, leaning forward and speaking with an urgency that rounded up my scattered wits and forced me to concentrate. 'You see, your "taking the rap" will achieve nothing at all if she goes on as she is: they would realize within a matter of days they'd got the wrong person. No, get her certified and safe and there will be no more murders – and so, no more evidence. Then the only suspicion you will have to counter is from those events you have already got covered, you see. But even that cover will be blown if you don't get her into care. This is it: you must convince the doctors, Harry – and fast.'

So together we went through the tale of Nemo's madness; I cannot remember how long we talked, but at some point Bertie pulled back the curtains, peered at me and said:

'You look really rotten, Harry – and you must be running a temperature. You can't do a thing if you're ill. Get back to bed now and I'll come and see how you are about nine. That'll give you time to sleep.'

'And you,' I said, getting up shakily. As he was going I had a sudden panic of misgiving. 'Bertie, you don't think I'm mad, do you? You're not going to go off and have us *both* certified as criminally insane?'

'We made a swop, didn't we? The truth for my silence?'

'And your peace of mind?'

'I didn't have that anyway. Mrs Boyce put paid to that.'

He went.

I was woken in the morning by voices in my study; there were mumbled consultations and heavy feet. Then Bertie came in and closed the door behind him.

'Harry? Are you awake? I've brought our GP to see you. And the Detective Inspector is here. I'll give him some coffee and keep him at bay.'

The doctor was coolly kind, asked some questions and ordered me to stay in bed for 'a few days'.

'You've got a severe chill on top of the symptoms of exhaustion, I'd say. There's no question of your getting up, or even teaching from bed. Complete rest – no question about it,' he pronounced, fastening his black bag.

'I must be up on Saturday evening,' I said.

'A pressing party?' he said raising thin sandy eyebrows at me.

'Very pressing,' I said. 'A matter of life and death.' I felt disembodied and irresponsible, and the melodramatic catch-phrase came out as a harsh whisper.

'I'll come in and see you on Saturday morning, and tell you if you can go.'

I heard him through the door he left ajar: 'Inspector, that's a sick man and I don't want him worried. Five minutes will have to be enough for you.' And Blunt came in.

'I'm sorry to find you ill, Mr Harris. Perhaps you overdid things yesterday.'

I tried to sit up – a defensive move: at least to be on his plane, however far below. But the undulations of the room pulled me back to right angles with the grey macintosh pillar and the distant bullet head. He did not even sit on my chair.

'I have not come to tick you off for giving our man the slip, however –'

'I can explain that,' I whispered urgently, and I was grateful for the long bus ride that had given me time to think even about such irrelevances as my Police Tail. 'I had to visit a girl friend in London.'

'As a result of your telephone call at lunch.'

'Yes, that's right. And I had to protect her identity, you see, because she's a married woman.'

'And you spent the afternoon with her?'

'Yes. And I got back here about – I don't know – about nine or ten. It was raining. I was very upset and felt ill. I don't remember how late it was.'

'Well, don't trouble yourself on that score, Mr Harris. That isn't what I came about. I'm afraid I have some bad news for you.' He paused to give me time to gabble my deepest fears. I resisted and sank lower beneath the covers. 'We found Dr Boris Goodie in his car. He was dead. I recognized him as an acquaintance of yours and thought it would be better to tell you in person.' In order to see exactly how you would react. I shook my head feverishly, playing for time. 'It was a call from the garage on the bypass. They found the car in the twenty-four-hour car-wash, and Dr

Goodie inside it. He appears to have died of a heart attack, or possibly a brain haemorrhage; we won't know until we get the results of the post-mortem. Tell me, do you know if he had a weak heart? Or anything about his movements yesterday?'

Again I shook my head. 'I didn't know Dr Goodie very well. But it's something of a shock to hear that he's dead. I didn't even know he was ill – ' I trailed away. Why should I tell him that, so far from delicate, Boris had been obscenely healthy? 'I'm sorry,' I added.

'Well, I thought I'd let you know: there don't seem to be any close relatives.' I closed my eyes and hoped he would go. 'Tell me,' he said, bending over me, 'can you think of any connection between Dr Goodie and Mr Maclean? Were they acquainted?'

'I don't know,' I murmured. 'I don't think so.'

He said something about making a quick recovery and I heard the door close quietly.

Later my scout came in with some breakfast. He brought another blanket for me, and took away my wet and crumpled suit to be cleaned. I dozed fitfully. Bertie visited me after lunch with the *Oxford Mail*.

'Boris is in the papers,' he said. 'No word about foul play.'

'The police must know by now,' I said. 'For all I care.'

I may have dozed off, but when I opened my eyes again, Bertie was still there.

'Look, Harry, with you like this – well, I feel I must do *something* – what *you* would do,' he went on quickly before I could protest. 'I think I should go and tackle Dr Boyce. I'll tell him you're ill, and that you're worried about his wife, about these headaches getting out of control, recurring so often. I could tell him how I'd gone out to look at the orchids – after all, he invited me – and how I saw Mrs Boyce all dressed up and behaving rather strangely – no more than that.'

'If you incriminate Nemo –' I said hoarsely, getting myself up on to one elbow.

' – I would be breaking my promise. No, Harry, I won't do that. But you will have to trust me: you've no alternative, have you? – now it's a question of other lives, surely.'

'Damn that,' I said. 'What about Nemo?'

'Look, I'll protect her; while you're helpless here, I'll do what you would do. After all, you agreed, didn't you? that it was no good your sacrificing yourself, taking the blame and leaving her, unless you first convince Dr Boyce and the medics that she genuinely needs care – or anything could happen. We've got to do what we can, for her, don't you see?'

I lay back. 'All right, Bertie. See where you get with James – if you feel you must. . . .'

I slept right through the afternoon and evening in a twilit nightmare world. Someone brought a tray of tea, but while trying to make the effort to pour the tea and lift the cup, I fell asleep and dreamt I had – but I could not slake my terrible thirst, for the cup was full of earth. Then a supper tray was in its place and the curtains drawn. I drank some broth and read a little. I wondered if the radio would say anything about Boris, but it was in the next room. I slept again. Hendry looked in later with a *Times Lit. Sup.* for me.

'I came earlier,' he said, 'but your scout was very firm. There's a notice on your door saying "Ill: Do Not Disturb" – in case you've been wondering why we were neglecting you.'

'I wasn't wondering,' I said, 'but I suppose I would have got round to it by tomorrow morning. It'll be Friday, won't it?'

And Friday passed in much the same way. Hendry had coped with my pupils and diverted phone calls to his room. He came to see me and made us both some coffee when he got out of Hall.

'A man called Blunt – Detective Inspector? – has telephoned twice to ask how you were. He wants you to contact him once you're on your feet again.'

He would, I thought. He might want to tell me that my friend Boris was murdered with something very long and fine and sharp, like an old-fashioned hat-pin; and did I know of a hat-pin that would fit.

Bertie came in and Hendry left.

'Well, I went to see Dr Boyce,' he said, sitting down, and I could tell by the droop of his shoulders that James had not been impressed. I said as much.

'Impressed? I should have saved my breath. He was in a hurry, to start with. "I can give you two minutes, dear fellow, but I've just put through a call to New York, and then I'm due at the Randolph – " etcetera and so on – and I'd made this appointment with him as soon as I left you yesterday – '

'I know, Bertie. A busy man. Too busy for a woman like Nemo – imagine . . . Well, you tried.'

'He was very concerned, if briefly, about *your* being ill, and touched that you should be worrying about his wife "from your couch of pain". I tried to tell him about going out there, and my encounter with her, but the transatlantic call came through at that moment. I waited doggedly – spent my time staring at a *Playboy* mag and trying to think how best to continue – but he rang off finally and opened the door for me in one fluid movement. "So good to see you again, Billie (sic), and don't you worry your head about a thing. And tell dear old Harry not to worry – just get better in time for the party." End of interview. So now perhaps the party is our only hope. At least I gathered he was at home most of today and all yesterday, and that Mrs Boyce is OK and enjoying a pleasant female flap preparing for Saturday. So. Here's the paper, by the way: lots on Boris, but nothing more about cause of death.'

'They must be keeping it under wrappers for some good reason,' I said. 'They might want to surprise me with it. Or perhaps I flatter myself: they may not connect me with it at all.'

'They must know he went out to Sutton Hamden.'

'And was seen to drive away,' I said. 'But they may have been questioning Nemo.'

'You'll know tomorrow,' said Bertie. 'I have a feeling – don't you? – that tomorrow will be significant; perhaps the "salon" may be the turning point, and Dr Boyce will see that she needs help. Sarah Moore could stage something dramatic for the occasion. She made her grand entrance at a party: she may even make her exit.'

25

The doctor came in to see me early, on his way to surgery. I was anxious to satisfy his requirements: I knew I must go to the Dower House, and had lain awake since five fretting and thinking of Nemo.

'So the fever has gone, but you aren't mended yet, as well you know,' he said. 'If you're determined to go out this evening you must rest all day beforehand; I'm giving you a sedative to make sure you do. I'd like your pulse to settle down a lot more before you go and get exhausted again. And you must come home early.'

When he had gone, I telephoned the Boyces. James answered.

'Harry! Yes, we're flourishing – just organizing things for this evening. What's this I hear about you being ill? Are you better? You'll be able to come? Good. Fine. Be seeing you then. Yes, she's flourishing. Why? No – haven't seen hide nor hair of them for days – should I say hide nor fuzz? They may have been tramping round the nearby woods, but not ours. Pity about the rain, eh? Mo's precious theatricals – now they'll have to be in the drawing room. And we had the lights fixed up on the azaleas and all – '

Then I had to ring Blunt. As I waited, I looked out at the sky. I hadn't realized it was raining; now I could see that there was a gentle insistent drizzle falling straight and almost as fine as mist.

'Mr Harris. Blunt here. Glad to hear you're better. I wanted to contact you about Dr Goodie. The post-mortem showed he had been murdered.'

'How awful,' I said. 'Have you found out how or why?'

'Yes: he was pierced through the left eardrum. There was no visible mark to suggest foul play on first inspection, you see. A clever murder, if I may so put it – and a very nasty one; the whole staging of it calculated to give the murderer a breathing space, not unlike the use of the ice-house, when you think about it. As to why, Mr Harris – if we knew more about his movements it might be easier. Can you tell us whether he was acquainted with Dr and Mrs Boyce?'

'No, he hadn't met them.'

'May I ask why you are so sure of that please, Mr Harris?'

'Because I had promised to introduce them. He was to go to a party there with me tonight.'

'Well, we have good reason for thinking Dr Goodie went out to the Dower House at Sutton Hamden the evening before he died.'

'I thought you said the car was found on the bypass.'

'It was. But someone in the village saw him turning up the lane, and leaving again later on. Do you think he might have had occasion to go out and visit Mrs Boyce prior to this party?'

'I have no idea, Inspector. Why not ask the Boyces themselves?'

'We will, Mr Harris. I wanted to ask you first.'

'Well, Inspector, I wish I could help you. I don't see how I can.'

'You can tell me why you wished, or arranged for, them to meet.'

'I thought they might like each other, I think. They had interests in common.'

'What interests, Mr Harris? Was it anything to do with psychiatry?'

I refused to have my plans for Nemo forced into the open before I was ready.

'No, Inspector. The supernatural. Dr Goodie and Mrs Boyce were both interested in it.' That would give him something to think about; and, in the end, it would all hang together.

'I see. And would you say Mr Maclean was also interested in the supernatural?'

'I think he would have shunned it, Inspector. He saw his writing as based firmly on science: the supernatural would have been an embarrassment to him.'

My scout herded me back to bed with a large tray of breakfast. I ate the greater part of it, obediently took my sedative and slept until two. When I woke the rain was still trickling down the window-panes. I had a late lunch from my chair by the fire, and read and slept away the afternoon. I went down to the Buttery for tea, to try out my legs.

'I say!' the Dean greeted me. 'Poor old Harris! Good to see you down, dear boy. Bit shaky on the pins, eh? Still, better off than this Dr Boris Goodie we've been reading about. Hendry here says he was a friend of yours.'

'I'm sorry about it, Harry.' Hendry came up. 'You'd heard already, had you? Now it appears it wasn't a heart attack: somebody killed him.'

'All of Harris's friends seem to be getting bumped off,' chipped in a young pharmacologist, an abominably perky lad still damp from his cocoon in darkest Durham. 'A veritable plague! Should we be warned, do you suppose?'

'I don't think you need lose any sleep, Whitworth,' I said crushingly. 'It's only contagious and I've never really fancied you.'

'Ooh – bold! Bold and fatal!'

He was uncrushable, and I turned back to the Dean. 'Yes, it's a terrible thing, Dean – I don't imagine there's any connection with the Maclean business, but it's a disturbing coincidence, even if the first murder was more than two weeks ago. No, Boris Goodie wasn't a particular friend; in fact – *de mortuis* – but I didn't even like him very much. I found him interesting. A very gifted man. Terrible thing.'

My staircase seemed endless, my knees made of rubber. I lay on my bed to recover and summon my resources for Nemo's party. I had not expected the police to release the findings of the post-mortem so quickly. They must have told the papers that very morning. But they clearly had made no mention of Boris's visit to Sutton Hamden on the evening he died: perhaps they considered that the connection with the Boyces was too tenuous to merit the ghoulish interest the Press would take in it. I fervently hoped so.

I was dressing at seven-thirty when Bertie knocked at my door. I was glad to see him. I had not properly thanked him for all he had done for me.

'It was nothing, Harry,' he said. 'At least, nothing beside what I didn't do – can't do to help. Talk is cheap, after all. How are you feeling now? You don't look too good.'

'I'm fine. I just wish I felt stronger.'

'So you're going to this party?'

'Yes, I must.'

'Let me come in Boris's place, Harry. I could drive you there and back and keep an eye on you. It isn't as if they weren't expecting someone, and we could explain. How about it, Harry?'

'You want to see her again. Is that it?'

'You know I do – but simply because I'm involved. Not as an ex-lover or a spectator sportsman. Harry – you must know that. I'm through with all that. But I feel deeply involved whether I have a right to or not. And I feel I might be of some use to you.'

'All right. I don't need to tell you that Nemo is potentially dangerous, I suppose. Well, we should aim to be there between eight-thirty and nine. I was going to telephone some of the Boyces' friends and get a lift, but now I needn't hurry. Go and change and come back for a drink before we go.'

I was ready far too soon and tried to sit and read while I

waited; but I was jumpy and restless and could not concentrate. I found I did not like being alone any more.

Privacy and freedom were perhaps the two things I most valued in my way of life – the same thing, really, since it amounted to the freedom to be private. The price was small: good times I would have wished to share, bad times of self-doubt and misgivings, when the isolation was not splendid, when a nightmare made me long for someone else beside me in the dark. My 'illness', diagnosed as exhaustion, had been in fact a continuous nightmare, and this I could not tell the dry cool GP: terrible dreams, while the exhaustion lasted, replaced by the waking horrors when I had slept my fill. Nor was it the comparatively simple retina-print of Sarah Moore, a physical tic, that haunted me now, but a rich soup of frightful images, so opaque as to obscure the deep-swimming shapes – I could never guess what the next would be, bobbing to the surface in the slow rolling boil.

Windscreen wipers and flashing lights, then suddenly Nemo's screaming wet face pressed against the windscreen blotting out the road ahead. A screech of brakes, a desperate fear that I had killed her – then she reared up and drove the long bright hat-pin at me through the glass that had turned to clinging plastic, wrapping my limbs so I could not move; and Boris uncurled slowly from his foetal position and caught at my ankles –

I would snap awake, sitting up, sweating, hearing the end of the terrible cry which was my own. And there was Boris lying sideways curled up on the end of my bed. When I put on the light, I pushed the mound of dressing gown on to the floor. But now I could see the black hood hanging on the door; it looked back at me from the hollowed and empty eye-sockets in its folds, and as I drowsed again, came spinning towards me along the side of the car.

Jerk my head up. Concentrate on the solid friendly brass rail at end of the bed, and as my sights narrowed with sleep, the slits of reflected light on it were Nemo's mad gold eyes glinting at me only a few feet away across Boris's head, and the head moved desperately from side to side as if he knew he was going to be killed and I could not save him but tried to reach out and grab him – and found myself clutching my own shrouded feet.

Fully awake, I could see the pattern on the eiderdown was like waving hair. So I would try to be rational. Turn on my side, switch out the light. And my newly cleaned suit hooked on to the wardrobe hung over me, square and tall as the Detective Inspector. Horizontal, helpless, eyes squeezed shut against the accusing shape, slip back into blackness – but there the worst things lay. It was I who was curled now, foetally, shivering with the cold of *rigor mortis* while the green yeti drummed on the windscreen till the glass gave way like clinging plastic and still I could not move because death makes all your joints so stiff . . .

Sitting in my chair, waiting for Bertie's return, it was only the waking variety. Trying to concentrate on my book, I had a sudden irrational feeling of panic urgency: there was something I had not done, something still to do – what had I forgotten? Had I left Nemo's file in the car? The spinning dark green shapes were closing in on me from behind now as I scrabbled at the back seat: I could see them sideways out of the corners of my range of sight. They were the tall macrocarpas of the wood, moving in. I dropped my book and looked round sharply, then felt a fool because only the familiar room was there.

Back to my book; and wading forward through the thick print, I caught sight of the lighted windows of the Dower House ahead. No – it was Nemo's eyes, with a fan-shaped broken vein under one of them. Had she been hurt? I waded on faster through the clinging gloom, and it turned into floating veils and smoke that choked me and made me gag and gasp and stand up, knocking my book on to the floor. And when I bent to mend the reeking fire – too much dust in the coal, I realized – and built it up to a blaze, I tossed some weeds on to it and heard her coming up behind me with a light stealthy footfall in the sodden leaves of last autumn and I did not dare turn round. But I held the fork, I knew, and I could swing round and pin him down into the soft loam. Poor Robert – he was so sensible and empassioned – eyes dilated, breathing rapid, lips moist . . .

Bertie poured me a drink and said, 'Are you sure you're well enough to go to this thing?'

I told him I was suffering only from hallucinations. 'It may just be a side effect of the sedative. What I need now is company.'

We went out to his small battered car, perched with one wheel on the pavement, like a mongrel lifting its leg. As I was getting in, I felt a tap on the shoulder. It was my faithful shadow from Bedford Square, Soho and points west.

'May I ask, sir, if you are proceeding to Dr. Boyce's residence? It would make my business a lot less arduous if you could see your way to informing me as to your movements, sir.'

Bertie was enchanted.

'Are you following him, then? Hop in and come with us – eh, Harry? No point in taking two cars.'

'That seems sensible enough,' I said, 'though I must admit I forgot to inform our host.'

'Oh, please don't put yourself out, sir,' said the Tail. 'I shall be more than discreet – blend into the environment, in a manner of speaking, mingle, as it were, with the throng.'

He folded himself into the small back seat, and sat with his knees under his chin and a fixed smile.

'And how shall I introduce you to Dr Boyce?' I asked, when Bertie had swung the handle and we were under way.

'Ben, sir.'

I did not know whether it was a surname or a Christian name, but left it at that. I apologized for escaping him in London, and said I hoped he had managed to finish his luncheon.

'Oh!' (he started most sentences that way – rather high-pitched for the bulky frame) 'don't distress yourself for a moment, sir – it's all part of the business. And if I may say so, sir, I fully appreciate your bid for privacy under the circumstances. I do not wish to speak out of turn, but the Detective Inspector implied it had been a matter of chivalry. Now I respect that, Mr Harris, sir. My fault that I was not entirely on the ball, so to speak. But as soon as I heard I said to myself, "Ben, that was an honourable draw." And I mean it, sir.'

Conversation ceased, for beyond the city limits, Bertie's banger doubled both its speed and its noise. The evening was clearing in the light of a spectacular sunset, with an egg-shell sky emerging above orange clouds. There were about ten cars parked ahead of us along the edge of the drive and a din of voices from the open kitchen windows. A small cluster of guests braved the soaking lawns to look at the view.

James broke away from the group and came to meet us. I had caught something of Bertie's euphoria as I bucketed along in his Tin Lizzie, worthy as Rosinante for this hallucinating don, attended by a giggling novice monk and a romantic plain-clothes policeman. I decided I must brazen this one out.

'James, you know Bertie Bull, of course – Nemo said I could bring a friend. And this is my official Tail, Mr Ben, who is going to blend into the environment.'

'My dear fellow – how splendid. Mr Ben, what is your tipple? Sherry? – chilled, of course. Or white wine? Or something more sustaining, like a gin and tonic?'

'Oh, gin and tonic, if you'd be so kind, sir – without the gin. Just a slice of lemon to lend artistic verisimilitude, in the words of the immortal Sir Gilbert O'Sullivan – '

I watched with fascination as James introduced him to a trio of Beautiful People. He did not precisely blend, but he was more than holding his own, and Bertie and I took our glasses out on to the west lawn. Here, as the orange faded from the sky and the river, and the bright flakes of the highest clouds chilled to grey, we could see that there were floodlights down in the hollow of the evergreen wood, and others far along the level lawn, shining up into the magnolia and the tulip tree. They strengthened in the growing dark with the special magic of the outdoor amateur production: that frisson of anticipation as the distances fade and the favoured greenery gathers in the light, artificially brilliant as an aniline dye, and casting long shadows towards obscure wings and entrances.

'It's a pity the ground's so wet,' said James, joining us. 'No acting in the clearing, alas – though I still say the drawing room is far better, acoustics-wise. Floodlights are nice, aren't they? Ah, there's Mo – full of the joys this evening – '

A bright figure flitted into the circle of light as we watched, trailing gauzy extremities like some tropical fish, and was joined by others – minor characters, one could tell at a glance: this was the star. She moved with that conscious charm and artifice I knew so well from my dark vigil; and we could hear admiring laughter as she flirted and caracoled among the sober-suited men of her retinue.

We all advanced towards the distant brilliantly lit scene as if pulled by invisible strings, and as we emerged into the glare, found ourselves suddenly playing our parts, holding our glasses high, greeting friends with elaborate courtesy, saluting Nemo with both the stiffness and the grace imparted by a sense of tight breeches or full periwigs.

She was superb – radiant with restless excitement, and those eyes picking up the dazzle like a night creature in headlights. When she took my arm and said sweetly, showing her little pointed teeth: 'Poor Harry – being so ill. And all on my account!' I was too enchanted to wonder. But later, as we walked back to the house, summoned for supper, I realized the implications of her words. She was in that dual role, as I had first seen her when I came back from America. There was still enough of Nemo in charge to know me and be fond, but it was Sarah Moore who alone – excepting only Bertie – knew the true cause of my illness and enjoyed mystifying her audience with her words. Indeed, one of my more jocular academic friends caught up with me to ask: 'So you got ill on her account, did you, you dark horse? May one ask how?'

'Gardening, George, gardening – and getting very wet.'

'Ah.' He was clearly disappointed. 'Your earthy game-keeper image no doubt – '

'No, just humble gardening, George,' I said.

In the big kitchen, eating sausages and hot pasties in our fingers, the formal dance-like party that had taken shape under the floodlit tulip tree broke up into a casual picnic. It was a quite different atmosphere from the first party, simpler, warmer and seemingly more relaxed. But Nemo, I saw, did not change her role. She sat enthroned in the big armchair, with a circle of her decorative London chums ranged round about her, and delicately nibbled at titbits from a proffered plate – arching her wrist, preening her finery round her and smiling down at Bertie Bull, as she used his knees as a footstool. I hardly felt any jealousy. I was too busy wondering at her beauty and how long this blaze of glory could last.

Meanwhile in all the hubbub and chatter and clinking, I saw another little group, noisier than the rest, of which my Tail was the quiet centre. I heard someone ask: 'But what do you *do*, Mr Ben, while you're waiting for something to happen?'

'He reads a folded newspaper, duckie – don't be silly – '
'Or a newspaper with two holes in it – '
'Which paper do you favour, Mr Ben? The *Sporting Times*?'
'Oh, the rag, so to speak, dear sir, is immaterial. I hold it there as a front solely.'
'As a front for *what*, Mr Ben? What nefarious doings – '
'As a front for the works of Mary Webb, Miss, since you so kindly ask. Last season it was Georgette Heyer. I found that lady somewhat on the superficial side – I trust I tread on no toes? – and felt I needed to return to the more deeply rooted sentiments of *Precious Bane* and *Gone to Earth*. . . .'
Then Bertie appeared with some pudding for me.
'So you managed to get away intact, did you?' I asked. 'I am surprised there are no singe marks.'
'I had to have one good look at her, Harry. What a fabulous creature – I thought she was quite something when I first met her, but I don't remember this dazzling *prima donna* at all.'
'Not at all, Bertie? Think back to the dairy then.'
He flushed. 'But she doesn't seem mad now – It's just a sort of nervous excitement, like she was on drugs.'
'I suppose the fire Sarah Moore releases into her veins must be more like a drug than anything.'
I spoke quietly under the din. It was hard to say that name in that house.

26

The big drawing room had been prepared for the recital. The body of the room was filled with sofas, chairs and cushions to take the audience, facing the great bow, the stage. Spotlights were trained on to this, and the uprights between the windows had been generously garlanded with swags of flowers and fruit – extravagantly, I realized, looking closer: they were cruelly wired. Florists' work; Nemo would never have done them like that. Or would she? Weaving the long silver wires into the juicy stems, piercing and securing the hard rosy apples.

A gilt chair and a music stand were arranged in the centre of the gleaming oval of boards; the violinist was on first. The gramophone in the morning room was to provide the incidental music for the dramatic fragments, and here a few people started to dance, while, in the kitchen, supper tailed off into second helpings. Large pots of coffee were heating on the Aga, and the two women who had come up from the village were clearing away the dirty plates and setting out cups and spoons and fresh glasses.

It was when I returned for a cup of coffee after a tour of inspection that I saw Nemo was not there. At once I tried to find who else might be missing, but it was an impossible task: they could be dancing, sitting talking in one of the other rooms, playing billiards or taking a turn in the cool night air. So might Nemo; but my sense of alarm would not be stilled – and where was Bertie?

There he was, crouching by the fire, toasting marshmallows for a straight-haired nymph in a brown satin nightdress. I did not disturb him, and went instead in search of James. He was not in the billiard room, nor in the drawing room organizing the last details of the entertainment, as I might have expected. An older woman, the wife of one of James's colleagues, was laying out props – fans, prompt books, music – and I helped her to find a record that, in the crowded morning room, had been overlaid by the sleeves of blues and rock-and-roll. When I got away and went out into the hall again, the front door was standing open. I closed it and started back towards the kitchen, when I heard James call me. He was on the landing above, and he beckoned me up.

'Mo seems to be ill,' he said. 'Came wandering in through the porch, holding her head, hair in a terrible mess, dress all crumpled and damp – must have collapsed outside – a sudden violent headache, I suppose. I don't want to leave her alone, but I really ought to get this damn recital under way – '

'Was no one with her?' I asked. 'I mean, hadn't she been out for a breather with someone? They might be able to tell you what happened, I thought.'

'I didn't see anyone else,' he said. 'Look, I don't think we need to bother people with this. If you could sit with her for a bit, I'll get the show on the road. Luckily Edna' (the capable lady with the props, I recalled) 'is *au fait* with the routine. We'll have to cut Mo's bit, I suppose, but there are plenty of folk-singing enthusiasts to fill the bill.' He hurried off.

She lay under the domed canopy with its silken drapes. The excited colour had gone from her narrow brown face; her eyes were closed; the thickly blackened lashes lay heavy without a flutter, and there was mud on one cheek. She seemed so much smaller lying there, all the animation that made her so dazzling, so dangerous, had gone, leaving only the fine bird-boned beauty, the lovely mask of Nemo.

I sat on the window seat and watched her, and wondered what had triggered this sudden collapse, this state of total withdrawal. Had something taken place to earth the electric storm that was Sarah Moore? And if so, might there be a casualty somewhere out in the dark garden? As coldly as I could I considered the time-scheme of rape and murder. I consulted my watch: it was over half an hour since I had last seen her, and I calculated I had grounds for hope that it might not have gone farther than stage one. I could not prevent myself wondering jealously who had been picked out for immolation in that candle flame.

Downstairs I heard sounds of movement: chatter and chairs and James's hearty bullying voice chasing up the stragglers. The heavy beat of dance music that came up through the joists, all melody drained away by distance, lath and plaster, continued a little longer. Then this too was stilled, and there was only the talk and rustle of the waiting audience. Silence, and the single clear voice of an un-accompanied violin outlining the delicate formal gateway to a Baroque set-piece. Nemo did not move. I folded back a half-open shutter and looked out over the wood at the western sky, pricked with low stars, and the distant lights of the ring road and the city. It was nearly one.

James came up about half an hour later, escaping amid the sounds of applause and loquacious reshuffling.

'How is she?' he asked.

'She hasn't moved at all,' I said. 'But her breathing is better, I think – more even. Look, James, have you ever seen her as bad as this?'

'D'you think it's bad then – seriously?'

'No, of course not – no question of death's door. But so completely exhausted.'

'Well, not precisely; but it's just an extreme case of migraine, surely – which I've seen all too much of, old man. This is just Mother Nature's way of coping with pain: retreat and rally. When she wakes up she'll be fine – weak, you know, but all right – I gathered from that nice boy –

Bull – that you were worrying about these headaches getting worse – '

'But James, *aren't* they getting worse? I mean, haven't you noticed any pattern of abnormal behaviour – what you call being "high" – repeating itself in quicker succession, a tightening spiral, as it were? I mean, this evening, didn't you find her, well, almost out of reach?'

'Communications-wise? Harry, let's face it, Mo and I don't spend much time communicating, except on a practical level. She goes her way and I – '

'Yes, but wouldn't you say, looking back, that the ups and downs are more rapid? That perhaps one ought to look for treatment, to break the pattern?'

'Well, I suppose one could resort to the head-shrinkers, now, since all the dope she swallows doesn't seem to do the trick. But isn't it a bit extreme, old boy? You see, I know I tend to opt out rather when she goes into a decline, but I feel – I may be old-fashioned – that analysis and all the gloomy heart-searchings that go with it are just what one *doesn't* want when one is out of sorts – '

'Out of sorts is surely an understatement – '

'No – listen, my dear fellow. We all get depressed at times, and you know as well as I that dwelling on it, examining it minutely, is no sort of answer. You've got to get out and *do* something. Trouble with Mo is that when she's low she doesn't feel like doing anything – and when she's up and full of energy and go, she seems to float off into her own world of make-believe, trailing about the wood in long dresses – '

'You've seen her, have you?'

'No – a couple of bobbies did and the whole thing was a bit embarrassing. I've sometimes found her still tarted up recovering from a migraine. It's these amateur dramatics that have gone to her head – and I thought they'd help keep her busy and happy for a while – but it really is too eccentric for comfort, I agree. I suppose one will have to do the fashionable thing – after all, no American society hostess is complete without her analyst, I gather. Look, I only came up to say – ' There was clapping and the opening of doors. 'I really should get back to the festivities. I'm sure she's OK – come down and see the fun.' Silence and some announcement. More clapping and the twang of guitars. 'Oh – it's the long-haired brigade now – with a protest song no doubt. Perhaps we're better off – '

'No, James – you go down.' I could see he wasn't really with me: the host in him was down there checking lighting and timing, testing the temperature of enthusiasm, however little he cared for the performance itself.

'All right – just for a while. I think I should give old Panoucik a drink before his intermezzo or whatever. He's quite a catch, actually. Did you hear the Bach Partita?'

'Yes, indeed – lovely. I'm fine here, James.'

'Well, I won't be long. Don't worry about Mo,' he said at the door. 'She'll bounce back – she always does.'

I watched her lying there in her crumpled finery; her stillness was like that of a coma rather than of healthy sleep. Where was Sarah Moore now, I wondered: where did she go while, according to James, Mother Nature was coping with pain – could one call it a self-inflicted wound? I saw them still as two separate beings, perhaps for my own sake; and even looked round with a start when the shutter creaked, moved by a light wind that whispered among the hollies. Separate beings; but was their separation diminishing? Nemo seemed to spend more of her waking hours being haunted even in the three weeks since my return; was there now any 'even keel'? Possession followed recovery faster, and recovery itself looked more like a mere withdrawal. I thought back to the days of autumn when Sarah Moore had first made her presence felt. How enchantingly mysterious the music box had seemed – how James and I had examined

233

it from all angles, and enjoyed our tentative acknowledgement that there are more things in Heaven and earth, Horatio . . .

Could I have averted the takeover? The day of the party, when Nemo played me the fading tape, should I not have taken more seriously her apparent submission to its whispered orders? 'I'm just doing what I'm told, Harry – setting the stage, to see what'll happen.' It had. And I realized now that I had seen not only Sarah Moore, on the dance-floor, but the new electrically charged Nemo: that vision of her through the kitchen window as I left, dancing an elaborate sarabande on the table with lighted sparklers fizzing in her hair.

Always I seemed to see her at one remove, as in a drama. Brightly lit behind glass, or appearing like a stage goddess through the smoke, and then retreating afterwards to a haughty distance and making a dramatic exit – always leaving me dazzled, stunned, in the cold.

There was one more drama still to play out.

I barely noticed the revelry below – noises off, voices and music, bursts of applause, laughter, loud farewells, a couple of cars leaving. Once Bertie opened the door softly, nodded to me and went away again. But through it all Nemo did not stir. James came and sat by her and together we watched her. He was restless, yet did not seem to want to talk. I realized it would be better to tackle him again at some less anxious moment about what, I felt, he must see as Nemo's illness. I knew I would have to bring up the whole subject of Sarah Moore, however rationally he might explain it. He must see how it had affected Nemo's mind – while remaining as sceptical himself as he chose to be. He had not been impressed by my ghost story; now I considered telling him about the tape, my other 'evidence', but I decided there would be time for that later and in the light of common day. I think, moreover, I felt implicated, guilty, an accessory before the fact: for now I believed I might have averted the disaster if only I had spoken in time.

Downstairs the recital seemed to be at an end. There was general movement and the beat of dance music. I left James having a quick dry shave and an alka-seltzer, and went down to stretch my legs. 'Mo may be like this all night,' James had said, 'though I've never known her quite so knocked out.' It might be all night, but I would wait to see her recover. Dimly I realized I was flouting doctor's orders. And I remembered Bertie; I looked for him and found him deep in conversation by the study fire.

'Ready to go, Harry?' he said coming out into the hall. 'I am when you are. Have you seen Ben, by the way? He was asking for you and I reassured him. He was a bit the worse for wear, I thought – grass stains on his dapper suiting; and it looked as if he'd cut his lip. I brushed him down and gave him a brandy, which he actually *drank*. But he wouldn't say what had happened – a man of mystery. Anyway he seems to be enjoying himself – all that was some time ago, before the recital. I think he's dancing now.'

So it was Ben that had earthed the charge? I wondered as I went in search of a long cool drink. Could Sarah Moore have picked on him? I realized it was perhaps more likely for her to choose not one of Nemo's friends but rather the stranger in their midst. I remembered her words: 'I suppose if I did have affairs, it would be quick casual stuff – I would prefer people I had never met before and would never see again.' If so Mr Ben would have had a party to remember. Georgette Heyer, even Mary Webb, would seem a little tame, I thought, after this.

I was having a breath of night air outside on the gravel by the front door, looking towards the paling eastern sky and wondering if this dawn might see the end of Sarah Moore, cut short her 'one more little life' and lay her to rest again deep under the laurel roots. In all the ghost stories I had smiled over indulgently, the Thing had fled at first light. But, snug in a living body – 'fur is warm' I thought, 'flesh is warmer' – might it stay on? And never go?

Then I heard a sudden commotion in the hall, and saw Nemo floating down the bright staircase. She was wearing the huge plumed hat – the grand entrance, smiling, bowing, to clapping and the upturned faces in the crowded hall. James was close behind her, and as she swept into the drawing room and silenced the dance music with a royal gesture, he pulled me aside.

'I couldn't stop her. She suddenly rose up' (it had a Biblical ring) 'and started fussing about with her hair, and got out this hat – '

We followed the crowd.

By the time the others had settled and made room, and, standing by the door, we could see her again, she was taking her place on the 'stage' in the bow windows. Behind her the shutters had been opened, the great full-length sash thrown up, and she stood out, lit dramatically by two candelabra 'footlights', against the utter darkness of the evergreen wall beyond. 'And now,' she was saying in a high clear voice, 'I will do a speech from *Macbeth*.'

And so she did – a very carefully rehearsed rendering, complete with hand-wringing: 'Here's a spot . . . out, I say! – One; two: why, then 'tis time to do't – Hell is murky . . .' And she was good; but the performance, in every detail, was so unlike the throwaway modern interpretations one was used to, or indeed Nemo's normally low cool delivery, that the audience, now packing the room (the front rows sitting at her feet) were transfixed. They realized at once it wasn't a joke – but goodness, so *original*! A surprise ending, a grand finale! They roared applause and 'Encore.'

Nemo bowed and curtsied elaborately, this way and that; then lifted one hand, imperious, commanding silence. She had not changed her dress, and her floating gauzy sleeve

236

was crumpled like a poppy. But she looked marvellous, fantastic, as she stood there: all the glittering animation had returned, and, even across the big room, her eyes were golden in the candlelight.

'And now I will perform my dance.'

'Let her be, James,' I whispered, 'it's doing no harm. It's magnificent.'

'Yes,' he said. 'And it might be a shock to wake her.'

Nemo started swaying and swirling to music only she could hear. Then we heard it too: the tinkling of a music box. Her swooping circles grew wider, the dance wilder, and I feared for the candelabra on the floor, whose flames flapped and guttered as she spun past, filling the room with flickering shadows. Suddenly the hem of her dress was alight, and as she bent, almost admiringly towards it, her floating veils and the plumes in her hat caught fire. For a moment she spun – a marvellous torch – transfigured, spreading her arms in a wide gesture of triumph and farewell. Then she turned and fled flaming out through the open window and down into the wood.

Those in front were on their feet, those at the back shouting and pressing forward. But no one could have caught her; for she moved with a swiftness not human, and in a straight line, like a brief falling star, right through the laurels, through the screen of hollies, and the wood swallowed her.

We found her in the clearing. The growing light in the east only barely sifted through the gloom as we stumbled headlong down the old paths. But high above the circle itself the dawn sky was clear, turning the spotlight on the azaleas to a sickly glare. There Nemo lay in her ring of fire like a burnt and broken moth.

EPILOGUE

Late summer, now; early autumn, as it was in the time Before the Fall, when, a year ago, Nemo searched through the overgrown tunnels of the walled garden for fallen apples and explored the orchard for blackberries to go with them; when she sat on the south steps in her Liberty print apron, sorting through her 'wild' potato hoard to find the smallest ones for our supper; and we sat drinking and watching her, and listened to 'The Four Seasons' and Mahler songs and the sounds of the pheasants below in the wood.

But I am alone here, as I was at the very beginning; a scholar gypsy, on the inside now, camping, roughing it humbly in the setting of past splendours, until another auction takes it from me – or it is sold by private contract. I believe a film star is interested.

I have written an account of what happened, as a record of the truth: the truth as I know it. On re-reading, I see the ending is very sudden. It was. There is nothing I can say to elaborate on the final horror, nor can it be neatly explained away. It happened, and so swiftly. I do not wish to linger on it – mouth meaningless words over it. I can see it when I shut my eyes; so I try not to shut them now.

Some explanation is in order, perhaps. Go to the police for that. As far as they are concerned the case is closed – not satisfactorily, but at least closed. They took down a lot of what I said; but they were more interested in Mr Ben's evidence, I think. 'A potentially murderous sexual assault' was his way of putting it, though I believe it meant more to his romantic heart than that admits. A good man, Ben. Went through the fire, touched Heaven and Hell; and after it was all over, dabbed some Listerine on his lip and handed in his typed report.

On the strength of it Nemo was deemed responsible, posthumously, and while the balance of her mind was disturbed, for Bob Maclean's death and, they presumed, for Boris's as well. They did not see how she could have driven the car to the northern bypass and have been at home in bed when James came back later that evening, weary of his strenuous blonde. I told them how, but they were taking so little notice of anything I said. I know they thought I was mad. They were very kind; and they dropped their intended charges when a greengrocer near the station told them he thought he had seen Nemo on the Monday Bob had disappeared. Anyway, they had realized they couldn't prove a case against me: the mileage on the Hertz car was nearly, but not quite, enough. They let my friends take over, and I was spirited away for a holiday near Grasse. Then I went home. But I had to come back before the house was sold.

Only Bertie believes me now, and he is shut up in his monastery in Wales. After a year he will have the choice to stay or go. I think he will choose to stay; but still I have named him as my literary executor. Perhaps he will refuse. You have a right, legally, to refuse such burdens.

Now I am going back to the big drawing room. I have not been in there since that night in May. There is a chain and padlock on the door; but I brought a hacksaw with me as part of my 'provisions', and have cut through the hasp that holds it to the door jamb.

She may not come at once. I shall probably have to wait. I have no music to summon her, and my candles at the window will not last very long. But I think she will know I am there. I have not been entirely alone in the house these past few days and nights: there is a restlessness here and I know it is not mine.

I feel, on the contrary, almost peaceful now – after that

first awful evening when the sun burned through the copper beech. Then the very house, unloved and deserted, seemed to ache like a beautiful neglected woman, and the feverish stillness oppressed me until I felt I had to escape. But why should I want to escape? All I feared and all I loved was here, I realized; it was only a question of submission. I must lay myself open to a visitation, call her to come back. And if I am answered, I can't tell if it will be the gentle Nemo, Latin for no one, or Sarah Moore all fierce and fiery in Nemo's skin, and thirsting for a little more life before the long cold night.

I would have liked to say something significant and profound; but it is all far too simple for that. Only the practical details concern me now: the hasp is cut; the fire in the kitchen grate is nearly out, and quite safe. The account I have written is on the table, in case anything happens to me; we don't want any more mysteries.

My mind is single and simple, too – narrowed to its purpose, to one strong overwhelming impulse; and I am nothing more now than that moth fluttering along the dark passage to the drawing room, where, in the big bow, the candle is burning.